Head to Heart Talks

Rediscovering Your Authentic Self!

VICKY KELM WILLIAMS

PUBLISHED BY FIDELI PUBLISHING, INC.

ISBN: 978-1-60414-720-9

Dedication

For all those willing to accept the Truth — To look "over their shoulder" at their life and courageously become their authentic self!

To all the brave Warriors who continue to move forward with hope, faith and unconditional love so Earth Mother can be restored to her original peaceful state!

To all those that honor the Creator/God who designed it all by living their lives as an example of the Divine Eternal Flame from which we all came forth!

To my family and friends who always believed and supported my dreams, and to the love of my life who never gave up — Love is not a big enough word for my gratitude for you all —

From my heart to yours!

Table of Contents

Introduction

Once upon a time, not so long ago, an old woman lived among the friends with whom she felt most comfortable — the trees (Standing Ones), squirrels, raccoons, creepy-crawlies, winged ones, those with many legs and no legs — all those who called the Forest home. An orange-striped cat she called "Gracie" and a stray dog she affectionately called "Tom" were among the domesticated creatures.

She lived most of her life in the rural countryside of the Midwest exploring the curves, caves, Forest and hills. Corn, soybeans and wheat blanketed the countryside in symmetrical designs, while farmhouses and silos dotted the terrain. The land she loved so deeply reminded her that just as the crops grew and multiplied, so did everything she thought, said, and did. It was a humbling reminder of the connection between all of life.

Throughout her life these gifts from the land were among her greatest teachers. They taught her to keep her roots firmly planted in the richness of that which nourished her, to rely on that foundation throughout her life, and to keep her eyes upward. She was, indeed, a very strong-willed woman who spoke her truth with conviction and a straightforward approach; and, yet, her tenderness of heart taught her how to have compassion for all of Earth Mother's inhabitants — including the humans.

When the old woman was a very young girl she had a dream of writing. She found written words a safe and easy way to express her feelings when the actions of people confused her. She discovered that after writing, she often felt *less* of the emotion that she'd had when she first sat down. Therefore, she learned early that one of her "gifts" to the world would be shared in written form.

As she developed this skill, she found herself even more fascinated with people and with what made them "tick." She found humans a most intriguing species, and the warmth she felt in her heart from making them smile, or somehow feel better, became her life's purpose. Her young heart resounded with a certainty that what she came here to do was to make people happy, even if it was only to put a smile on their faces for a brief moment.

Of course, as life teaches, no person can make another "happy;" however, she did her best to let people know they had gifts within themselves that were of great importance to the world. She had a knack for "seeing" the authentic person buried beneath the veneer of his or her life experiences. For some this was refreshing; for others it was quite disconcerting.

She watched her own children come into the world expecting unconditional love and asking for what they wanted and needed. As they grew and entered the world outside their home, she observed how they, like so many children, learned that in order to "earn" the affection or approval of those outside the family, some sort of behavior or action was generally required on their part.

Her years in education helped her gain even more understanding of how modern day "civilization" trained and, indeed, programmed young souls to abandon their intuitive, divine natures that sought only to give and receive love, and instead, learn to follow the rules so that they might receive "love." She observed that as children learn these "societal norms," unconditional love becomes a distant memory. Instead, after numerous attempts and receiving only conditional love, a young soul would eventually turn away from giving love as well. Ultimately, young souls learn that in the process of becoming human they must move from their *heart* centers and turn to their *heads* for answers and solutions.

From these observations, the old woman did what she could to teach these "growing souls" that people had a choice as to what they wanted their lives to be. She did her best to help them rummage through the old "tapes" and "recordings," and retrain their thinking to focus on what they wanted to see more of in life. She offered them the opportunity to see the "flip side" of any situation so they might really "see" what was being taught. To do this, they had to reconnect to their heart centers and listen.

She reminded these students that it takes commitment, time, and energy to make changes, but that the results are well worth the effort. Sometimes the fact that she knew everyone had a choice would make people feel "uncomfortable;" and yet, the old woman held true to her knowing.

You see, the old woman had learned through her own life experiences and those of the thousands of young people and their families she had worked with, that each person is ultimately responsible for his or her own life and what it becomes. For it is in the experience of what we *do not* want that we find what we *do* want, and in the sad moments of life we learn what it means to be happy! The old woman would often say, "My best teachers have been nature, my children and my students!"

Some would take these teachings and begin the journey to wholeness; others would discount them as the ranting of an "adult." However, the old woman knew her only responsibility was to plant the seeds of truth. For just as the farmer cultivates the soil and plants the seeds, nature has the ultimate influence on the overall development of the seeds that have been sown. She knew all too well that environment had a great deal to do with the final product. However, without the truth planted, tended, and cared for, there would be no food to feed the soul of the community!

As the old woman continued to examine her own heart, she allowed nature to teach her the simplicity of doing what is innately natural. She had learned that if she were to be of service to others, she had to stay intimately connected to her own heart.

She found that solitude supported her heart, so she chose to move to the quiet, serenity of the Forest to complete her years on Earth Mother. The wisdom the old woman carried within her heart was, indeed, gleaned from her retreats into nature throughout her entire life. Regardless of the circumstances, whether personal or a concern of a student, the critters, birds, trees, creeks, oceans or mountains always offered her a lesson in every situation.

Some described the old woman as too direct, since she was not one for dancing around situations. She did not accept excuses or explanations. She merely listened to their hearts as they spoke, zeroed in on the "heart" of the issue, then reflected back to them what she heard them say.

Since many people are far removed from their true emotions, hearing them reflected back was not always something they really wanted to hear. Those ready to take responsibility for their lives found her reflections refreshing, for they knew what the old woman said was true. Others who were not as eager to take responsibility for their actions often found themselves thinking she thought she knew it all.

By the time the old woman moved to the Forest, she had learned to not be attached to what others thought. She knew the truth and that was all she needed. You see, the old woman had learned that each person must find the "sacred truth" within, and that searching for that truth from others would delay the path to their heart — to the place where their personal truth resides.

Respect and love: those are the twins needed to be a sacred human being! Without both life will be a constant source of "seeking," for as the old woman knows all too well, "you cannot give to others what you do not give to yourself!"

Every visitor to her cabin was allowed to ask only *one* question. It is the old woman's wish that through the stories that follow you move closer to your heart, to the place where you know exactly who you are, and what you came here to do. Your "head" is the mechanism you learn to rely on to gain the love you seek; and yet, it is also the obstacle that keeps you from the place you yearn most to be: *Home in your Heart.*

Reflections Pages

His Holiness, the 14ᵗʰ Dalai Lama ended a public talk with, "Perhaps there is something I've said you would like to 'think some more about,' if not, well that is OK, too." That seemed an excellent idea, so here is an option for you!

As we begin our journey with the old woman who, much like the spider, weaves a web, it is wise to pay attention to the *Truths* woven within each story. Therefore, a *"Reflections Page"* concludes each Season's stories. This is a grand opportunity to pause and reflect as you honor both your HEAD and your HEART, and consider what truth lies within each story for you.

Our HEAD is where our Reality is created. For as the Bible (KJV) says in Proverbs 23:9, "For as he thinketh in his heart, so is he..." Or, as James Allen, author of *As a Man Thinketh* observes, "A person is limited only by the thoughts that he chooses."

Our HEAD constantly tells us what is going on around us. That is, what someone meant by what they said, why they said it, what we did to "cause it," who was "right" and who was "wrong." The stories we tell ourselves are most generally based on assumptions we make about each experience, rather than on the truth. Unfortunately, most of us create these stories before even checking with those directly involved in the situation. No doubt about it, our mind is quite the storyteller!

Our HEART then interprets these thoughts (stories), and then responds to them with emotional reactions we call "feelings." We respond to life's many situations based on these "feelings." It is most interesting how we create and react to a story based solely on our thoughts, without even so much as asking the other person(s) for clarification of their words or actions!

So, if we want to change our feelings, we must begin by changing our thoughts! While this sounds simple enough, in reality most of us have no idea about the continual chain of thoughts that roll along the tracks of our minds 24/7.

The "Reflections Pages" are designed to help you begin to pay attention to this internal dialogue, so you can pause and reflect before exhausting yourselves with "what ifs" or "yeah, buts!"

The old woman hopes you will pause after each story and think about the *Truths* revealed. Then, pause again, and allow the stories to really settle into your heart.

Use whatever method works for you, to hit the pause button in your HEAD, so that your HEART can "hear." Or, consider this simple technique:

> Put your mind in your pocket, place your hands on your
> heart, and take a few deep breaths. Tell your mind that its
> job is to simply remember what it hears when your heart
> "listens" to the teaching in each story.

Here we go! Time for some "HEAD to HEART TALKS!"

Spring is a time of birth, newness and growth.

The natural order of life springs forth
before the divine whispers of love
are even heard.

It has been said that life is like a circle. We start our life as innocent beings, fully present in the moment with little concern for tomorrow. We are just happy to play with our toes, stick our fingers up our noses and explore the world around us. Everything is new and fresh, waiting to be discovered!

Spring is precisely like that! All the plants that have been snuggled within Earth Mother have been waiting within the safety of her womb for the moment when life is ready to receive its beauty! Every plant, blade of grass, leaf, seed and critter, awaits that divine moment of birthing. The warmth of the sun helps the plants to grow, as the clouds, rain, and wind provide the nourishment needed for them to grow strong and sturdy, and add to the beauty of this world. Spring is a time of newness, growth and abundant possibilities!

THE EAST

As we look to the East, we see Grandfather Sun bring light to our darkened world. He heralds in a new day as he teaches us how to take our gifts out into the world, and how to see the next steps in our lives. And, so, the Circle of Life begins in the East, where we are given the opportunity to choose what we want to experience. What marvelous choices we are given to "turn a corner," "begin anew," or "open another door," as we leave behind that which no longer serves us.

As the Eagle and the Condor fly high in the sky, so also we are given an example of how to "step back" and see the big picture without getting caught in the details of life! This we do each morning as we face the East and offer our prayers to the Creator — to the great, unknown mystery of Life!

"When you see a new trail, or a footprint you do not know, follow it to the point of knowing."

— Uncheedah, The Grandmother of Ohiyesa

Morning Song

Her heart stirred as *I love you* ran through her thoughts and she felt a quickening from within. "Grateful for all of you, for my life and for sweet Mother," she softly whispered as her eyes opened. She felt her toes wiggle as her body began to stir from a restful night's sleep. She moved from a fetal position and gently pulled the covers snuggly around her as in a lover's embrace.

Good morning, my friends. Thank you for a good rest, were her thoughts as she yawned and stretched from her toes to her fingertips. She moved the covers and rolled to the edge of the bed. *I am so grateful for this comfy bed.* A fluffy cream-colored rug welcomed her feet to the floor. *OK, body, let's see what magic awaits us today.* She slipped into a very worn robe and tied the belt snuggly. *I love your well-worn feel, my friend. Let's get the day started.*

The old woman moved slowly as she reached for the sage smudge stick, lit it, and then whispered, "To all that is sacred, may my actions show your love." She then moved from room to room and blessed every inch with divine love. After she finished in the kitchen, she returned the smudge stick to its proper place and went back into the kitchen to prepare the coffee for brewing.

Looking out the kitchen window, she spoke to the morning light. "Grateful for another day to be of service. Thank you for supporting the dreams of all Earth Mother's inhabitants." The sky was a bright orange as Grandfather Sun began his ascent. She took a deep breath and marveled at the contrast of the greens and browns of the trees against the backdrop of orange hues.

A pewter dish filled with water sat by the coffee pot, and the old woman dipped her first finger into the water, then bent, touched the soles of each foot and said, "Where I go in the world." Then she dipped her second finger into the water, touched the palms of each hand and said, "What I do in the world." She dipped her third finger into the water, touched her mouth and said, "What I say in the world." Finally, she dipped her fourth finger into the water, touched her forehead and said, "The Christed One." She placed her hands to her heart and whispered, "Ah ho, Mitayke Oyasin." As if on cue, the coffee pot beeped, telling her the coffee was ready, and the old woman smiled.

As the old woman approached the porch swing with her morning coffee in hand, she noticed how exceptionally still it was. "Good Morning," she softly said to her friends that lived outside the cabin. "You're mighty quiet this morning."

She sipped her hot coffee and gave the swing a gentle nudge with her foot. The rhythm of the porch swing seemed to harmonize with the morning's peaceful stillness. *Don't want to wake anything up,* she thought as she held the morning brew between her hands. *Better allow my friends the quietness of the morning.*

It's been a good life. Lots of adventures, lots of discoveries and more trouble than I needed. A mischievous smile deepened the lines and creases on her face that reflected a life fully lived. *Reckon I've lived life exactly as I wanted, regardless of what others thought. I pretty much drove my family crazy; but, what the heck? They needed some adventure too!*

The steady movement of the porch swing seemed to pick up speed as she continued reminiscing. *I remember starting school and wondering what the heck I was supposed to do in a dress every day! Back then, girls were only allowed to wear skirts or dresses. I remember figuring out that I could wear pants under my skirts without too many complaints from the "adults."*

Heck, I wore dresses to church; wasn't that enough? With four brothers, pants were the most appropriate attire that would allow me to keep up with their shenanigans.

The hawk greeted her with a "Good Morning" caw. Squirrels began to peek their heads out of tree holes, as rabbits emerged from behind the cabin.

"Well, good morning, sleepy heads! I was beginning to wonder if you were going to sleep all day!"

As the critters began their morning activities, an old, orange-striped cat crept from the side of the woodpile. "Good morning, Gracie. How are you this fine day?"

As if the cat understood human words, Gracie stood still, licked her front paws and stared directly at the old woman. The old woman said, "Doing your morning primping, huh? Well, you look beautiful, as usual, Gracie!" Gracie finished her preening, glanced at the old woman, then turned and headed to the woods.

Hmm, Gracie must have a new boyfriend, she giggled. *Reminds me of my younger days! Being a tomboy worked until I hit fourteen, then being a girl became more important. Jackie Smith, an Italian boy, and cute as a button. How smitten I was with that lad. That is, until Dad met him, and then it was all over! "He's too dark skinned," Dad had said, "Don't mean to be prejudiced, but what would it look like to our family, not to mention the church members?" Well, it was just as well; there were lots of boys from which to choose, so I enjoyed pickin' through them all!*

The old woman scanned the Forest display in front of her, picked up the pace on her swing and looked out at the various hues of green bursting from the branches of the awakening trees. *My second favorite time of year!* she reflected. *Watchin' everything come alive after a long, slumbering winter sure brings hope and newness to my heart, not to mention warmth to these old bones!* Taking a very deep breath, she continued, *Do believe I'll have my usual second cup with a biscuit out here this morning so I can enjoy the beauty! Why, you can practically hear things growing!*

She rose from the swing, steadied herself a few moments, and then entered the cabin. *Think I'll just heat up a biscuit from yesterday; it doesn't appear anyone is coming today,* she thought, retrieving a biscuit from a brightly painted breadbox.

She wrapped the biscuit carefully in a small piece of aluminum foil and moved toward the stove. After setting the temperature to 325 degrees, she glanced out the kitchen window and noticed something move. She moved closer to the window and saw that it was the stray dog that appeared fairly regularly. She had affectionately named him "Tom" when he first showed up some six months earlier. He was a shorthaired yellow mutt that looked as old as the old woman.

She tapped on the window, and when he looked up she gave ol' Tom a wave. Tom stared at her for a few moments as if to say, "Yeah, yeah, I see you. Let's get to the important stuff: got any leftovers?" The old woman turned to her refrigerator, retrieved a small bowl covered with waxed paper and placed it on the counter. She turned to the stove, placed the foil-wrapped biscuit in the stove, then grabbed the bowl and went outside. She leaned over and removed the waxed paper, displaying a plethora of leftovers the old woman had obviously been saving. Tom followed his nose to her gift. "Oh, boy!" he seemed to say, his tail rapidly wagging as he devoured the food.

"You're a good boy, Tom, and you know I always have a little something for you," she said as she patted his head. "You have a good day. Now I need to get to my own breakfast." She turned and entered the cabin, "Mmm, that biscuit smells ready!" she said as her tummy growled in agreement.

She took a saucer from the cupboard, retrieved the butter and a knife, and placed them all on the counter. With a very worn hand-crocheted potholder, she retrieved the delicacy from the oven and gently removed the foil wrapped around the biscuit. Steam rolled out with the delicious aroma of freshly baked biscuits. She split the biscuit in half, smothered it in butter, and then poured another cup of coffee. She placed both on a small tray, placed her hands over them, and thanked Earth Mother for the nourishment provided for both her body and soul.

With tray in hand, the old woman took a seat on the porch swing. She sat down, scanned the Forest and observed, *Everything is awake.* She savored the warm and tender first bite of her biscuit. *There are some things you don't share in life, and this secret biscuit recipe is one of those things!*

Her thoughts were rich and full this morning as she remembered what a great cook her mama had been. She could make meringue pies that stood six inches high. *It didn't matter if the cupboards were bare; Mama always had a meal on the table for all of us. Being raised on a farm, there was always an abundance of eggs and milk, so Mama could create something that filled our bellies and tasted delicious.*

She sipped her coffee as she surveyed the spring growth around her. *We loved roasting hot dogs and burning marshmallows black for dessert.* "We never got tired of that dinner," she said out loud as a chicken scurried to the front of the cabin.

"Well, what are you doing here?" she asked the chicken. "You're supposed to be laying eggs!" The chicken looked at her as if to understand what she said, then turned and headed back to the chicken coop.

We'll have fresh eggs for dinner. Maybe I'll try making that "eggs a la golden rod" Mama always made.

The old woman finished the biscuit, washed it down with the last of her coffee, and said, "OK, let's see what needs to be done today."

Scanning the woodlands in front of her, she could almost hear the trees telling her, "Sit and be with us today." The old woman sat very still with the tray balanced on her lap. She surveyed the beauty around her, took a few deep breaths and said, "You know, that is a great idea. I have that quilt to finish that David asked me to make. Maybe I'll just sit right here and work on it."

Pausing to smell the freshness of spring, she closed her eyes, sniffed the air and felt the moisture of spring caress her body. *After a very cold winter, this warms my bones! What a delightful morning!*

She listened to the symphony of sounds around her. "That's a mighty fine idea my friends, mighty fine! I'll be back directly." She rose from the swing and carried her tray into the cabin.

The sun peeked through the billowy white clouds that began to take shape in the morning sky. The air was crisp and the wind gently blew a warm breeze through the still bare trees. The old woman walked onto the porch with a brightly colored quilt of various sizes and shapes sewn together. The back of the blanket was a solid green and between the layers was a cotton batting that was certain to bring warmth to the one wrapped within the quilt's caress.

The old woman's hair was tied back in the usual braid, and she wore a hint of pink lipstick and a slight peach blush on her cheeks. She wore black wool pants that looked as though they had seen many winters. She had on a soft pink furry turtleneck with tiny flowers dotted around the collar and a burgundy sweater tied snuggly around her waist. On her feet were very worn black suede moccasins. She was a sight to behold on such a cool crisp spring day as she carried her bundle to the porch swing.

She spread the quilt carefully across her lap, fastened a hoop around a section and secured it in place. She then placed a small basket on the table beside her and pilfered through it until she pulled out a large needle, some yarn and a pair of scissors. After setting the items on the table, she closed the lid to the basket and retreated back into the cabin. Within twenty minutes she re-emerged with a large glass of water.

"OK, I think we're ready to get started," she told herself. "If we are lucky, we can just about finish this today."

The old woman looked to the trees that had beckoned her presence and said, "I think we have everything we need. Thank you for making the request; David's birthday is in a few weeks, so I'd better get this done."

She turned and took her place on the swing and began tie-knotting the quilt as a melody of songs became softly audible. With the hum of love streaming from within the old woman's heart, the needle moved down and up through the layers of fabric and batting. The old woman pulled the yarn through, clipped it, and then tied it into several knots. She repeated these steps for nearly an hour until her body told her it was time to move.

With a few deep breaths, the old woman paused her handwork as she placed the quilt beside her on the swing. "My bones need to move!" she said as she slowly steadied herself to her feet. Reaching for the heavens, she stretched upward until the heels of her feet lifted from the ground. "Oh, how grateful I am for this sturdy body!" she continued.

As she settled both feet down onto solid ground, she took several more deep breaths. "There's nothing like fresh air to clear one's head." With a twist to the left, then to the right, she continued limbering up her stiff body from sitting for so long.

"Are we ready to touch Earth Mother?" she asked. Without a moment's hesitation she stepped off the porch onto the ground, closed her eyes and, with her head tilted back, took a big whiff of fresh air. "Good day, sweet Mother. How you bless our lives with such diversity. One day may be warm and sunny, the next cool and cloudy. Thank you for reminding me to be grateful for all the experiences placed in front of me."

As if to respond to the old woman's words, a warm breeze blew over her body. "Thank you," she whispered, "this old body needed that warmth."

Feeling the blood moving through her body, the old woman turned and moved toward her garden space. Bare from the winter's rest, a rich brown section of soil seemed to be beckoning to her to take notice.

"I see you, my dear friend. Looks like you made it through another cold winter. From the richness of your color, it appears we'll have another good year of planting." She bent down to Earth Mother, touched the soil with leathered hands, lifted some to her nose and took a big whiff. "Oh, you smell so good; so full of life, so ready to be of service. What an amazing teacher you are. Thank you for helping me remember my work here on this planet at this time."

With that, she closed her eyes and placed her hands to her heart. "May all that I am be an instrument for you to help all my relations on, sweet Mother. Thank you, heavenly Father, for supplying all that we need. Thank you for showing me how to find balance within myself so that I may stay clear."

The old woman walked the perimeters of the garden space three times, then touched Earth Mother and whispered, "Thank you for showing me how to hold the space for those seeking growth in their lives. You are a faithful servant to the seeds dropped upon you. You never complain, judge or rebuke any of them. You simply offer them a place to plant themselves, provide whatever nourishment they need to grow and mature, then offer them a place to rest when they have completed their cycle. You are a very good teacher for me. Thank you!" She paused for a few moments to allow the connection to deepen.

"Today, Mother, my heart is heavy. There are so many humans conflicted within their hearts, concerned over many things in their lives. They come to me with stirrings within that ask to be noticed. I know it is their 'root system;' they have not remembered where their place of strength resides. In our world today we have taught our children to focus on tangible things. They are taught to compare themselves to others, to look outside themselves for direction, to measure their worth by what they can accumulate, attain, achieve. In all of that, they have lost the ability to be content in the silence, to know that their Creator resides within them at all times and that they already have everything they need."

The old woman closed her eyes for a moment as she sat down on the ground and continued her heart's song. "What I request, dear Mother, is assistance with staying centered and peaceful, as you do. I know everything unfolds precisely as each person chooses, and that despite the many choices any person makes, they will find their way. For today, Mother, I ask for my heart to reconnect to that place of knowing. For as

I have told you before, being in this human body presents opportunities for emotions to take us in many different directions."

She settled herself solidly on Earth Mother, and then raised her eyes to the heavens. "Father, send down your loving energy so that it might work with Mother to rebalance and re-center my heart."

Without a moment's hesitation a ray of light filtered through the Standing Ones that surrounded the cabin. The old woman felt the warmth of Grandfather Sun's rays embrace her with love as she closed her eyes and allowed the energy to penetrate every cell in her body. As she sat in the warmth of love, knowing her prayers were being answered, her mind began to clear. The ruminating thoughts and concerns that had taken hold in her head began to soften like butter on the warm biscuit she'd eaten that morning. She felt the inflowing of strength and truth permeate her being as she felt a quickening in her heart. *Thank you*, was all she could say within the silence of her heart.

After a few deep breaths, and what seemed like only moments, she heard her heart speak. *For it is only with the heart one can see clearly; what is essential is invisible to the eye.* It was a phrase she recalled from "The Little Prince," by Antoine de Saint-Exupery, that had embedded into her heart and forever changed her connection to life.

Tears fell down her cheeks as a smile spread across her face. Every inch of her body was being fine-tuned, and she welcomed the healing. As the heavens continued to send her healing love, she felt them enter the top of her head and move downward through her body into the ground below. From the soil, she could almost hear the energy piercing upward toward the heavens. It was a circular movement from Heaven to Earth and back to the heavens as the old woman became one with the infinite. The old woman's heart was being resuscitated and her prayers answered as she sat still in the moment. Thoughts of yesterday and concerns for tomorrow disappeared as she continued to breathe in and breathe out with the rhythm of love.

Within a few short moments, the soft touch of a furry creature brushed across her hand and she slowly opened her eyes. Gracie sat close to her and began to purr as soon as the old woman's eyes were completely opened. It was a melody of love that harmonized with the old woman's heart.

"Thank you, Gracie," the old woman said as she gently stroked the cat's back. "I see you heard Mother call to you to help me find my heart's natural rhythm." With warmth in her heart, she felt restored to her natural rhythm with life. As she continued to stroke Gracie's fur, she said, "You certainly have great advantage over we humans! Thank you, Gracie, for being such a gentle teacher."

After a few moments, the old woman pulled a small leather bag from her pocket, opened it, took out some tobacco, kissed it, and then placed it on Earth Mother. "A very small token of thanks for what you have given to me. May my life continue to offer the same for those humans brave enough to make their way here. Thank you for realigning me to the truth so that I may continue to be of service. My heart is full!"

The old woman rose from the ground, returned to the porch, and resumed her position on the swing. "Grateful for the realignment, now I can continue working on this quilt with peace and love, so David can feel that every time he wraps himself in it." She took her needle threaded with yarn, and, with her hands, began to weave her heart throughout the quilt as part of her *Morning Song*.

Honoring Our Instincts

As the weather turned from winter to spring, Earth Mother began her great thaw. The winter had been a cold one with an abundance of snow and strong winds. One had to pay very close attention on the path to the old woman's cabin; the awakening ground left puddles of moisture hidden beneath the branches that covered the path. Roughly three inches of moist soil lay soft and "goosy," making for a good half inch of mud on a traveler's boots.

The young man had been told to "follow the trail to the cabin." However, it was summer when the person who told him had made her visit; what did she know about the muddy path in front of him? There was no question the rich soil smelled of newness, and sprouts of green dotted the trees and bushes along the path. Even with the pull of the mud at his feet, it felt refreshing to the young man to have such a reminder of what "newness" smelled and felt like. *I am very ready for something new to be in my life*, he thought, as he carefully watched each step along the path. *I have been stuck in the past long enough!*

As expected, the old woman was working in her yard. She was picking up fallen twigs and branches, which looked like an insurmountable task from the young man's perspective. *She will have quite a stack of kindling once all those twigs are gathered, and she'll have a sore back in the morning to remind her of the task.* The look on the old woman's face suggested that she seemed quite content with the task at hand, almost to the point of enjoying what she was doing.

He neared the cabin without saying a word; hearing the noise from the crackling of fallen branches under his feet would alert her that someone was approaching. *Besides, she is supposed to be intuitive; she should know when someone is on her land.* His thoughts were in direct correlation to his doubts about this old woman.

He coughed a few times and cleared his throat, and still the old woman never looked up from the task in front of her. She continued to pick up twigs and stack them in piles, and hummed some familiar tune that he could not quite put his finger on. The young man sat on the top step of the porch for what seemed like thirty minutes (in reality it had only been about five minutes), when the old woman stopped, put an armful of twigs on yet another pile, dusted off her skirt and wiped her hands on her apron. The young man rose from the step and the old woman passed by him, took her place on the porch swing, and picked up the bag that held her handwork.

The young man just stood there and waited for her to acknowledge him. It was a very awkward moment for him since he did not know what he was supposed to do or say. She pulled out her handwork and began "curling thread," so the young man took a seat in the chair closest to the porch swing. *This is the darnedest thing! What am I supposed to say?*

About that time the old woman said, "Are you going to ask your question?" Like so many before him, he was very irritated and wondered why he had made this trip, when she began her story:

"Once upon a time, many years ago, there was a family that lived in the city. They were a young family with three children, Fred, Bill and Susie, each two years apart in age. The mother worked at the school caring for the lunches of the students, and the father was a TV repairman.

"This family was very old-fashioned, and they enjoyed doing 'family' sorts of things. For example, they liked to visit their church each Sunday, return home to a family dinner, and watch TV and eat popcorn later in the evening. This was their 'routine,' and they enjoyed knowing precisely what was going to happen every Sunday.

"On one particular Sunday as they were leaving church, the youngest child, Susie, said she had to go to the bathroom just as they approached their car, and quickly raced back to the church without giving her parents a chance to respond. The other two children took their places in the backseat as Mom and Dad took theirs in the front. They waited and waited for what seemed like twenty minutes. Of course, Mom and Dad took turns looking toward the church to watch for Susie's return, until finally Mom said, 'I don't know why this is taking so long; I'm going to check on Susie,' and with that she left the car.

"Now, Dad was not one for patience, and he quickly became irritated that things were not 'on schedule.' He complained that dinner would be late, and, if they did not hurry, that it would probably also be overcooked. He was so irritated that he began to complain about what the boys were doing in the back seat. They were typical boys and were busy making paper airplanes out of the church bulletins; of course, they knew not to let them 'fly' anywhere.

"After what seemed like forever, Dad grumbled something under his breath, opened the car door and told the boys that he was going to see what was taking Mom and Susie so long. So, the two boys sat in the back seat and decided that it was OK to fly their paper airplanes.

"After a few moments and a lot of giggles, the boys began to settle into a quiet space. Bill finally said, 'What do you suppose is taking so long?' Fred said to Bill, 'I have a bad feeling,' to which Bill blurted back, 'Nothing is wrong; let's play. You are always looking for things to be bad.' Fred immediately became angry and told Bill to 'stick his head in a toilet,' and Bill said, 'Make me.'

"The next thing they knew they were wrestling in the back seat, when someone tapped on the car window. A man in a dark coat and hat was standing by the car window on Fred's side, and motioned for him to roll down the window. The man's face was not very clear, since the sun was shining just behind him, but Fred responded, 'We are fine; our parents are in the church.' Bill just sat there staring at the man and thought, *Something is very wrong,* and he clicked the door locks.

"Fred said to the man, 'What do you want?' Bill whispered to Fred, 'Don't talk to him; he is not a nice man,' to which Fred responded, 'Now, who is the scaredy cat?' Bill snapped, 'I'm telling you, he is not a nice man,' as his eyes welled with tears, 'Please, Fred, tell him to leave.' Fred turned back to the man and said, 'Our dad will be back in just a minute, and he can help you if you need something.'

"About that time Fred and Bill's dad came walking out of the church, and the man who had been talking to the boys seemed to disappear. Their dad arrived at the car and Fred unlocked the doors. Bill began to cry as his dad got into the car. 'Where is Mom?' Bill sobbed, 'I want to go home.' To which Dad said, 'Susie has gotten sick; they will be here shortly.'

"Dad then said, 'I thought I saw some man talking to you all; what did he want?' Fred said, 'I don't know; he felt creepy, so we locked the doors.' Dad replied, 'That was good thinking.' About that time Mom and Susie came walking toward the car, and out of nowhere, the man in the dark coat came running from just behind the family car. He grabbed Susie, turned, and ran toward his car. Mom screamed and Dad jumped out of the car and yelled, 'Hey! Stop! Let my daughter go!' and he ran toward the man who was making a mad dash to his car. Susie screamed her lungs out as she kicked her legs and flailed her arms in the air. The man in the dark coat let her go, and ran down the road, leaving his car behind.

"As Susie approached the family car, Mom jumped out and took her daughter into her arms. Dad took down the license number of the man's car, and looked inside the car to see if the keys were in the ignition. Sure enough, they were, and Dad took the keys and put them into his pocket. As Mom held Susie, Fred and Bill leaned over the front seat to comfort their sister. Dad got in and started the car, and took off as he handed his cell phone to Fred. 'Dial 911, Fred, and tell them to meet us at our home.' Fred did as he was asked, and by the time he finished giving them their home address, the family pulled into their drive. Within fifteen minutes the police arrived and the family told their story.

"About two days later the man was captured, and it turned out that he had escaped from a jail just thirty miles away. The family gave thanks to their Creator for the instincts each of them had honored. Susie started it all by having a 'sick' stomach; something within her knew something was about to happen, and she could not 'stomach' the idea. Mom knew that Susie had taken too long, so she went to assist her. Had she not done so the man may have entered the building instead of approaching the car. Dad sensed that something was up and went to check on his wife and daughter. When he was assured they were fine, he returned to the car, and had he not done so the boys may have been in a very precarious situation.

"Fred and Bill both sensed this man was not someone they could trust, so they let the stranger know their parents were just inside the building, and had the good sense to lock the doors. Susie knew to flail and kick when abducted; Dad knew to take the keys and write down the license number; and finally, they knew to report the whole situation to the police so the man could not harm anyone else.

"We are given a gift that is as instinctive as taking your hand off a hot stove; sometimes we second guess ourselves and kick the old 'head mind' into action by explaining, rationalizing and doubting what our 'gut' knows. This is a natural gift our Creator built within each of us. It is something many people take for granted, but thank goodness this family honored their instincts and took action."

The young man looked at the old woman who was busy curlin' thread and asked, "What does this have to do with me?" To which the old woman, biting the thread in two and tying a knot in the end of the tatted chain, replied, "Perhaps it would be good for you to consider what you are afraid of, and what you know instinctively to be true that you are running from." She completed the knot and handed the tatted work to the young man, and then said, "It is time for you to quit being afraid. You have good instincts, so stop doing what everyone else wants you to do and trust what you know is for your highest and best good. It is time for you to come out of the shadows of fear that you will make a 'wrong' choice, and simply take action." She paused a few moments, puts her handwork into her bag, and rose from the porch swing.

As she sauntered to the doorway to her cabin, she hesitated and said, "Gathering twigs is good for the soul; it helps one pay attention to the task at hand and not listen to all the chatter in their head that likes to put doubts into one's mind. You might try it sometime." And with that she opened the door, turned and said, "These are my words." Then she entered the cabin and closed the door behind her.

The young man was bewildered. *What just happened?* He placed the tatted chain in his coat pocket and just sat on the porch looking out toward the Forest. About that time a squirrel scurried up to the porch and climbed the timber rail that ran between the posts along the porch. The squirrel carried something in its mouth, its jaws bulging on both sides. The young man sat as still as possible, hoping to not the scare the squirrel. As he watched the squirrel scamper along the rail, he wondered, *What am I afraid of? Why do I always question decisions I make? Could it be that I am afraid of making the wrong choice?*

As he sat in the chair, he heard the old woman stirring inside the cabin, and she was humming a tune. *That's the same tune she was humming before … what is that tune?* he wondered, as he noticed the squirrel had disappeared from his view. *Well, darn; I never did see where the squirrel was taking that mouthful of goodies.*

Suddenly, the young man realized what the old woman was humming; it was the old hymn, "Amazing Grace." *That's it,* ran through his head. *I am so busy doubting myself and looking to others for guidance that I lose my focus on what is in front of me. Then when things turn out differently than I wanted I blame others rather than spend the time to change what I don't like. It has always been easier for me to let others make decisions for me and then go about blaming them, rather than trusting my own instincts about what I know is best.*

The young man got up from his chair, dug in his pocket for a gift to leave the woman, and placed it in a gifting basket woven from twigs that sat by the steps. "Never again!" he said out loud. "I have missed too many opportunities by not trusting my instincts. That old woman is right; I have good instincts, and it is time for me to *Honor my Instincts*, and to wake up and know without a doubt that whatever I choose is precisely what I need to experience. Just as that family stayed safe, and did not point fingers at someone else for 'victimizing' them, I need to take responsibility for my life right now!"

As he walked toward the path, he stopped in his tracks, closed his eyes and asked Creator to help him trust again. He had lost his "gift" by giving it away. It was not anyone's fault that he was not doing what he loved; it was his lack of faith and trust in the gifts he knew he had, even back in grade school. He continued along the path, pausing from time to time to watch a critter scurry about the Forest. He said out loud, "It is time for me to play, to have fun, and to enjoy being in this world. There is no reason to fear anything; I have the God-given gift to know what makes my heart sing, and it is my responsibility to share it with others." And, with that, he made a promise to all who would listen, to pay attention and do what came naturally, without hesitation.

This Moment

Good! I can check that off my list, ran through Lynn's head, as she placed a bright purple check mark next to an item on a very long list. "I love seeing that purple on this page! It means I've accomplished something," she proudly stated. She held up the burgundy leather binder that held the buff-colored writing tablet and continued her thoughts, *Rich: that's the word that describes what the blend of colors create together.* A smile widened on her face and she concluded, *Rich is good! It brings even more beauty to the world!*

Lynn was quite pleased with herself. She had been very diligent throughout her life. Sure, she would definitely make some different choices now; however, she also realized everything she had chosen made her the woman she was today.

She carefully placed the purple pen in the designated space in the binder, and then counted how many items on her list still needed to be completed. "One, two, three, four, five, six, seven." She curved her lips to one side, *Well, seven's not bad.* She straightened her lips, moistened them with her tongue, and nodded her head. *Yep, out of twenty-five items, seven is very doable!*

Feeling a sense of accomplishment, Lynn folded the binder and carefully placed it neatly into her metallic gold tote bag, next to a buttercup yellow clutch bag and matching umbrella. She glanced at her wristwatch and thought, *Better get on the road so I'm not late. GPS or not, I want to make certain I'm on time. I'm really not perfectly clear where this cabin is located. Better get the lead out and get on the road.* Lynn grabbed her jacket, keys, and slipped a shiny blue foil-wrapped package adorned with a bright red bow into her tote bag.

It was an unusually warm day for early March in the Midwest. People were busy working in their yards collecting twigs that had fallen from winter's wrath. It was apparent that everyone was most grateful to be working in the sunshine as they scurried about like ants about an anthill.

Lynn enjoyed the drive along the back roads as the warm air stimulated her skin, awakening it from the long winter's freeze. She took a big whiff of fresh air, thinking, *I can smell the fresh dirt. This is why people live in the North; the change of season brings a sense of newness to life.* "How I love the aliveness of spring!"

She admired the bursts of green hues springing forth on the bushes and trees, as critters scampered around plant growth like kids frolicking on a playground. *They must be as excited as we humans to be out in the fresh air warming their bones! No doubt they are exercising their bodies in preparation for a busy gathering season for next winter.*

Deep in her thoughts, Lynn was brought back to the road in front of her by the voice from her GPS. "Turn right in fifteen feet," the voice said. *Wow, that was a quick drive.* She glanced at the clock on her dashboard and said, "Well, I guess it hasn't been that quick; I've been on the road nearly forty-five minutes." She continued, "That GPS devise estimated it was fifty minutes from my house to the cabin." As she made the turn she wondered, *How do they know that?*

She wheeled her car onto the clearing per the GPS instructions, placed the gearshift in park, got out of the car and clicked the key lock. Then she carefully placed the keys in their assigned spot in the gold tote bag. *Well, here we are! And, we're fifteen minutes early; that's good!*

Lynn started out at a brisk pace, and then slowed herself as she caught a glimpse of the cabin. *I still have ten minutes, so I guess I can slow down; don't want to interrupt what she's doing. I don't like being interrupted, and I don't imagine she does either.* A blue jay caught her eye, and she paused for a moment, readjusted her tote bag, smoothed her hair and took a deep breath. "You are a pretty one," she told the blue jay. "Bet you're getting ready for 'baby' season!" As if the blue jay understood her words, he hopped to the next branch where a gray-colored blue jay sat on a nest.

"Well, I'll be darned," Lynn, said, "You already have 'em 'cookin!'" *What a sweet sight. A mama and papa waiting for their babies!* She felt warmth in her heart, while butterflies took flight in her belly. *I sure hope Tom plans to be involved with our babies,* she continued. *He says he will, but we'll have to see; guess time will tell!*

Lynn stepped onto the porch as the front door of the cabin opened. The first thing she noticed was a bright orange cloth covering a tray that was held by two tiny, leathered hands. Within a split second deep purple sleeves appeared, and the old woman stepped fully onto the porch. She was wearing a pair of very worn blue jeans, a bright yellow tee under a purple shirt, and black suede moccasins that appeared to have seen many a mile. Lynn stopped to give the old woman plenty of room to carry the tray and offered, "May I help you with that?"

The old woman mumbled, "No, thank you," as she carefully placed the tray on the small table between the swing and willow branch chair. "You may have a seat," she told Lynn, as she removed the orange cover, folded it neatly and placed it on the side of the tray.

Lynn waited for the old woman to take a seat before she sat down, and then placed her gold tote bag on the porch beside her chair. "I appreciate you taking the time to see me today; you didn't need to go to any trouble," she said as she smoothed her hair, settled into the chair and accepted the lemonade the old woman offered.

"Thank you very much; this will be quite refreshing on a warm day like today," she said as she took a sip. *Wow, this is the best tasting lemonade*

I've ever had; and it's so cold. Just what I needed! She looked over at the old woman and noticed her snow white hair. *Her hair's so shiny. I wonder what she uses to make it shine like that?*

The old woman sipped the lemonade and stared out at the Forest in front of the porch and said, "It was no trouble; all I had to do was pick up another glass." Her hair was tied behind her head and a long braid hung off her left shoulder. She appeared to be in her early to mid seventies and was quite attractive for her age. Lynn noticed her fingernails were neatly groomed, and she wondered how they could look so good considering all the yard work to which she apparently tended. *Maybe she has someone who does the manual labor?* Then she quickly corrected herself. *No, she seems the type to do that sort of work herself.*

As the two sat sipping lemonade in silence, Lynn felt an awkwardness about when to ask her question. Being a thoughtful person, she didn't want to interrupt the old woman's thoughts, but she also didn't want to take up too much of her time. As if the old woman could hear her thoughts, she said, "Now would be a good time to ask your question." The old woman placed her glass on the tray, picked up a black velvet bag and began her handwork.

Without a moment's hesitation Lynn asked, "How does one know if one is doing the right thing in life?" She squirmed in her chair, clearly aware of her discomfort with the question. *Did I ask that correctly?* "Is that question clear?" she asked the old woman. "It sounds rather vague now that I've said it."

Without a moment's hesitation the old woman began her story:

"Once upon a time, very long ago, there lived a community of horses that wandered the lands to the West of here. Legend has it there were hundreds of wild horses that traveled together. They lived deep in the high mountains during the warm months and headed for the valleys during the cold winters. Each season brought new adventures for the community as the weather brought a variety of challenges and opportunities. The warmer seasons provided the community ample time to play, graze, birth new colts and teach the young ones the ways of survival. The role of the elders in the community was to lead by example, so the skills necessary to sustain the community were taught and carried on to the next generation.

"As in all communities, there were leaders who were naturally groomed for such a role. They earned their positions by diligently paying attention to those already overseeing the well-being of the community and honoring the ways they were taught. As in all communities, there were those who wished to hold such a position of authority, and so they would sometimes create situations that brought focus to *their* physical strength, hoping to overshadow the strengths of the one being groomed for leadership.

"Among that particular community such behaviors were viewed as disrespectful, so the one acting in such a way would be taken aside by some of the other elders and placed away from the community. After a day or two had passed, the elders would fetch the separated one and bring him or her back into the community for a feast. The one returning was allowed to eat until his or her belly was full, and then the other members would once again begin playing and showing affection for the one that returned.

"Our actions reflect the character we hold within. If someone is held accountable for their actions, they will realign to what is for the best of the community because they are loved and accepted as a valuable member of the family in which they live. Forgiveness is a vital component to the overall peace and harmony in a community."

The old woman lifted up the chain, looked at its length, and then resumed her tatting. "We could learn much from the horses. They carry the medicine for learning how to develop one's personal power. They are extremely resourceful and willing to do whatever it takes to serve others — and not just of their own kind. The horse has offered much to the human race that has made our lives much easier. Can you imagine how the work would have been done had we not had horses to carry our necessities as well as us?

"The trouble with our current civilization is, many forget the support we are given by the Creator of the universe. Many are so focused on the future they have forgotten who helped them get where they are today."

The old woman took a deep sigh, looked at the beauty of the landscape in front of her, then continued, "If our communities are to work together in a peaceful way, there must be respect for all living things; humans and non-humans. Respect is the key that brings harmony to all of life. With respect, every rough spot can be made smooth and all of the community will feel safe. When every being feels valued and loved it feels a part of something greater than itself — it realizes its 'gifts' as unique and, therefore, adding value to the community."

The old woman bit the end of the thread, tied a knot in the end, and placed the chain in her lap as she neatly placed the handwork materials back into the black velvet bag. After placing the bag on the edge of the porch swing, the old woman held the chain between both of her hands and looked straight ahead. The moment of silence that followed seemed to extend beyond current time and space as Lynn sat very still and watched her.

"All we have is this moment," the old woman continued. "If we choose to be part of a community that is peaceful, we will honor the ways of those that walked before us — our ancestors. We will listen to the stories told with an open heart, willing to really hear what the elders are saying beyond just their words. There is much in an elder's heart that needs to be heard and respected as part of his or her unique story, and from that place we can learn 'why' such ways were created and imbedded in the community. As the elders leave this world and become the ancestors, the next generation of members can discern what ways need to be changed in order to accommodate the new ways unfolding on the planet, and adapt those changes so that the community will continue to grow in peace and harmony."

The old woman rose from the porch swing and stood in front of Lynn. "If we can stay connected to our hearts, we will choose ways that enrich the community; if we find our actions are not adding to the peace and overall well being of the community, then we simply choose another action." She leaned over and handed Lynn the chain as she concluded, "Every action that is taken from a heart that lives in the moment, is always for the highest and best for the community. We are not responsible for how someone accepts that; we are responsible only for the way in which we choose to deliver the action. Remember, 'it is not what you do, it is the energy with which you do it that matters.'"

With that, the old woman wrapped her hands around Lynn's and said, "These are my words." Then she gathered the items on the tray, covered them with the orange fabric and carried them back into the cabin.

Lynn sat clutching the chain in her hands for what seemed like half an hour. With tenderness in her heart she thought, *I love you, Tom. Thank you for being so patient with all my fretting!* Tears ran down her face as she felt her heart pounding in her chest. Sobbing with joy, she placed the hand holding the tatted chain on her belly. *Everything will be good, little one. I promise you, no matter what happens, you will be loved and cherished. And, when the time comes that you choose to exercise your individuality, we will love and respect you so you can stay connected to your heart.*

She took a couple of deep breaths, wiped her eyes and whispered, "This moment. Not tomorrow, not yesterday, but this moment is all we need to stay in our hearts."

Lynn gathered her gold tote bag, pulled out the shiny foil box with the bright red bow, and dropped it in the twig basket sitting at the edge of the porch. *A very small token for a very large gift you've given me.* She murmured "Thank you, thank you," as she touched her heart and began her walk back to her car.

I don't want to think *about this,* Lynn told herself. *I want to* remember *this, right here,* she said as she kept her hand on her heart. *Always, I want to always remember my heart.*

She arrived at her car and, once inside, removed her cell phone from her clutch bag. She retrieved a name from her contact list, pushed the call button, and when the lady answered the phone, Lynn said, "Hey, Grandma, it's Lynn. How would you and Grandpa like to come to dinner one day this week?"

Grandma quickly answered, "It is good to hear from you! We'd be delighted. We could do Thursday evening if that works for you. But you don't have to go to any trouble, Lynn; we know you're a busy lady. Is everything OK?"

Lynn replied, "Thursday sounds great, Grandma, and things have never been better! I do have a lot of questions for you and Grandpa, though."

As Lynn drove the road toward home, she noticed the beautiful gold tote bag that held the colorful assortment of items she needed to keep her life in some semblance of order. *I am grateful for an organized mind and for having a great appreciation for beauty.* She kept her eyes on the road ahead of her, and the colors of the landscape seemed to have intensified since she had last seen them. *I wonder if the colors are brighter, or if I'm just seeing them more clearly? Or, did I even notice the landscape on the drive here?* As quickly as the thought appeared, it was replaced with the flutter in her belly. *OK, I haven't forgotten about you!* She patted her belly as her heart seemed to beat with the rhythm of the baby growing inside her.

Lynn took a few deep breaths, ever so grateful for the moment, and for the realization that this little one was already teaching her how to stay in the moment. *My organization has kept me in my mind, which takes me back and forth from the past to the future. Guess you are going to teach me how to come from my heart and be in the moment,* she silently told her little one within.

A smile widened on Lynn's face as she felt the love and partnership with both Heaven and Earth. *I promise to teach you how to be in the world, if you will remind me how to bring the gifts of heaven here. Together,* she thought, patting her belly, *we'll find the balance needed to have peace and harmony inside and out. And, maybe, just maybe, we can help others in our community do the same!*

Lynn glanced at her burgundy notebook and said, "OK, we can mark one more thing off our list!" She looked back at the road, then glanced quickly at the gold tote bag and said, "But, we have a couple of others things to add to it! One of them is to breathe and notice *This Moment!*"

Shadows

"Really? You are going to follow me to the old woman's cabin?" Ralph spoke out loud. With his lips pursed tightly, he shook his head from side to side as he watched for the turnoff to her cabin. "I mean, what the heck do you want from me? Why do you always show up everywhere I go?"

Ralph took a deep sigh to calm his already anxious stomach. As he spotted the turnoff his tummy growled, reminding him that he had not taken care of feeding it. "There it is," he said as he flipped on his turn signal — and slowed his truck as he took a quick glance in his rearview and side mirrors. All was clear, so Ralph pulled over at the clearing into the parking space.

Well, here we are, he murmured within. *Guess we are ready to find out what to do with you all!* And with that, he felt a strange stirring within his belly. "Hmm," he spoke out loud. "This is strange!"

Then he immediately felt a settling in his belly. What? No anxiousness, no concern for what's about to happen? It was an "odd" feeling for him since most of his life he had felt "anticipation" in his belly, *Hmm, this is very odd.*

He grabbed a bag and his cell phone, locked the truck door and stepped toward a downtrodden path. "This must be the clearing to her cabin," he speculated. "Here goes nothing." And "nothing" it was for Ralph. He had spent most of his life with an "unsettled" feeling in his belly, and for some strange reason it was no longer present.

Thoughts ruminated through his head as he meandered along the trail enjoying the new growth on the path. *Nothing like spring*, he mused, *and watching everything come alive after being so dormant over the winter! How I love it!*

The day was cloudy, and Ralph buttoned his jacket and lifted the collar to protect his neck, as the cool morning winds blew from the North. Then he plunged his hands into the soft flannel pockets. *Good ol' Mom, leave it to her to purchase the perfect jacket to keep me warm! Whatever would the world do without moms?*

As he entered the clearing of the old woman's yard, he was mindful to carefully stay on the stone steps that had been strategically placed so as to keep the yard well groomed. He glanced on either side of the front porch and admired the burst of color from the budding bushes that adorned the perimeters of the cabin. As an environmentally conscious man, he noticed the care and tending of such beautiful plants and trees.

A large oak tree stood tall to the right of the cabin. *That tree must be 200 years old or better.* He strained to get a clearer view, and noticed some sort of "knot hole" with a unique shape. *What is that shape? Hmm, from here it looks like a heart?* Then he quickly pooh-poohed that notion. *Nah, that can't be what it is.*

He turned his eyes toward the porch, where he spotted the old woman sitting on the porch swing doing something with her hands. As he approached the porch, he took off his hat, made the step up onto the wooden floor and said, "Good day! You have a lovely place."

The old woman glanced up at the gentleman and said, "Thank you. Please have a seat." She placed her handwork to her left, then carefully lifted a purple towel from the top of a tray that sat on a table between the porch swing and the chair where the gentleman was to be seated.

The smell of coffee filled the air as a coffee pot, two cups and saucers, and an orange basket were revealed. The old woman poured coffee into each cup, handed the gentleman a colorful cloth napkin, pointed to a set of silver dishes and said, "Help yourself to cream and sugar, if you would like." She then removed the cover to the orange basket and the most exquisite fragrance of freshly baked biscuits filled the air.

Ralph's stomach let out a growl as he sniffed the air and said, "Oh, my goodness! What a decadent smell!"

The old woman handed him a saucer and said, "Help yourself to butter and jam if you wish," as she pointed to a small yellow ceramic container to the left of the orange basket.

Without hesitation, Ralph helped himself to the sugar and cream and took a big gulp of coffee. He then promptly retrieved a biscuit and smothered it in butter, placed it on the saucer, and sat back in the chair to enjoy his morning treat.

The two sipped coffee and munched on hot biscuits for a bit until the old woman placed her saucer and cup back on the tray and retrieved her handwork. Ralph helped himself to a second biscuit, this time smothering it with strawberry jam before leaning back to enjoy his second helping.

"My goodness, this is quite a surprise," he said. "I had no idea I'd have my belly filled with such goodness this morning." He leaned back in his chair to savor every delicious bite as he glanced over at the old woman. *This is a pretty interesting place. And, you know, my belly has felt fabulous since I arrived. Now, what do you suppose that's all about?* And, with that he quickly dismissed the question.

The sun was well above the top of the trees to the East as critters scampered about the Forest. The faint sound of a rooster could be heard in the distance, and Ralph thought, *Well, you certainly are a sleepy head this morning!*

He could not believe how peaceful he felt. It was a very "odd" feeling, as it had been years, if ever, since his belly had felt so calm. He had struggled almost his entire life with an impending sense of doom, or that something "unpleasant" was about to happen. Why he felt that was a mystery to him. His friends referred to him as a "worry wart," and often told him that all his worrying would one day materialize into a "real" situation if he did not change his ways. While Ralph heard what they said, he simply could not understand why he fretted as he did.

The old woman examined the tatted chain, then returned to moving her fingers as she began her story:

"There are mysteries in life that cannot be explained. Try as a person may, the mind cannot comprehend all the influences that surround us each day. Human beings seem to think everything in the world can be understood if they spend enough time *thinking* about it. But the truth is, what a person 'thinks' about is precisely what will show up in their life.

"I knew a man who constantly lived in fear of what 'might' happen next. He spent most of his life concerned that something tragic or sad was just around the corner. This man we will call 'Larry', was constantly plagued with feelings of impending doom.

"If you were to ask him why he fretted, he would only reply, 'It's just something I feel in my gut.' It seemed the more he tried to *not* think about negative things, the fear that something would happen intensified.

"One day, Larry was working behind his house cleaning debris, when he felt as though someone was watching him. He turned to see if his neighbor had come to ask a favor, but when he looked no one was there. It was at that time he came to visit me.

"Let me tell you what I told Larry." The old woman paused her handwork, took a few deep breaths and looked straight ahead toward the Forest. She sat perfectly still for about five minutes, as though she was waiting for something. Ralph began to feel a bit uncomfortable. And, yet, unlike his normal routine, it was not his belly that felt "uneasy;" rather, it was something within his heart that felt a quickening.

Hmm, Ralph observed, *my gut feels quite calm. What is this feeling I have in my chest?* He took a few deep breaths, felt his feet beneath him, and noticed that his heart seemed to be pounding. *Hmm, most peculiar ... I don't feel anxious, nor unsettled, but just a sort of curious 'quickening.'* He gently readjusted himself in his chair as he consciously chose to be as quiet as possible in order to not disturb whatever the old woman was doing.

The five minutes had now stretched into about fifteen, and Ralph realized his heart had found a steady, even beat. As he sat in the stillness, with only the sound of the birds moving from branch to branch in the trees, he noticed a humming in his ears. It was a soft, steady sound that seemed to harmonize with the beat of his heart.

As he sat very still, his head asked him, *What about your belly?* So, Ralph did a quick "check-in," only to discover that it was still very calm and peaceful. He was baffled by the situation. *How come my belly feels calm?*

As quickly as he asked the question, he felt the beat of his heart intensity. So, Ralph asked his heart, *What's up?* Without a moment's hesitation he heard, *I'm here, waiting for you!*

What the heck? Am I making up this stuff?

The old woman returned to her story as if on cue. "Everything in life has two sides. There is dark and there is light, there is good and there is bad, there is up and there is down. Every creation requires both a male and a female to bring it forth.

"Dualities are equal partners in life, and each adds something unique to our understanding. The problem with humans lies in the interpretation of such dualities. Unlike nature, humans wish to control what happens by making the situation something that can be explained — they seek the 'black' and 'white' of all situations.

"The truth is, it is all the same *stuff!* Everything in life offers us an opportunity to grow, expand, contract, and settle in. The problem with dualities comes when we try to categorize, label, and judge something that ultimately separates us from the experience. Imagine, if you will, what the world would look like if we simply observed each unique experience and looked for the *gift* it offers."

The old woman returned to her tatting, and continued, "Life was not meant to be controlled; it is simply an opportunity to, well, experience it! To observe our feelings, we can take flight with the hawk and soar above the situation so we can get a better view of the *big picture*, in order to not get caught up in the details.

"There is a shadow side to all of us; it is the great mystery, the powerful unknown, that can make humans *run for cover.* Truth be told, the shadows that linger in our belly are often the thing we need to love the most."

Ralph sat forward in his chair and said, "May I ask a question?" To which the old woman nodded her head.

"I know all about that foreboding feeling in your gut that can make you think something *bad* is about to happen. I have lived most of my life with that feeling. While I do think I am an optimistic person, I do feel my gut helps me stay alert to the possibility that something may happen. So, how can that be something I need to love?"

The old woman bit the thread in two, tied a knot at the end of the chain and said, "Most of the 'what ifs' in our life are based on our fear of not being loved. We can call it insecurity, we can blame it on our parents, the world situation, or a dozen other descriptive words; but the simple truth is, we either feel loved or unloved. Anything that takes us away from love makes us feel afraid, for the only real fear we have is of being unloved.

"Those knots in your belly, or voices in your head that say, 'Yeah, but ... ' or 'What if ... ?' are only there to keep you separated from your authentic self." She turned to Ralph and looked him straight in the eyes. "Your belly has felt calm and peaceful since you stepped onto this land because love is what is firmly planted on this sacred place. While I respect the teachings the 'shadow side' offers, I have chosen to look the darkness straight in the face and firmly proclaim, 'Love is all there is.' In the light of these words, darkness is illuminated."

The old woman handed Ralph the tatted chain, placed her hands over his and said, "Choose wisely and with clear intent, so there will be no separation within you. Your belly will be at peace, as your heart beats with the light of love. That 'voice' you heard awhile ago was your heart … the place where love resides. The darkness keeps you from your heart.

"Just as the perimeters of this home are adorned with beautiful shrubbery and flowers, so our hearts must be protected with the light of our Creator. Each day you choose what you will bring into your life. It is time to wake up and make that choice a conscious one." She released his hands, gathered the dishes, returned the purple towel over the top of them, carried the tray to the door and concluded as she entered the cabin, "These are my words."

The winds now blew a warm breeze from the South as the sun moved toward the West. Rabbits scurried about the edge of the Forest as squirrels emerged from the trees in search of fallen 'goodies' from winter's fury.

Ralph observed the movement of the early budding branches as the warmth of the sun seemed to awaken new growth from within the trees. Daffodil blades emerged from the ground, and spotted areas of grass began to surface. *It is a time of great awakenings!* He unbuttoned his jacket. *And I am certainly one of those 'blades of growth!'*

He stood and stretched his arms toward the heavens as he stepped toward the twig gifting basket, and set the bag he had brought beside it. For a moment all Ralph could do was breathe deeply as he popped and twisted his body in preparation for the walk back to his truck. *I wonder if everyone feels so peaceful when they leave here?* He answered his own question with a wide grin. *Of course they do, or they wouldn't keep telling other people about this place.*

When he arrived back at his truck, he observed the colors that seemed to have burst forth in the couple of hours he had been gone. *It is simply amazing how, once the decision to grow is made, everything bursts forth! Oh, let that be true for me!*

Ralph unlocked his truck door, and as he opened it he caught sight of a dark object. At first he felt a flitter in his belly, to which he quickly responded, *Oh, no! I am not going there!* Then he felt his heart beating in his chest. *Good! I like that much better, thank you! I guess I have made each of you separate entities from me — that is no longer true.* He stood up straight. "We are in this together, and I am determined to be whole and unified!"

He stepped into the truck and, just before sitting down on the seat, he noticed a single feather. *Hmm, and where did you come from?* To which he quickly replied, "Where do you think? It is Creator letting me know he hears my heart!" He lifted the feather and carefully examined the bluish, black color. "What do you want to bet this is a raven or crow feather?"

As he carefully examined the darkness of the feather he remembered hearing that raven represented magic. *At least, that is what I heard was the Native American teachings of the raven. I believe they called it the "medicine" of the raven. And, crow medicine had something to do with seeing both worlds — the spirit world and the physical world. Hmm, I like that! Black means magic, and magic is what I feel here!*

Ralph took a couple of deep sighs, and then said out loud, "What I really like is the blending of both worlds! Oh, that brings my heart such a good feeling — such a solid, unified feeling!"

As he settled into his seat, he placed the feather on the console beside him and said, "Thank you! There is no need to be frightened by the *Shadows* any longer. What did the old woman say 'Light always illuminates darkness?' Or, something like that." A smile widened on his face as he shook his head in amazement. "How does she do that? Well, makes no matter to me; what is important is that I do my part. And, I'll do my best to add to the *magic* of life!"

The Wooden Box

The morning was rich with stirrings; critters scurried to prepare for the day's activities. Birds flittered about in anticipation of Grandfather Sun's ascent as the Standing Ones waved goodbye to Grandmother Moon. The balance of life was in full view as winds stirred the stillness of night and the movement of morning activities began. Nocturnal beings settled in for the day's rest as the daytime creatures yawned and stretched from their slumbering state. It was a time when the movement of life was gentle, not yet filled with the busyness of the day. Each activity was intentional as the natural ebb and flow of morning life heralded in another day. There was no one being "in charge;" rather, the community came together to contribute their gifts to the Earth's early morning activities.

The old woman watched from her favorite position, the front porch swing, as all her friends in the Forest set about their morning tasks. She watched the squirrels scamper about in search of walnuts, hickory nuts, acorns, and other precious morsels gifted by the Standing Ones to those that needed "fruits" to sustain their existence. A raccoon lumbered clumsily through the securely held recycling bin in search of morsels of leftovers. The old woman spoke to him in her mind. *You know I keep that closed tightly; there'll be a few goodies left by evening, especially for you.* As though he heard her thoughts, the raccoon looked in her direction and scurried back into the woods.

The corn plants had emerged from the soil and were nearly a foot high, and a solitary pumpkin vine meandered among the rows. *Volunteers, I see you have returned,* the old woman observed. *I guess you want to be among the sweet corn this year.* As she looked a bit further, she noticed a single cornstalk that stood among the bush beans, and a tomato plant emerged from the cucumber vines. *It's a succotash garden we have this year!*

She sipped her morning coffee and closed her eyes for a moment as she breathed in the fresh air. How she loved the rich smell of Earth Mother, of morning dew, and the feeling of everything coming alive! Her tired bones needed the stillness of the morning to wake up so she could move about her garden this beautiful spring day. *Guess I have become as routine as the morning songbirds; I do love the calmness of morning that awakens this old body.*

She opened her eyes, scanned the yard and said, "Thank you, my friends, for being a part of me. You have taught me how to be peaceful, and to move with the ebb and flow of life. And, most importantly, you have shown me how to honor every moment for the sacred gift that it is; I am honored to be your sister." With that, she touched the shawl wrapped around her shoulders and said, "Thank you for keeping the morning chill from my bones! My heart is full."

She moved her hand to her hair and pushed it out of her face as a hawk sounded a cry that moved her eyes to the heavens. "Thank you, great messenger, for allowing me to assist those that walk the trail here to find their path home; home, to their hearts. For those that seek truth, whether in the form of prayer, tears, or by actually walking the trail here, I pray for your continued guidance as I witness their heartsongs."

She opened her eyes, stood up, walked to the porch steps and opened her arms. "May all that I am be a hollow bone for your truth to touch their lives. Thank you for your unending love, patience and compassion." She raised her arms to the sky and said, "As above," and, pausing a moment to bend down, she touched the ground with both her hands and said, "so below." She bowed her head in reverence to all that is divine. "Ah ho, Mitayke Oyasin" (which means "Blessings to All My Relations").

And so, another day had begun in this old woman's life as she returned to her cabin. Once inside, she moved about with fluidity and purpose as she prepared for her day's work. Slipping from her bedclothes into work clothes, she hummed a tune that seemed to call to the birds perched on the windowsill just outside the kitchen. The hummingbirds danced around the feeder, adding a soft melody to the old woman's tune as they harmonized together to greet the new day.

The old woman surveyed her food supply. *Better make some biscuits; I have a feeling someone's coming this morning.* With that, she pulled a large mixing bowl off the shelf, gathered the necessary ingredients and placed them all on the kitchen table. With waxed paper in hand, she tore off a couple of sheets, placed them on the table and dusted the top with flour. She then moved to the large mixing bowl where she placed flour, baking powder, and salt, then cut in shortening to make a coarse texture. Finally, she added rich buttermilk to the mix. As she stirred the mixture to soft dough, she pondered, *Wonder how many buttermilk biscuits I have had in my life? Granny taught me how to make these when I had to stand on a chair to see what she was doing.*

As she rolled the dough onto a floured sheet of waxed paper, she sprinkled extra flour sparingly on the dough so that it would be pliable to the touch and not stick. The old woman then took an old glass jelly jar and dipped it in the extra flour piled on the edge of the waxed paper, then placed it firmly down on the dough. She carefully lifted the cut-out rounds of dough and placed each gently on a lightly greased baking sheet. She dipped a table knife into some melted butter and carefully buttered the top of each biscuit.

"Granny, your secret is safe with me," she said as she completed the task in front of her. Using a potholder that looked like it had baked hundreds of biscuits, she carefully placed the baking sheet into a hot, 425-degree oven. She glanced at the clock and mentally noted the time.

No need for a timer; my great sense of smell will let me know when these are done.

About fifteen minutes later she removed the hot baking sheet that displayed the golden brown biscuits and placed them on the wooden table in front of the kitchen window. As she set down the sheet, placed the potholder back near the stove and wiped off her hands, she noticed movement just outside the kitchen window. *Sure enough, here comes someone! Guess I am not the only one with a keen sense of smell!* She placed the coffeepot on the stove in preparation for her "guest." "We have us an early bird!" she said to the robin just outside the kitchen window.

The young man who meandered his way toward the opening to the old woman's cabin carried something in his left hand. *Not sure why I brought this thing,* thought the young man, *but we will see if this woman really is as wise as they say. If she can tell a good story about this, I will be a believer!* He made his way to the cabin porch in long strides.

Just shy of the last few steps, he stopped in his tracks and noticed a big buck staring at him just behind a flowering lilac tree. He sniffed the air and thought, *Wow, this smell certainly takes me back many years; and would you look at the rack on that buck! You can tell you have outwitted many a hunter, look at that sag in your back and the width of that girth.* Standing very still and staring directly into the buck's eyes, he stood his ground, *Well, you have met your match, my friend; we will see who moves first.* He took shallow breaths so as to appear motionless. *OK, Grandfather, let's see if I still have the "gift" you taught me!*

The two locked their eyes for what seemed like five minutes. A faint sound could be heard to the left of the young man's view. He tried not to move his eyes as he listened with his keen ears to discern precisely from where the sound was coming. Within two seconds the deer pointed his ears straight up, lifted his neck, then turned on a dime and shot straight back into the dense Forest.

"Aha! I knew I could out-stare you! My grandfather taught me well," the young man said, as he turned to his left to see from where the sound was coming. Then he looked back toward where the deer went and said, "That creature has a great sense of hearing, and certainly knew how to 'disappear!'"

The young man turned toward the cabin, stepped up onto the porch and, as he approached the front door, it opened ever so slowly. The first thing he saw was a wooden serving tray covered with a dishtowel moving toward him. He pushed the door open to help the old woman manage the tray through the door onto the front porch.

"Need any help carrying that?" he asked the old woman. She shook her head and made her way to a wooden table that sat between the porch swing and the willow branch chair. She balanced the tray filled with "goodies" ever so gingerly, and set them on the table. The smell of freshly baked biscuits filled the air like an intoxicating whiff of something magical. The young man closed the door behind the old woman, moved the item he carried to the side of the willow branch chair and again asked the old woman, "Do you need help with anything?"

The old woman just pointed to the willow branch chair, then took a mug from the tray, filled it with coffee and offered it to the young man. "Thank you, Ma'am," he said as he accepted the hot cup of brew.

The old woman then removed the colorful dishtowel, revealing the piping hot, golden brown, three-inch-high biscuits. The young man's mouth watered as his stomach growled with gratitude for the delicious smelling morsels in front of him. He graciously accepted a biscuit smothered in butter that was presented to him on a blue willow saucer. "My grandmother had dishes just like this. Thank you so much for this treat." With that, he quickly took his first bite.

"These melt in your mouth; just like my grandmother's. No matter how much biscuit companies try to copy these old-fashioned biscuits, there is nothing quite like homemade ones. Again, thank you so much," he said through a muffled mouthful of biscuit.

The old woman took her place on the porch swing, ate the last of her biscuit covered with grape jelly, drank down her coffee and wiped her mouth with a beautiful purple napkin. She placed her napkin, mug and saucer on the wooden table, then dusted off her hands and grabbed her black velvet bag to begin her handwork. As she began tatting away with the thread and shuttle a chain began to emerge.

After he finished his second biscuit, the young man wiped his mouth with his shirtsleeve and leaned back in his chair. Savoring the remains of the rich biscuit that lingered in his mouth, he looked down at the item he had carried to her cabin. "Guess it is time I get to the question," he said as he lifted the cloth from the item and revealed a small wooden box.

It was a simple, unadorned box, about the size of a small cigar box. One could tell from the way in which the young man had covered the box with fabric that it was not just any old box. There was some sort of etching across the top of the box that was not clearly visible. The careful cleaning and polishing of the box over the years had worn down the rudimentary carving; and, yet it carried a richness of warmth.

The young man sat in silence for a few moments admiring the box before he spoke. "I am curious what you can tell me about this box." He held it toward the old woman who never took her eyes from her handwork.

She just continued to gently swing and move her hands with a rhythm that could almost be heard, and without taking her eyes from her work, she began her story:

"There are places in the heart that only silence can describe. People try to attach words to these feelings and emotions. They write songs, poems, and even stories to explain events that bring about stirrings within the heart. There are paintings and movies that attempt to depict situations that contribute to this mysterious occurrence. Try as they may, there are no words to describe what the heart knows to be true."

She slowed the pace with which she was tatting until she completely stopped. Looking out toward the Forest, she seemed to be lost in the silence that hung in the air. She gazed toward a large oak tree just to the left of the cabin where two cardinals were perched on the same branch.

One of the cardinals was a beautiful bright red, with a spot of black around the beak and white at the tip of his head. The other was a grayish color with black and white markings very much like the brilliantly colored one. As the old woman stared at the pair, the young man took his eyes from her mature face and looked in the direction she was staring. As he, too, looked at the pair, he noticed that each took turns flying away, and each time returned with a new twig, leaf or piece of dry grass from the yard. One would go, returning only to have the other repeat the process.

They are building a nest, the young man realized. *It is time for babies to come into the world.* Without saying a word, the old woman and the young man watched the pair diligently carry out a natural spring occurrence. "It is nesting time," the young man said. The old woman never moved a muscle. She seemed to be lost in the event directly in front of her.

As the old woman and young man continued to watch the "couple," the two cardinals seemed oblivious to the "observers." Instead, they busied themselves with creating a perfectly woven nest. As one would return with an item in its beak, the other seemed to be sharing comments about how things were going by making chirping sounds to the other. It was a picture of cooperative team effort and what can be accomplished when a task at hand is allowed to just "happen."

The nest was near completion; both birds now stayed on the branch and picked and pulled at the "finds" they had brought to the branch. As they carefully placed the pieces of twig, leaves and grass, one could see an occasional piece of string being woven into the nest as both cardinals chirped and picked at the details of their new babies' "home." It was a magical experience to behold.

The old woman took her eyes from the tree as she began moving her fingers once again. "It is in the dance of life that we find our dreams, our passion, our purpose. It is in the simple acts of love that what is important is revealed. When we discover the truth of life, we treasure the memories that are not easily explained with words. It is through our actions that we show what is in our hearts; and, when that truth is fully expressed, one's heart feels complete."

She bit the string, tied a knot in the end and placed the shuttle back in her black velvet bag. Placing the bag to the left of her on the porch swing, she handed the tatted chain to the young man and said, "Allow your heart to guide you to what you seek. You will know it when you listen with your heart. These are my words."

She rose from the porch swing and moved to her garden, leaving the young man to ponder what he had experienced. The young man sat perfectly still as he considered what he had witnessed, in actions, in words, and in the silence.

He looked down at tatted chain he held in his left hand, lifted the lid of the box, placed the chain inside and closed the lid. As he looked to the far right of the porch he saw the old woman walking among her flowers. She seemed to be humming; or, perhaps the birds were singing to her. It did not matter; what he knew for sure was that something very magical had just happened, and there were no words for what he had experienced.

Being a very thoughtful man, he wrapped the box in the fabric and placed it on the willow branch chair, then moved toward the wooden table. He carefully gathered the used mugs, saucers and napkins, placed them neatly on the tray, then covered them with the dishtowel. He moved the table that held all the items to the right of the front door. *That should make it easy for her to take them inside,* rambled through his head. *What an experience!*

He returned to the willow branch chair to gather the fabric-covered box and moved toward the steps of the porch. He dug into his pants pocket and pulled out an item that he placed securely in the twig basket by the steps. *A very small token for what I received today ... thank you!* Then he moved toward the path to his truck.

He could hear his heart as he walked to his truck in silence. It was a strange feeling to actually "hear" his heart; and yet, he knew that was what he was hearing. Something inside him said, "Yes, you will find the love you desire. Stop 'thinking' about it; throw away the mental list, and just 'be' with the person."

He held the fabric-covered box tightly as he remembered the stories his grandfather had told him. His grandfather described how the wooden box was all he could make to show his wife how much he loved her. Grandmother would give him the devil for not saying "I love you" often enough, so Grandfather used scraps of wood from the fence he had built around the farm, and etched the word "Always" across the top with a screwdriver. A year or so after his grandmother had died, the young man began dating, and his grandfather took out *The Wooden Box* and told him the story about how he had met his wife.

The young man felt his heart beating a deep tone that seemed to reverberate within every cell in his body, until he finally arrived at his truck, opened the door and said out loud, "OK, Grandfather, I get it; I know what it feels like to love. Thank you for showing me what you could not describe in words." He held the fabric-covered box to his heart, and then placed it on the seat beside him. Taking one last glance toward the old woman's cabin, he said, "And, yes, I am a believer."

Giving and Receiving

Storm clouds filled the sky as Gary made his way through the Forest to the old woman's cabin. *I knew I should have brought my umbrella,* he realized. *I just know it's going to begin pouring down rain at any moment. Whatever was I thinking?* Pausing only a second, he quickly continued, *Now, that's a silly question; obviously, I wasn't!* As the thoughts rambled through his head, he ignored the critters that observed him from the Forest. A pair of deer stood wide-eyed, watching the two-legged creature hurry past them, and a raccoon perked up his head to take a good look at the human. With wide strides Gary picked up his pace in hopes of reaching the porch before the rain began.

There it is. He proclaimed, *Oh, dear Lord, give me a few more minutes and then do whatever you want!* The wind began to stir the trees, causing branches bearing tiny green buds to sway in the air. *I know it's spring and time for the rains, but just hang on a few more seconds,* raced through his head as he reached the clearing to the cabin.

As he stepped onto the clearing he stopped dead in his tracks. A very large skunk stood to the right of the cabin, and seemed to be as surprised to see Gary, as Gary was to see him. The skunk stretched his head upward, raised his tail in the air, turned, and looked Gary directly in the eyes.

Oh, dear heavens, ran through his head as he stood very still, *what in the world do I do now? Maybe if I stand still enough he won't see me.* As if some divine force of nature had intervened, the skunk turned and lumbered off to the woods with his tail waving. *Whew, dodged that one! Thank you, Jesus, for making me invisible!*

When the skunk was clearly out of sight, Gary completed his steps to the cabin and walked to the door. The door opened just as he raised his hand to knock, and an old woman dressed in a rainbow of colors stood before him.

"Good day, Ma'am," was all Gary mustered up. *Really, is that all you have to say?* Gary searched for more words. *Well, I'm speechless,* he chuckled. *I'm never speechless!*

With an orange shawl around her shoulders, purple pants tied snuggly around her waist, and a sky blue tee shirt tucked neatly inside them, the old woman stepped out of the door. Gary noticed her bare feet and wondered if she was going to slip on some shoes, but instead, the old woman simply moved past Gary and went in the direction of the porch swing. Gary watched her move with the agility of a young woman, while the rainbow of colors gracefully swirled about as she cleared the table between the swing and a willow branch chair.

No words were spoken, and Gary thought it most interesting that the woman seemed to act as though he were invisible. Thoughts ran through his head as an air of awkwardness took center stage. *So, what am I supposed to do now?* Less than a second later the old woman drifted past him and Gary noticed her long braid. *What beautiful hair; you don't often see women wearing a braid these days.* He watched her enter the cabin, leaving the door open behind her, and stood perfectly still, uncertain if he was to follow her or wait for her return.

The gray skies had now become a dark charcoal color as the winds became frighteningly calm. *Hmm, what is it they say, "The calm before the storm?" I feel as though I've entered the Twilight Zone.* He became aware that he was holding his breath. *Breathe, Gary,* and with that he took a deep breath in through his nose.

Gary felt the warmth of the air fill his nostrils as he closed his eyes and allowed the in-breath to move up from the ground through the bottoms of his feet, up his body, and into his heart. He held the breath in his body for a few seconds, then parted his lips as he released the breath slowly through his mouth. *Relax, relax, relax,* Gary told himself as he exhaled all his breath.

He felt very present with life; very in the moment in such a way that he nearly forgot where he was until he heard a noise that brought him back to where he was standing. He slowly opened his eyes as a vision of color took shape. The old woman had returned to the porch carrying a fabric-covered tray that she placed on the table between the swing and chair.

She removed the fabric and two coffee cups, a coffee pot, and a wicker basket were revealed. As the old woman uncovered freshly baked chocolate chip cookies Gary's nose caught the scent. "Mmm, that smells great! Can I help you with anything?" he asked.

The old woman replied by handing him a freshly poured cup of coffee and a napkin. "Help yourself," was all she said as she took a seat on the porch swing.

Gary accepted the cup, took a seat in the willow branch chair and reached for a cookie. "Thank you very much; you didn't need to go to any bother for me," to which the old woman simply replied, "I didn't. It was time for my mid-day treat."

Rumbles of thunder filled the air with electricity and the winds began to pick up speed as Gary and the old woman sat watching the squirrels and rabbits scamper about. They seemed to be in as much a hurry to get to a safe place as Gary had been while walking the trail to the cabin.

"Looks like we're in for a gully washer," Gary said as he finished his first cup of coffee. "Is now a good time to ask my question?" He looked over at the old woman, who was now working her magic with some white thread and a wooden shuttle.

Gary took her silence to mean it was OK to ask his question, so he began. "How does one know where the balance is between giving and receiving? I've observed many people who are very generous with their time and money, and yet they rarely allow others to give back to them. I often get confused as to where the balance is between allowing oneself to be cared for and being independent enough to not be beholden to anyone."

Lightning rolled across the sky as thunder shook the ground, and rain came down in sheets. Gary stood for a moment to survey the porch and wondered if they needed to take their conversation inside the cabin. "Excuse me," he said, "I'm going to check and see if we're going to stay dry; looks like we're in for a fierce rain storm."

The only movement made by the old woman was the rhythmic motion of her hands as she orchestrated a delicate chain of white thread. Gary moved from one side of the porch to the other, slowly surveying the rain's pattern. "Looks like we'll be OK," he said as he returned to his chair.

"So, where was I?" he continued as he leaned back and nestled into the chair. His thoughts quickly shifted and he said, "You know, I didn't think this chair would be so comfortable, but I was wrong. It's darned comfortable."

Feeling cozied into the chair, he said, "At any rate, it seems to me there are givers and takers, and I need some help knowing how to work with people who do not know how to receive." He removed his cap, scratched his head, adjusted the cap back onto his head and said, "I think some people just like to be martyrs. They seem to enjoy pointing out all they do for others and how no one's ever there for them. It's a really frustrating situation, because if you point out that they declined your help, they seem annoyed that you even brought it up."

About that time an old orange-striped cat leaped onto the porch. She looked like a drowned rat after being soaked from head to toe in the rain. She moved to a comfortable, dry place beneath the porch swing where she began preening herself dry.

The old woman paused her hands, looked down at the cat, and simply said, "Hello, Gracie." The cat stopped her preening and, without moving her head, turned her eyes upward to look at the old woman as if to say, "Hello." After just a few moments, both the old woman and the cat put their eyes back on what they were doing and returned to their work.

Gary poured another cup of coffee, grabbed another cookie, and took a big bite. "Wow," he muffled, "these really are great cookies."

The storm was still moving across the sky as the old woman began her story:

"Once upon a time not so long ago, there was a beautiful woman walking along the beach. She loved everything about the ocean; the smell, the feel of the sand under her feet, the sound of the ocean moving to and from the shoreline. Even the feel of the salt air on her skin made her feel alive. It seemed that no matter what the woman was confronting in life, she could always find solace at the beach.

"Now, this woman was one who let very little get under her skin. To her, life was a series of opportunities. Sometimes finding them was simple, other times it was more challenging. But one thing was for certain: there was always a solution — some way to move around, through, above or below a situation. Most of the time this woman, we'll call her 'Mae,' met life's challenges with a positive attitude. She had a gift for turning everything she confronted into an opportunity to grow, learn, or create something beautiful.

"Every day that she visited, the beach offered a new 'view' of life; some days the sands would be firm with a narrow shore line, while other days it would be fluffy and wide. There were days when shells were abundant, and other days when there were few from which to select.

"Mae never knew what the beach would have to offer her until she arrived each morning, and that prospect alone offered her hope. For you see, Mae had a sense of adventure. She was not one who wanted every day to be the same. Just as Mae viewed each person as a unique human being, she saw each day in the same manner. To Mae, Earth Mother and all her inhabitants were as sacred and special as were humans.

"There were many teachings Mae received from her daily visits to the beach, and one day she received a very big lesson. On this particular day, Mae approached the sandy terrain of the beach to find a plethora of shells blanketing the shoreline. *Oh, so many gifts! I may have to walk a bit slower this morning; there might be something wanting to go home with me!*

"As she found her slow, steady pace, she scanned the mounds of shells, searching for some special ones she enjoys collecting. A few 'gifts from the sea' in particular represented the Creator for Mae, specifically the corkscrew, hollow tubes, and the spiral patterned ones some call 'devil's eyes.' To Mae these special shells are 'God's eye.' She loves to gift these to individuals with whom she works as an outward reminder that God is always waiting to be of assistance.

"To Mae, Creator is a loving being that wishes only to give to us what our heart desires to keep us feeling loved. When Mae meets people feeling lonely, discouraged, or seeking to find a richer meaning in life, she loves offering them some gift she has found from the beach.

"To Mae, the ocean is a gift-giver — a fluid, flowing, manifestation of God's abiding love. On this particular day she heard a message as she walked along the shoreline. *'Every day people walk the beaches; some days there are many shells, other times only a few, and yet there is always some sort of treasure laid before those who take the time to pay attention.'* Mae is one who takes the time to notice, and yet this was a moment in which she realized how often she may not notice those treasures when she's somewhere other than the beach."

The old woman paused her tatting, examined the length, and then continued her work along with her story. "When Mae receives these gifts from the ocean, she always kisses them, touches them to her heart and says, 'Thank you.' Then she touches the ocean and sends a blessing for its well-being, for the creatures that live within its boundaries, and for the teachings she receives. Mae only picks up the shell that speaks to her heart. While she is clear that every shell is a gift, she also knows someone else may be looking for that particular one. As a result of the teaching she received, she now uses the same form of 'thank you' when she notices the many gifts given by Creator in the many other places besides the beach."

The old woman stopped tatting, bit the thread and tied a knot at the end. She placed her tatting supplies back into the black velvet bag, set it aside on the swing, then rose and walked toward Gary. As she placed the tatting into Gary's right shirt pocket, she said, "Mae has learned that she is a vessel by which the Creator can offer a gift to someone else who may be too busy to notice. She has learned there is an abundance of love, support and healing, if we take the time to notice, and really use our senses to discern how the gifts are to be used. Mae only picks up what she knows are to be taken, and always, always, gives something back to the Creator. For she has learned that to take without giving back is to not truly honor the gift. It is a wise soul who can really 'see' the gifts in front of them and allow their heart to give back something in return."

With that, the old woman reached into her pants pocket, pulled out a "gift," placed it in Gary's left hand and said, "Thank you for caring enough about others that you came here today to find your balance. We cannot give to others what we do not give to ourselves." She closed her eyes, patted his hand and said, "These are my words."

The old woman then placed the fabric back over the tray, turned and carried it into the cabin. The skies were beginning to lighten as the rain subsided and the winds calmed. Gary sat perfectly still, holding the gift in his left hand and looking at the tatted chain that hung from his right shirt pocket. There were no words in his head, only silence, as he felt warmth from the item in his hand. He felt a vibration within his palm that seemed to be directly connected to his heart; he could feel his heart pulsating through the gift in his hand, as though his heart and the gift were on the same universal stream of life.

He took a few deep breaths, as every cell in his body seemed to be singing a melody with the symphony of life that harmonized with all that is divine, and closed his eyes as tears began to flow down his cheeks. As he tasted the salt from his tears, the scent of ocean air filled his nostrils. Like the rhythm of the ocean, Gary could feel the waves of emotions as they rose and receded with each breath. He could feel the movement of sand beneath his feet as he sat perfectly still with the moment. From a distance he could hear the wings of the seagulls as they soared above the ocean in search of food. The warmth of the sun caressed his skin and Gary felt rays of hope embrace his heart.

Surely goodness and mercy shall follow me all the days of my life, and I shall dwell in the house of the Lord forever, sang through his heart. "Amen," Gary heard himself say out loud as he felt the stirring of life bring him back to the porch. As he gently began to move, he slowly opened his eyes, and looked down at his hand to see a "God's eye" shell resting in his palm. Joy filled Gary's heart as he parted his lips and whispered, "Thank you, 'Mae,' thank you."

He took one more deep breath and got to his feet. "Wow!" was all he could say as he surveyed the yard in front of him. *I do believe the grass has grown greener from that rain. Or is it just that my eyes can see more clearly?*

A hum hung in the air as the squirrels and rabbits emerged from their "safe places" and began to play in the moist grass. The squirrels glided along the wet ground from side to side as though using the moisture for their afternoon bath. Birds took flight from their nests in the trees to peck at the ground and find an evening meal for their babies. Gary watched as a bright red cardinal yanked and pulled until a fat worm popped from the rich soil. *Ah, you gotcha one! Your babies' bellies will enjoy that juicy morsel!*

Gary scanned the porch to see if there was anything he could do for the old woman before leaving. Although the sky was a lighter gray it was clear the rain would return. *Looks like she has everything under control,* he thought as he glanced at the twig basket by the porch steps. He reached into his pants pocket, withdrew some cash, and dropped it into the twig basket as he stepped off the porch.

He scanned the yard once again and this time noticed a neat stack of split wood sitting beside a pile of wood waiting to be cut. *You know, I believe the rain is a few miles off; I can take care of that.* He moved toward the woodshed, retrieved a maul and began to split the wood.

Gary swung the maul with strength and speed, and within fifteen minutes all the wood was split, stacked, and the latch secured on the woodshed from which he had retrieved the maul. Dusting off his clothes and hands, Gary moved along the yard to the trail that led to his car, pausing a moment as he turned to the cabin one last time.

"Thank you, Ma'am," was all he could say. He had no idea what she did or what had happened, but he knew his life would forever be changed. Gary moved along the path as he considered, *It matters not what others do; I'm accountable for me. I need to keep myself in check to make certain I am both giving and receiving. I am the one who has cheated others of the opportunity to give. I have always felt good inside giving to others; it makes me happy. The truth is, I've been selfish.*

A gentle rain began to fall, and Gary's thoughts continued as he picked up his pace. *When I don't let others give to me, I cheat them out of having the good feeling I get when giving to them. Well, doggone, I never thought of that before.* He got into his car, secured the door, put the key in the ignition and said out loud, "I have a lot to learn."

Just then, something caught his eye, and he glanced to the edge of the Forest. Standing beside each other were two magnificent deer. Gary watched the two stand perfectly still, as if to be hiding from his view. *Hmm, maybe they think I won't notice them if they stand still long enough. Wonder where they came from? They sure weren't there when I arrived.* He then remembered being "invisible" to the skunk ... or, was he?

The rain began to come down more steadily, and, when the automatic windshield wipers began to move the pair disappeared into the Forest, frightened by the movement. Gary put his car into gear, pulled out of the parking area, and headed down the road. *That "Mae" knew how to see the divine in all things. What else can I do that shows respect for things "not human?"* he wondered.

"I know," he responded, "when the apple trees in the backyard bear their fruit I'm pickin' some and taking them to everyone I know. There is no sense in having them go to waste like they usually do."

As he rounded the corner that led to his home Gary felt a smile widen on his face. "Speaking of *Giving and Receiving*," and he thought of his wife. *Mary Louise, you're such a jewel. If you want to make me more apple pie, I'm going to accept that, too. So what if I gain a couple of pounds? I'll just have to work out more.* His smile took a different shape as his mind took a "mischievous" turn. *Bet between the two of us we can find some ways to burn off those calories!* He chuckled as he accepted yet another gift — he allowed the rain to gift him a clean car!

High Noon

Blue skies blanketed the horizon as Elizabeth neared the clearing to the old woman's cabin. Leaves waved to each other throughout the Forest as a gentle breeze stirred the trees. It was late spring and the April showers had fed Earth Mother well. Birds sang of summer, as rabbits scampered hurriedly along the trails.

It appears babies will be abundant this summer, Elizabeth thought as she watched pairs of rabbits hop along the trail. *Multiplication,* she considered, *that's the word used to describe rabbits and spring.* Spring was alive with newness and growth as Elizabeth walked the path through the Forest.

As she stepped out of the Forest onto the clearing to the cabin her thoughts continued. *It's a good thing people don't populate as quickly as rabbits do, or we would be in a real mess!* She paused a moment to survey the lay of the land as her thoughts shifted to the colorful display of flowers and shrubs that caressed the cabin's porch. The backdrop of blue skies filtered through the treetops as dark brown branches covered with various shades of green veined through the sky. "A masterpiece of artistry," Elizabeth said aloud. Then her observations resumed in her head. *What a beautiful place; I wonder if she keeps all this up herself? And, I'll bet that old woman only goes to town once a month or so, given this walk!*

Elizabeth shifted her handbag from one shoulder to the other as she stepped along the cobblestone path that led to the porch. She was just shy of the porch when the front door opened and out came a woman carrying a fabric-covered tray. She was a colorful old woman, dressed in purple pants with a yellow sweater over a polka-dotted blouse, and leather strapped sandals on her feet. *She's a vivid display of late spring*, she observed, *almost as colorful as the flowers in her yard.*

The old woman placed the tray on a table between the porch swing and a willow branch chair, as Elizabeth stepped onto the porch and asked, "May I help you with something?" The old woman simply shook her head and nodded toward the chair.

"Well, thank you. That chair is a most welcome sight after that lengthy walk," Elizabeth said as she set her handbag beside the chair and removed her jacket. "The day has warmed nicely, but then, it is high noon, and that is when the sun is most intense."

She placed her jacket on the back of the chair and waited for the old woman to take a seat. "My name is Elizabeth, and I'm most grateful to be here today. You have a lovely place."

As though she heard nothing, the old woman removed the fabric from the tray, revealing a beautifully painted teapot along with two dainty cups and saucers. A small wicker basket, matching sugar and creamer holders and two delicate spoons were also waiting to be used. *Oh, those spoons look like the ones in Europe.* Elizabeth thought. *Hmm, I wonder if she's traveled abroad?*

After the old woman took a seat on the porch swing, Elizabeth took her place in the chair. "It was very nice of you to bring out some tea. You must have sensed someone was coming today?"

The old woman poured each of them a cup of chamomile tea, placed one close to the edge of the table closest to Elizabeth, then took the napkin covering off the wicker basket, that revealed freshly baked peanut butter cookies. The scent was delectable!

"Oh, my goodness, those look as good as they smell! That was most kind of you," Elizabeth said as she picked up her cup of tea. "It's almost as though you knew someone was coming."

Sipping a bit of the tea, Elizabeth noticed the old woman's hands. Much like the old woman, they were dainty and petite. The blue veins were visible on the top of her hands, as were several scratches and calluses, no doubt from working in her yard. Her nails were neatly trimmed with the cuticles pushed back, and a small golden band adorned the ring finger on her left hand.

Hmm, she must be married. No one mentioned she had a husband living with her. Elizabeth watched as she sipped her tea and munched a peanut butter cookie. *She reminds me of my granny; such a strong and powerful woman who spoke her mind. It didn't matter what a person thought, Granny always told it the way it was. There was no "neutral" ground as far as Granny was concerned. It was precisely as Granny saw it. Period. End of discussion. If you had a different opinion, that was fine, but you may as well have kept it to yourself, because Granny had no time for "idle chatter" about things that made no sense to her.*

Looking out at the yard in front of them, Elizabeth considered her granny. *Wonder what she's doing in heaven? No doubt busy making things, fixing them up, gardening, and ... oh, I am certain she's also showing people how things really need to be done. I wonder if she thinks of me? Oh, how silly is that? I know she does! I can hear her telling me how proud of me she is, all the time.*

Her thoughts were interrupted by birds who squabbled loudly as they attempted to secure "the best spot" for their nests. After a moment's pause she said, "Good grief; that huge oak tree, and they all want the same spot."

The old woman put down her cup, wiped her hands and mouth and picked up a black velvet bag. "Well, sometimes people want what someone else wants just because the other person wants it," the old woman commented, as she pulled out a wooden shuttle and some white thread and began to tat. "Even the animal kingdom has contrary characters to contend with," she concluded. "Makes no difference to some folk what they do have; they want what the other person has."

The sun hung high in the sky as the air filled with the warmth of the day. A tall cluster of sunflowers stood facing the sun as if to say, "Thank you for your warmth."

Elizabeth's eyes darted to the right as an orange-striped cat pounced onto the porch. "Oh, my goodness, you scared me to death," Elizabeth blurted out, as she gulped the last of her tea and placed the cup back on the saucer that sat on the table.

"Now, Gracie, that's no way to welcome a visitor," the old woman said, "I've told you to be a little more subtle when we have company. I don't get scared by your shenanigans, but others might be taken by surprise." Gracie leaped onto the swing, nestled up next to the old woman and began to purr as if to say, "Sorry about that."

"Atta girl," the old woman said as she paused her tatting and stroked Gracie for a few moments. "I need to get back to my work, and you behave for our company," she said as she tenderly patted Gracie on the head. The cat was most obliging and curled up in a ball beside the old woman.

The warmth of the sun penetrated Elizabeth's thoughts as she took a deep breath and reminded herself that she had made this journey for some assistance. Yet, Elizabeth wished only to savor the moment as she took yet another deep sigh. The smell of freshness filled her nostrils as she leaned back in her chair, closed her eyes and let out a long breath. She heard Gracie purring beside her friend, and chipmunks scurried about the yard as the birds now chirped a peaceful tune that seemed to indicate that all had found their "special" place to build a nest in preparation for the babies to come.

I wonder how life would be if every day were like this one. I wonder if the peacefulness of nature can teach me to find my "nesting place?" With her thoughts came a mental picture of a nest woven neatly into a circular pattern with bits of grass and pieces of string.

I suppose, like the birds, we do squabble and fuss, only to resign ourselves to a particular place. Fuss as we may, each of us does eventually acclimate to our surroundings — some of us more than others — but we do eventually "settle in."

As Elizabeth pondered such things, she heard Gracie uncurl from her balled up position. She looked over at Gracie just in time to witness as she arched her back high in the air, giving it a good stretch, and opening her mouth wide as if to yawn. *I suppose that is a yawn, huh Gracie?* She looked over at the old woman, who continued serenely tatting away as a white chain emerged beneath her hands.

"So, what do you suppose Gracie is thinking about?" Elizabeth asked the old woman, to which the old woman replied, "Probably not a thing. We humans seem to be the only creatures that live our lives thinking all the time."

Elizabeth thought about that and responded, "I suppose that's true."

"Of course it is," the old woman said. "Humans spend most of their time, both waking and sleeping, thinking about things. What they need to do, what someone said to them, how they are going to pay the bills, when they need to visit their sick friend, how they can stay healthy, when they are going to take a vacation or read a book or listen to some music ... and the list goes on. Trouble is, nothing's really getting done but the thinking. More time is spent fretting about what they have to do, should do or want to do, than in actually getting those things accomplished."

Silence hung in the air as the sun moved toward the West. The warmth of the afternoon was thick as the air became very still. *Wonder why we need to think all the time,* Elizabeth pondered. *I suppose it's because that's what we've been taught to do.*

As if reading her mind, the old woman continued, "We are taught to think all the time. Fact of the matter is, we are rewarded for being good thinkers. From the time we get up until we go to bed we are thinking, and most of the time it's the same stuff. We're thinking about what we have to do, what we did and what we have yet to do."

The old woman paused for a few moments, looked up at the sun and said, "There is much we can learn from the sun about such matters. Consider how the sun just moves all day, in a slow and steady pace that never changes. The sun is not in a hurry; it has its rhythm with life and moves with the ebb and flow regardless of what is happening in the world. Even if we can't see the sun it is still there, moving across the sky."

Elizabeth thought for a moment. *Yes, but the sun doesn't have to deal with other influences like we humans do. The sun doesn't think; it has no brain, just as it has no emotions. It's all part of why we are different from the world of nature.* She paused as she looked over at the old woman. *But, I sure can't say that to you; you'd probably think I was being disrespectful or something.*

The old woman tatted the chain until it seemed a foot long. She held it up, looked it over and bit the string loose from the shuttle. As she knotted the end, she said, "Every living thing has intelligence. The Creator gave everything the inner 'know-how' to do what it came here to do.

"The same thing can be said about how events and situations affect the 'feel' of things. Take that ol' sun. It moves around Earth Mother, shedding light everywhere it goes. Some days it is very visible to the inhabitants of Mother, and other days it is covered over by clouds; and, yet, we feel its presence. When it is visible we are warm, when it is covered we are cold, and still it's the same: it is the unchanging creation it was designed to be. It is only our *perception* that changes things."

Elizabeth thought for a moment, then said, "I don't think I understand that. How can our *perception* change the sun?"

"That's just it, it doesn't," the old woman replied. "Most humans are so busy thinking, they don't consider the sun unless it's high noon and the sun's burning rays are beating down on them. People notice the sun then." The old woman paused a moment and said, "People would otherwise give little regard to the sun, even though it is one of the steady and constant things in a person's life."

The old woman rose from the porch swing and stood for a moment scanning the beauty in front of her. "People are in all sorts of crazy-making business. Truth is, they don't really know what is real; the only thing they know is what they *perceive* to be real. It's really pretty funny if you think about it. Most people have no idea what they came here to do, but they think they are more intelligent than nonhuman creatures, and they certainly do not realize that nature is very smart!" She hesitated a moment, then concluded, "Smarter than most of us!"

As she moved toward Elizabeth, she continued, "The sun begins and ends peoples' days, and yet few even take the time to notice. What is *real* is that sun hanging in the sky each day, and the moon taking the sun's place at night. All that thinking stuff only detracts humans from those realities. Humans are so busy thinking that they forget to notice what is real. They 'think' those ideas are real, when in reality they are merely illusions, because they are based on what the human *perceives* to be real. And you know, all that thinking comes from reflecting on the past and fretting about the future. Seeing and feeling the sun's rays puts a person smack dab in the moment; then they can notice what is real and not something they've 'thought up.'"

As she extended the chain to Elizabeth she concluded by saying, "It's a very funny world we live in; makes my belly sore from laughing at all the silliness. But then, if we didn't have something to laugh about it would be a pretty boring world."

Elizabeth opened her hand to receive the gift, and the old woman placed it in her palm as she said, "If you want more of what you've experienced here, try thinking more about thinking less." She patted Elizabeth's hand and said, "These are my words."

Within the blink of an eye, the old woman was off the porch and heading to her garden. As she approached the rich green leaves of the vegetables she began to hum. The tune was familiar to Elizabeth and struck a chord in her heart. *Oh my goodness, Granny hummed that tune!*

The old woman had tied her hat on her head, slipped her gloves on her hands, and had begun to hoe the weeds from around the plants as the tune's melody stirred Elizabeth's heart. Still sitting quietly in the willow branch chair on the porch, she felt the warmth of tears emerge from her eyes. *This I know to be real, Granny — you are here with me at this very moment. Thank you!*

She held the tatted chain to her heart, thanked Creator for bringing her to this place, then gathered her belongings and set them in the chair. Elizabeth then took the fabric and covered the tray that held their midday treat. She picked up her things, walked to the edge of the porch, dropped a gift in a twig basket and headed down the path to the Forest.

The sun was now descending in the West, and Elizabeth noticed its beauty. "Thank you for your warmth today," she whispered as she stood at the edge of the Forest and turned one last time to look at the cabin.

The old woman was busy weeding the garden, in her purple pants, polka dot blouse and straw-brimmed hat. *I guess that yellow sweater isn't needed anymore,* she noted as she took in the beauty of the old woman's home. *The bright sun has taken care of keeping you warm now.*

Elizabeth felt the warmth of love flowing through her veins as she began her journey through the Forest. It all seemed so new, like she had never been on that trail before. *Goodness, this trail doesn't look familiar, but I know this is how I got here. Well, I guess I'm noticing the Forest now, whereas before I was too busy just thinking.*

She had to giggle at herself as she neared the clearing where she had parked. "Well, for heaven's sake, that wasn't such a long walk," she said. "Why did that seem like such a long walk before?"

She settled into her car and giggled again. "I've been sleepwalking through life with all my thinking." As she turned the key in the ignition, she glanced to the West to speak to the sun that burned brightly.

"Thank you, for getting my attention and for helping me find the *High Noon* in my life! The place that is *real* — the present moment; the NOW! As she continued to glance at the sun, she concluded, "Thank you for being a constant light to this world!"

Spring Reflections

"It is in the dance of life that we find our dreams, our passion, our purpose."

— These are her words.

HEAD TALK

What from this Spring season would you like to know more about?

Or, is there one thing you would like to *"think some more about?"*

What do YOU suppose you might discover in the Summer season?

HEART TALK

Of the stories in this season, pause and consider what Truths were revealed.

What of these *Truths* apply to YOUR Life right now?

As you consider the Spring of YOUR Life, what "jumps out" as a theme?

What can you learn for your own life from the Teachings of the East?

Summer is a time of warmth, playfulness,
and basking in the joy of outdoor activities.

Fed by Grandfather Sun, gardens abound, as nature mirrors the gifts
provided when living life in Faith, Trust and Forgiveness.

Summer is a time of youthful carefree play, where we can use our imagination and creativity to explore life. Through the spontaneity of play we learn how to laugh with life. During this time we observe the different lifestyles outside of family, develop relationship skills, and explore the possibilities in front of us. Through the actions of others we learn about duality: the difference between hypocrisy and integrity, being loved and unloved, trust and mistrust of others, fear and courage.

Through adolescence we begin to question what we were taught as children, and through trial and error we begin to exert our independence. After falling down and picking ourselves up, we ultimately learn how to forgive others and ourselves for choices made, and with the resiliency of youth, we learn how to move forward, allowing our experiences to teach us.

THE SOUTH

As we turn our face toward the South, we greet the teachers of faith, trust and forgiveness. With the help of mouse, we begin to notice the details of life as we begin to develop skills of discernment that help move us into our adult years. Once our roots are firmly planted into the richness of our faith in our divine Heavenly Father and Earth Mother, we find the Center point needed to trust the flow of life. And, with the help of dolphin, we find the "inner voice" that keeps us connected to our true self as we learn to move through the waters of life with grace and beauty.

"Now faith is the substance of things hoped for,
the evidence of things not seen."

— Hebrews 11:1 KJV

Standing in the Truth

It had been a while since the old woman had had visitors; a season had come and gone since the last young lady had appeared on her porch. Her garden had been planted and was reaching the peak of fullness. As the cornstalks reached to the heavens, zucchini and cucumber vines snaked along the mounds of soil, intertwining with the ever-so-full green bean bushes. The heat of summer ripened the tomatoes as red and yellow dotted the tall, lanky plants. Tied securely with strips of fabric, the green vines were supported on wooden stakes that leaned from the weight of the vegetables.

It was a tapestry of mosaic design, as the seeds that had initially been strategically placed in the soil in a manner that allowed space for growth, now wove a pattern of community as they grew toward one another. The old woman tended the needs of her garden with much loving care, as was evidenced by the abundance of fresh vegetables. Much like her squirrel friends, the old woman gathered and stored the fruits of the season for use in the winter months ahead.

As the old woman filled her apron with yellow summer squash, she caught sight of someone walking along the path to her cabin. Keeping her rhythm, she continued gathering ripened vegetables until, like the squirrel's chubby jaws, her apron could hold no more. As she straightened herself preparing to carry her riches to the cabin, she noticed that the young man who approached did not seem in a hurry, which told her much about him.

When he arrived at the porch, the old woman had already dusted off of herself the remains of her work and sat serenely on the swing. He walked up the steps and sat down on the willow branch chair closest to her. After clearing his throat, he came directly to the point and asked, "How is it that I can feel so much peace, and then all of a sudden things can change and I feel anxious and concerned?" He settled himself into the willow chair as he continued, "This most often happens with those I love; I seem to handle other people's challenges more easily." He adjusted his ball cap and leaned forward as he continued, "If you could help me understand how to keep that peace, especially when it is most needed, I would be most grateful."

The old woman took her hands from her lap, gathered her bag of handwork and began twirling the thread as she began to tell her story:

"When I awoke this morning the dark skies were clear. Stars dotted the darkness like diamonds on a black velvet cloth. As I listened to the early morning creatures and the dew dropping from the trees, peacefulness hung in the air. I gathered the lighted kerosene lantern, opened my writing journal and began recording the words of my heart. There is nothing like the early morning, when the night creatures are preparing to sleep and the day beings begin to stir, one's soul begins to speak. It is the time when the veil between the worlds is very thin.

"After writing awhile I turned the lantern off and looked outside. A mist had moved in and no stars were visible. Billowy clouds hung in the sky, as though someone had covered the night sky with a down comforter. The cool air moved, sending a shiver throughout my body; I reached for a blanket to warm myself. It was then I remembered that when Grandfather Sun is fully in the sky, the mist will be cleared away, warmth will follow and clarity will once again prevail. I know this to be true because I have seen this hundreds of times."

She paused for a few moments, put her handwork in her lap and gave the swing a push with her bare feet. The young man simply watched her and said nothing. A cool breeze stirred the warm air as the wind blew the lush green branches of the trees just off the porch, which was welcome in the heat of the summer day. As the swing became still, the old woman returned to her handwork and continued her story.

"Observing this typical morning routine provides great wisdom for all of us. Life can appear to be very clear and peaceful, and then an event in life occurs to change that peacefulness in the blink of an eye. We can take our eyes away from the task we are doing for just a moment, and something can happen that affects our peacefulness. We can feel the chill from the event, reach for something to comfort us and wait for the sun to appear, because we know it will. We can hold that space of knowing that peacefulness and clarity are still there; they are simply hidden by the event. If we can remain still and wrapped in the warmth of that knowing, we will assist with holding that peacefulness until the event passes.

"If we 'forget' and engage in the event, we merely add to the lack of peacefulness. It is always best to be in the moment of knowing 'this too shall pass' rather than to fuel the event with our human emotions. Unfortunately, it is easy to be drawn into emotions, especially when people we love become unhappy, or sad. And yet, it is precisely then that we are most needed to hold a space of peacefulness, trusting in the wisdom that there is a divine order to life. The event is merely a 'bump in the road,' an opportunity to pause and allow all that is divine to handle the event without our human emotions.

"This is a basic truth. We are given many opportunities during our lives to practice standing in the truth, by showing respect for the divine flow of life. When we are observers, these events will pass more quickly and with less intensity for all those around us. It is our choice; it is our opportunity to remain in that divine knowing that all is in perfect order.

In doing this, we add peacefulness to the 'time in between.' It is always about remembering the truth and honoring it, and that can only happen if we stand in the truth and stay in the moment.

"The trouble comes when we become fully engaged in someone else's 'drama.' We cannot think for someone else; we each have our own sacred way of living life, and we cannot choose someone else's destiny. If we engage in this, our 'head mind' pulls up old memories from our past that may, indeed, be similar to those of our loved ones.

"However, our old fears become the focus and they carry us into an endless stream of possible negative outcomes. This, of course, puts us smack dab in the future and our present moment peacefulness is gone. Why? Because this thinking is based upon fear, and that always thwarts our thinking. We become focused only on our 'head mind,' and our loved one's heart is completely ignored. When we do this, we actually fuel the fire of fear in our loved one's life.

"If we can merely look over our shoulder at our life, we will realize we lived through our choices, and that what happened in our past actually made us stronger for having experienced it. With this action, we will use our past as our 'advisor,' and with that assurance will know the same will be true for the one we love.

"Thus, we must trust the divine and natural law of the universe and get our human emotions out of the way in order for that unfolding to occur. Standing in the Truth is about honoring that everything we experience strengthens who we are—*at this very moment*. The truth? Why, it is very simple; Grandfather Sun is present, whether we see him or not, and sooner or later, he will be visible. Then, and only then, will clarity and warmth restore peacefulness to those we love who experience the 'event.' We offer our loved ones more assistance by holding that truth during their personal 'event' than by engaging in human emotions and reactions." She paused and said, "These are my words."

With that the old woman bit the end of the string, tied a knot and handed the tatted chain to the young man. She placed her handwork back in the bag, got up from the porch swing and walked to the garden. The young man had a smile on his face; it was true, this old woman had great wisdom. He was in no hurry to leave, this place felt sacred and he wanted to breathe in every ounce of truth he could take in. He knew he was firmly *Standing in the Truth*.

After some time he rose from the chair, walked to the steps, and dropped a gift in the twig basket. He said, "What an amazing day. Thank you, Grandfather Sun, for always bringing warmth, clarity and peacefulness—even if I cannot always 'see' it." And with that, he walked the path that led him home.

What's Love Got to do with it?

The scent of pine filled the air as the elderly gentleman placed his car in park, turned the key off and pulled it from the ignition. He paused for a moment, looked in his rearview mirror, and noticed the "aged" face that looked back at him. "What are you doing in my car, Grandpa?" he said to his reflection. "Dad always said I looked just like you, and darned if he wasn't right!"

"OK, so let's get this done, whatever it is we are doing here. Can't believe a man my age is coming to speak to a woman about his life." He picked up his bright yellow ball cap and placed it securely on his head. "If I lose any more hair, I will have to move the notch on this cap yet again." He fumbled with his keys as he placed them in his vest pocket. "Well, let's get this over with," he mumbled to himself as he stepped out of the car, clicked the car locks and headed down the path to the old woman's cabin.

He sniffed the air and said, "I love that smell! There is nothing like fresh pine to bring back memories I've had stowed away for a long time." As he moved along the path, he caught sight of a "mama" deer and her two fawns. *There was a time you would have run if I were in the area*, rambled through his head as he paused to watch the three of them. *Guess it's a good thing I don't hunt anymore.* After a few moments of stillness, *Never did really notice what nice looking creatures you are.*

Adjusting the cap on his head, he continued his thoughts. *Well, on to the task at hand.* He looked toward the path as he heard the deer tromping over twigs that had fallen from the trees. As he turned to look, all he saw were three white tails bobbing in the air. "Dang, those things are fast," he said, as he continued along the trail.

As he approached the clearing of the old woman's cabin, he noticed how neatly the yard was groomed. Flowers dotted the entire yard in no particular order. It was as though the old woman had scattered seeds and let them land wherever they chose. *Glad I don't have to mow this yard with all the curves and swerves around these plants.* As he walked among the daisies that trailed the stone walk to the porch, he took off his hat and gave a holler, "Good day, Ma'am."

She made her way to the porch with an armful of freshly cut daylilies. To the right of the steps was an old glass milk jug. The old woman bent down and placed the daylilies in the makeshift vase, and fluffed and shuffled those elegant creations of nature.

The gentleman politely stood by the willow branch chair until the old woman took a seat on the porch swing, and then took his seat in the chair. *Dang,* he relaxed back, *this is one comfortable chair; I would have figured it was stiff.* With that, the two sat in silence for a few moments. The old woman picked up the bag holding her handwork and began to "curl thread." The gentleman knew this was her "cue" for him to ask his question.

"Well, Ma'am," he began, "Guess you're wondering why a man my age would be coming here with a question." The old woman never looked up, but just kept moving her hands as the gentleman continued, "Reckon I am at the place in my life where I have time to ponder what my life was about. What with working long days and tending to repairs around our home, there has been little time to consider anything else.

"My wife used to ask me all the time, 'What do you really want from your life?' and that used to bug the heck out of me. Darned if I knew what she meant. I did what was expected, tried to be a decent person, a good provider, and treat people the way I wanted to be treated. Reckon I just thought each day was my purpose."

With that he leaned forward in his chair, pulled a toothpick out of his vest pocket and stuck it in his mouth. "My wife has been gone about five years now, and I have found myself thinking about that question... What do I really want from life?"

He relaxed back in his chair, looked out at the splashes of color before him and said, "You really have a lovely place. My wife always liked flowers and would forever ask me to help her plant some in the yard. I would complain that it was more to mow around, and the subject was dropped until the next spring season. For thirty-four years my wife asked me to plant flowers; and, for thirty-four years the answer was always the same." He paused for a moment and felt the silence around his words.

As the warm air caressed his skin, he caught a whiff of the scent of roses and began again, "My wife loved roses; she loved violets too." He paused a moment, then continued, "Always roses, always violets. Since she didn't have any in her yard, she had them plastered all over the house. I would come home from work and she would have another new 'find,' like some china teapot with tiny roses or violets around it, or a picture with violets plastered in the center. Sometimes, when the grass was getting tall, she would cut some of the tiny little violets out of the yard and place them in some teacup or an old jelly jar. Yes, Ma'am, she was forever finding something with roses or violets on it." With that he took a few deep breaths, "Dang, haven't thought about that in a long time."

Stillness hung in the air as the old woman kept twirling thread around her fingers. The gentleman closed his eyes as he remembered the day his wife passed.

He was on his way home from work when something told him to stop and get his wife some flowers. During those thirty-four years he had done that from time to time, but usually it was after he had done something that made her mad. This time something just told him to buy her some flowers on his way home.

As he took the roses to the counter to pay for them, his friend Roy, the clerk, looked at him and said, "Well, Andy, guess you did something to make Loretta mad again, huh?" To which he replied, "No, just being a thoughtful husband," and he winked at his friend. As he reached in the pocket of his jeans for his wallet, his cell phone rang.

Standing in front of his friend, he heard on the other end of the phone, "Mr. Hayes, I am sorry to have to tell you, but your wife has been in a terrible accident." His mouth went dry. "Is she OK?" to which the voice on the other end replied, "I am sorry to tell you, she passed away."

He remembered feeling nothing. Absolutely nothing. He thought he should be feeling something. But he didn't. When he tried, he could not think of any word or feeling for what he felt ... maybe numb? But numb isn't a feeling, he thought, so what's wrong with me? The only thing that broke the "numbness" was Roy. "Andy, are you OK?"

The question snapped him back, as he pulled the money from his wallet and handed it to the clerk. He mumbled something like, "Yeah, I'm OK," and headed toward his car.

The sound of a woodpecker pecking away at a huge oak tree just in front of the cabin brought him back to the present moment. He focused his eyes on the tree and remembered where he was. He turned to his left and noticed that the old woman was still moving her fingers and swinging.

"Guess I let my mind wander," he said, "Sorry about that. Now, where was I?" He placed another toothpick in his mouth, took a good look at the old woman and observed the contours of her face. *Bet she was a real looker in her day. Wonder if she had a husband ... Surely she did; she is such a nice looking old woman.*

His thoughts were interrupted as the old woman placed her handwork to the side of her swing and moved toward the cabin. As she entered the cabin, he wondered if he had said something that offended her. *Surely not. I was really just off daydreaming.* About that time she returned with two glasses of lemonade, one of which she extended to the gentleman. As she took her place on the swing, she said, "What I hear, sir, is that you loved your wife very much."

He swallowed a large portion of the lemonade, wiped his mouth with his hand and said, "What's love got to do with it? I was just talking about your flowers, and how my wife loved flowers." He stopped for a moment, and said, "I did love my wife, though; she was a good woman. Had to be to put up with me." He gulped down the rest of the lemonade and said, "That's really good stuff, thank you."

He noticed a birdhouse sitting on a post just to the left of the path he had taken to get to her house. As he watched the birds moving about — standing on the post, going in and out of the house, nibbling some seed on the tray around the house — he once again thought about his wife.

She had decided to take some painting classes one year. It seemed like every week she was asking him to make something in his wood shop that she would paint and place all over the house. Of course, it was mainly flowers, roses and violets, which she painted on the items. She had a birdhouse just like the one in the old woman's yard; except, of course, that it had violets painted all over it.

Realizing he had drifted away with his thoughts again, he asked, "So, how do you like living out here? Are you married? Do you have children?" The old woman sat quietly, just twirling her thread for what seemed like ten minutes. The gentleman was beginning to wonder if she had heard him, when he realized he had asked too many questions. He quickly said, "Never mind those questions; I forgot that I am only to ask one question." He adjusted the cap on his head and said, "I really don't know why I came here today. I heard about your stories and have seen people change their life as a result of coming here; they seem to be happier. So, I figured I would come here and see what story you have for me."

He sat back in his chair, extended his legs straight out in front of him and said, "I do feel very comfortable and peaceful here. I can understand why you live here. So, let me just say I realize I have held onto a lot of regret that I did not do more for my wife. Like I said, for thirty-four years she asked for flowers in the yard, and, for thirty-four years I ignored her request. But then, I already told you that. Reckon I wish I had let her plant those flowers. I can see how lovely your yard is with them growing everywhere. So what if I would have had to mow around them? Sitting here on your porch, drinking this good lemonade, listening to the stillness and smelling those flowers, I realize life is very good."

With that he crossed his legs at the ankles, tilted his head back and looked over at the old woman. She seemed to be lost in the work she was doing. He continued, "Guess I just never realized my wife really loved those flowers; I thought she just thought they were pretty. It was more than that for her, though."

He paused and moved the toothpicks in his mouth from one side to the other. "Reckon love had everything to do with it. All I knew about love was how it existed between a husband and wife, not something as simple as flowers. Truth is, I had no idea who my wife was as a person. I just knew she was kind, she cared about people, and took real good care of me. She wasn't one for lots of conversation; she preferred working in her house, painting flowers on anything she could." He paused for a few moments, feeling a pull at his heart; he realized he missed his wife.

The old woman broke the silence and said:

"Flowers put love in one's life. They touch the human soul to such a depth there are no words. Flowers ask nothing of anyone; they snuggle deep in the ground during the winter months allowing the stillness to feed them. In the quietness of Earth Mother, they dream — they dream of what will come after their rest. Flowers do not ask a lot of questions; they do not ask where they will go when warmth revisits Earth Mother.

"They waste no energy asking questions that only the Divine knows. Instead, flowers trust the natural order of life. Without question they know that their Creator, the one who created their beauty has everything in perfect order. If winter seems extremely cold, or extends longer then the previous season, flowers do not disrespect the Creator by asking why, or what they did to deserve the long winter.

"They surrender instead to the natural flow of energy that exists within the Earth Mother. They have no fear, no doubt, that when the time is at hand for them to emerge, all that is in harmony will nudge them from their rest. Flowers know within their core that they are a part of something greater than themselves — that they are the outward expression of their Creator's love."

The old woman held the tatted chain to her teeth, bit the string and knotted the end securely. She placed the chain in her lap as she put her shuttle and string back in the black velvet bag that held her handwork. She lifted the chain and said, "There is no human being on this planet that can craft such beautiful creations; there is no inventor who can dream of such intricate designs, colors and textures as those you will find with flowers. The most amazing beauty of it all is, if they are allowed to do what comes naturally, they flourish year after year. Humans can learn much from the flower family, if they will pay attention, trust, and respect these amazing teachers."

She handed the gentleman the beautiful chain and said, "Love has everything to do with what you and your wife shared; she is in her resting place, waiting for and trusting in her next divine unfolding." With that, she closed her eyes, sniffed the air and said, "These are my words."

The gentleman extended his hand and received the tatted chain with the warmth of knowing; it was his wife's heart he accepted. Tears burned his eyes as the scent of roses caressed him in a fragrant embrace. His head seemed to be spinning as he felt the ground move beneath his feet. Like waves on a turbulent sea, emotions surfaced that he could not control.

The humming in his ears was like bees pollinating flowers; swirling and turning, he felt as though another dimension was opening up as he felt the tender touch of his wife's lips upon his cheek.

As tears streamed down his cheeks, he spoke, "Thank you for learning how to love so well, my beautiful Loretta." He sat in the chair for a few more moments, not wanting the experience to end.

He looked over to the porch swing and the old woman was gone. As he felt the ground beneath his feet, he allowed his eyes to focus on the landscape directly in front of him. He took some deep breaths, pulled a handkerchief from his pocket and wiped his eyes. He realized, *That was a long time coming,* as he took yet another deep breath and felt his emotions calm. *It is time for me to get home before dark. I have a lot to do to prepare for tomorrow.* He moved to the porch steps, dropped a gift in the twig basket, and started down the trail.

As he reached his car, he turned once more toward the old woman's cabin. "Thank you so much," was all he could say, as he got into his car, turned the key and drove off. "I know Gibson's Landscape will be open tomorrow; I'll get there first thing in the morning."

As he looked down at his left hand where his wedding ring was still in place, he said, "*What's Love Got to do with it?* It's everything! We're getting that flower garden going, Honey. And I'm starting with roses and violets!"

Wisdom

Hues of red ascended from the horizon as the darkened skies awakened from the slumbering night, as though someone had taken a brush and painted streaks of red and orange across the sky. She remembered, *Red skies in the morning, sailors take warning.* "Reminds me of summers on the bayou," she said, "The damp air would penetrate your skin like static clinging to your skirt showing every curve in your body."

As she pulled her truck off the road onto the slightly graveled parking spot, she spotted the walking path to the old woman's cabin. "There is something about early morning that stirs my soul," she said, as she stepped out of her truck. She reached up toward the heavens and lifted her feet from the ground in a luxurious stretch. "Good morning, everyone!" she said out loud. "Looks like we'd better 'make hay' while the sun's up, because rain's a-comin'." With that she stepped onto the path and began her journey to the old woman's cabin.

As she approached the clearing, she noticed the cabin was dark. *Gee, is the old woman even up yet? Seems to me a wise person knows morning's the best time of the day for communicating with all that's divine, because this is when the veil between the worlds is thinnest.* "We'll see what she knows," she said, somewhat skeptically.

Just shy of the porch, she could see a light filtering through a window; as she got closer she noticed a candle lit on the table. Just to the right of the candle was a leather bound journal, a fountain pen and a single feather. She strained to get a closer look at the feather without getting caught peeking. *Is that a hawk or a falcon feather?* She stared more intensely. *Surely it's not an owl feather; that could be some very powerful medicine. Wonder if she's aware of what she's working with?* Realizing she was intruding on this woman's personal space, she pulled back from the window.

The sun's ascension was evident as light filtered the cloud-filled sky. She surveyed the old woman's landscape. *Very nice. Looks as though someone has helped her arrange her flowers in precisely the best way for pulling the energy into her home. Wonder who she hired for that? No doubt someone who understands those techniques, although I can see they don't completely understand the teachings of proper arranging.*

As she headed toward the front porch, the old woman came out of her cabin with an armful of rolled up newspapers. The woman said, "Good day, do you need any help?" to which the old woman extended her arms, accepting the offer. The woman put down her large bag and took a handful of the rolls. She then followed the old woman to a wooden container located in the back of the yard just to the right of a shed. As they approached, the old woman moved her armful of newspaper rolls to her left and lifted the lid with her right as she placed the rolls onto an already tall stack. She held the lid up and moved aside, allowing the woman to place the rolls she carried into the container. "Thank you," said the old woman in a soft voice, as she closed the lid.

As the woman followed the old woman back to the front of the cabin, she noticed the old woman's garden rich in color from the abundance of vegetables! Her eyes glanced to the right as she surveyed the planting utensils, neatly arranged on a wooden stand full of clay pots, troughs, spades and various sizes of glass jars. *Hmm. I wonder if she does all that herself? Seems like an awful lot of trouble for a single person.* As they reached the porch, she noticed the old woman's bare feet. *My goodness, she needs a pair of shoes for working in the yard.*

The old woman turned and pointed to a willow branch chair and said, "Have a seat, I'll be back directly," as she wiped her feet on a rag rug just in front of the door and entered the cabin. As the screen door slammed in the wood frame of the entryway, the woman took her seat. *Wow, it's been a while since I heard the slamming of a screen door; reminds me of Granny's farm.*

Within a few moments the old woman returned with a tray full of goodies. There were cups, a small ceramic teapot, a glass jelly jar holding something red, and a small wicker basket with a blue cloth wrapped around some mysterious goodies. The woman's mouth watered as her stomach growled, reminding her it was time for breakfast. As the old woman set the tray on a small table on the porch, the woman noticed that the old woman's feet were still bare. *She's feeling the ground under her feet; that's a good teaching to follow.*

The old woman moved the table between the willow branch chair and the porch swing, paused, and placed her hands over the food basket. *Oh,* the woman realized, *she's blessing our food; that's a good teaching to know.* The old woman then handed the woman a cup of hot chocolate and a saucer with a napkin on it. She then took a saucer for herself, placing on it a steaming hot biscuit from within the blue fabric. She buttered and jellied it, then placed her napkin over it and took her treasures to the porch swing. She placed the napkin-covered saucer carefully on the seat of the swing and returned to the small table, where she poured herself a cup of hot chocolate and took her seat on the swing. Carefully balancing her morning delights, she closed her eyes, took a deep breath and mumbled a few words. As she opened her eyes, she lifted the hot chocolate to her lips and, ever so carefully, blew on the hot brew, then took a small sip.

The woman watched her as she gracefully and almost reverently swallowed the brew, repeating the ritual for several moments, until she placed the cup on the swing and picked up the napkin-covered saucer.

She then continued this ritual with the biscuit in nearly the same manner. *Hmm, that must be some special ceremony she's learned. Wonder what tradition that is from.*

Then the woman turned her attention to her own cup and began sipping the hot chocolate. *Well, it might be a warm morning, but this hot chocolate tastes exceptionally delicious today; wonder what her recipe is. After a few more sips she continued, There is something very different about this brew; wonder what it is. Maybe some magic potion that helps one find answers within? That is what this woman does; at least, that's what I've been told. Wonder what the ingredient is.*

She was interrupted from her thoughts as the old woman spoke, "What brings you here?"

The woman licked the chocolate from her lips and said, "I'm really not certain. I feel very strong within myself, have studied with some amazing teachers, and have practiced many different ceremonies and rituals from a host of indigenous tribes. So, I do know many amazing truths from around the world."

She took another sip of her hot chocolate and said, "By the way, my name is Marissa, and you have a lovely place. I was wondering what special ingredient you have in this hot chocolate. It is my understanding that you help people find new purpose for their life, and I was wondering if there is something in this hot chocolate that allows that truth to become clear."

With that, Marissa drank the rest of her brew and said, "May I have some more, or have I had enough?" She looked at the old woman, who was finishing her jam-covered biscuit.

The old woman wiped her lips with her napkin, then picked up her cup and took a sip. "If you want some more, help yourself. There's more in the kitchen."

Marissa sat there trying to be very still and notice if she felt any difference. *Do I feel a bit woozy?* Then she looked at the old woman and said, "Well, does it take two cups to bring the visions for clarity, or will one cup do it? I'm really not feeling anything but a desire for a second cup," to which the old woman replied, "Then drink another cup."

Without hesitation Marissa poured herself another cup and repeated her statement, "So, does it take two cups to bring visions for clarity?" The old woman responded, "What clarity is it that you seek?"

Marissa downed her second cup and, without even taking a breath, said, "I am curious about what teachings you have that might assist me along my path." As she wiped the remaining chocolate residue from her mouth, she continued, "I feel a sense of curious peace after drinking that potion. May I ask what ingredients you use?" She settled back in her chair, closed her eyes and did an "internal" scanning of her body. As she began a series of deep breathing exercises, she made some sounds as she held her thumbs to various fingers on each hand.

The old woman stopped her handwork for a moment and glanced over at Marissa, then promptly returned to her tatting. The wind stirred the still air and the scent of rain hung heavily in the air. The distant rumbling stirred Marissa from her silence, "I do believe it's going to start storming; I need to get about what I came here to do." With that she pulled a smudge stick from her bag, lit it with a match and began fanning it all around herself. She extended the stick to the old woman, who never so much as lifted an eye to acknowledge what was occurring.

It was then Marissa began, "I have studied the indigenous ways of many cultures, through diligent reading, searching the internet for facts, researching various teachers of many forms of worship, and traveling all around the world; I have developed quite a 'medicine bag' of tools. I have great respect for all those seeking to live their lives in peace and harmony. It has been my life's mission to gather all the various tools used in ceremonies from all over the world."

She paused for a moment as though gathering more "evidence" of her wisdom, and continued, "You know, I have thirty-five various shapes and sizes of rosaries, and six different forms of scriptures that have been translated and interpreted by the most scholarly theologians of the world. I am proficient in several languages so the interpretations are not lost. It has been my passion to learn these ways, in order to write a book that offers all the shared wisdoms to others, so they can also grow in wisdom and reach enlightenment."

Marissa put her smudge stick and matches back in her bag, and then pulled three sets of beads from underneath her shirt to display the ones she wore around her neck. Then she pulled what looked like a scarf from her bag and said, "This has been blessed by His Holiness, and these beads were gifted to me by a priest, a monk, and a High Priestess of the highest order." With that, she closed her eyes as she touched the pieces that were, indeed, sacred to her.

She opened her eyes and looked at the old woman as if anticipating a response. When the only response she received was silence, Marissa looked at the old woman and said, "Have you heard what I have told you?"

The old woman continued tatting, curling the thread with a rhythm that was almost intoxicating. As Marissa watched her hands, she wondered, *Why isn't she talking? Does she not understand what I am telling her? Perhaps she does not realize the many beautiful forms of worship that exist outside this dense Forest. Perhaps she's spent her entire life knowing only what is here.*

She cleared her throat as she stood up and reached for her bag. "Perhaps I've made a mistake in coming here. Apparently you do not care about the many beautiful forms of worship eighty percent of the world shares. I have heard of your work and am confident that you have helped others, so I felt it my duty to see what I could learn about another way of gaining wisdom. I do thank you for your time and for the work you do for others. No doubt, they needed whatever you had to say."

With that she stepped off the porch. She paused for a moment and turned to the old woman, "What is the practice you use that makes people change their life? I simply cannot leave without knowing something. I most certainly respect what you do; just give me something I can take with me."

Without hesitation the old woman bit the thread, slipped a knot on the end and extended the beautiful tatted chain to Marissa. "Wisdom comes from within, from having a personal relationship with your Creator. Words merely fill the air; it is love from the heart that springs forth compassion that changes lives. And, it is the courage within each person to examine his or her own heart and to take action accordingly that brings wisdom." She placed her handwork in the black velvet bag, set it beside her and got up from the porch swing. "These are my words." And she headed toward her garden.

Marissa was dumbfounded. She watched the old woman, with her bare feet, walk to her garden. *Perhaps I don't understand what she does,* ran through her head as she moved back to the porch and dropped a gift in the twig basket sitting by the porch steps.

The clouds had become quite thick as the rumbling of thunder became louder. *The storm is very close; time for me to leave.* She quickly walked along the path back to her truck. *There are mysteries that cannot be explained but only experienced. Perhaps it is time for me to stop asking so many questions and just listen. I am tired. I would love to just enjoy the space in which I live.* She felt a sadness, *I am never there; I am always living out of a suitcase, always sleeping on yet a different bed. It's hard to imagine sitting still.*

She unlocked her truck, and, as she opened the door, out fell a brochure. It was one she had just picked up at the metaphysical bookstore in town. As she positioned herself in the truck she felt the comfort of the cushion she had purchased to support her back. She took a deep breath as raindrops began to fall ever so gently on the windshield. She examined the brochure; it was about an upcoming trip she could participate in that would take her through the sacred caves just outside Utah. *Only $1,500 plus the cost of travel, accommodations, food, and, of course, the purchase of the spiritual teacher's book. What a bargain!* she thought as she tossed the brochure in the passenger's seat. Then she said, "Just what I need: another 'retreat.'"

She started the truck, put it in gear, and headed onto the main road as she said out loud, "I *am* tired. I have learned so many different truths, and they are all mixed up in my mind. Perhaps the old woman is correct; it is time for me to just 'be' with myself. Sit with all these teachings and allow my heart to discern what is comfortable for me."

She looked down at her left hand and noticed her wedding ring. *George would be happy if I stayed home more, if I asked fewer questions and just listened to him tell a story or two. He's really an amazing man; I am most grateful for his patience.* And she lifted her ring to her lips and kissed it as she said, "I love you George, you are *Wisdom* in action." As she felt tears roll down her cheeks, she realized, *You know, George, I really know nothing of what you dream for your life or what you believe to be true. I have made my life about me, without regard for you.* As the tears continued she said, "Time for me to listen to your heart; I'm certain you have wisdom waiting to be shared."

With that she proceeded home — to the place she knew little about. However, that was about to change! *How does that old woman do that?* she wondered. Then she quickly answered her own question with, "Who cares? It works!"

Love Birds

"Would you look at that corn!" the young man said to his wife. "What is the saying about the Fourth of July?"

Emily was busy filing her nails as she commented, "Come on, John; I guess you have been in the city too long. You remember how the saying goes: think!"

John looked down at his odometer and said, "I think we are nearing our turn. Would you double check our directions, Em?"

Emily put down her nail file and pulled a sheet of paper from the console between them. "Let's see: it says to turn right at mile marker 376." She looked up quickly and continued, "Slow down a bit, John, I need to read these road signs."

As John slowed down, he commented, "And it's knee high by the Fourth of July."

Emily pointed to a small green sign they were approaching and said, "I think that says 376. Yep, that's it, John, put on your turn signal."

John snapped a look at her and said, "Already a step ahead of you, thank you very much." Grateful he had learned to control his Irish temper, he threw her a smile to make certain she knew he was merely playing with her. He maneuvered the truck to the right at the green 376 sign and said, "OK, there's the turnoff to the left that Mom told us to watch for, and I think we have found our parking area."

Emily put her manicure tools in her purse, then quickly looked into the mirror and said, "Don't know why I care what I look like; your mom said this old woman is 'a la natural.'" She moved her bangs to one side and said, "Remind me why we are visiting this lady?" as she opened the truck door and stepped onto the land.

John closed the door of the truck, clicked the key locks, and responded, "We are here to learn how to be good parents. How come you don't remember that? I thought this was your idea, anyway."

Emily reached for John's hand as they started down the path and replied, "Oh, don't pretend you aren't as interested in knowing how to be a good parent as I am. We have had this conversation too many times, so quit pretending you don't care." She squeezed his hand, then stood on her toes and gave him a peck on the cheek. John felt the warmth of her words almost as much as he felt her kiss.

He stepped a bit ahead of her. "I'll take one for the team so the cobwebs won't hit you. How's that for being a 'thoughtful' guy?" he said as he reached for a stick to wave in front of him to knock down the cobwebs. "It sure feels good to be in the woods. Remember how much fun we had as kids exploring the woods behind your grandparents house?"

He stepped around a pile of deer droppings and said, "Watch your step, Em." As they swerved around the fresh droppings, he continued, "Good thing your grandparents didn't know everything we did in those woods, or we would have been in big trouble!"

Emily giggled, and said, "You certainly are right about that!" She looked to the right and saw the movement of something very colorful. "Did your mom say that old woman wore brightly colored clothes?" She strained to look more closely and then stopped. "No, that's not the old woman; whatever is that, John?"

John stopped and looked back at Emily to see which way she was looking. Then he turned and looked in the direction she was staring.

"What the heck is that?" He strained a little more and both of them stopped dead in their tracks.

"Well, I'll be darned, Emily, people really do still hang out their clothes to dry! Look at those clothes blowing in the wind!" There was an excitement in John's voice that Emily had not heard for a long time. She smiled, looked at John and said, "You sound like you are sixteen again!" She came up behind him and hugged his back.

John smiled and reached his arms behind to hug her arms. "I do love you, Em; and, you know," he turned around and touched her face tenderly, "I feel sixteen again!" With mischievous eyes he said, "Want to 'revisit' some old memories? We have plenty of time." He wrapped his arms around her waist, then leaned down and kissed her on the lips, softly but passionately.

Emily responded to his kiss and then gently leaned back and said, "What a lovely thought, my sweet; maybe on our way back." John smiled at her and said, "You sure know how to light my fire! OK, I'll hold you to that!" With that he kissed her again, turned toward the clearing and said, "Glad you are so practical. I guess if you're going to be a doctor, you'd better be the one who is!"

Emily smiled and sighed, "Only one more year of residency and then we can begin to breathe!"

As they approached the cabin the colorful clothes waved in the wind. "Mmm, nothing like the smell of clean clothes," Emily said, as she led the way to the porch. John eyed the split wood neatly stacked in preparation for the approaching cold weather and said, "Someone cares greatly for the old woman; look at all that wood!"

The front door opened and out walked a small, gray-haired woman carrying a rather large wooden serving tray neatly covered with a bright orange fabric.

"Hello," said Emily, as John moved to hold the door open for the old woman. "Can I help you with that?" he asked. The old woman moved passed him as though she did not hear him, and placed the tray on a sturdy wooden table. She responded by pointing to a chair on the other side of the porch swing and said, "You may move that chair closer to the other one," and she nodded to a willow branch chair sitting by the wooden table. John quickly moved the chair close to where Emily had taken a seat.

The old woman removed the orange fabric to reveal a pitcher of lemonade, glasses and a basket filled with sugar cookies. The scent of the cookies filled the air as John's stomach began to growl. "Wow, that's one delicious smell you have there," he said, as he reached for the pitcher and poured a glass for Emily, the old woman and himself.

"That's quite nice of you to bring us such a delectable treat," he said handing Emily some of the "goodies" the old woman had provided. As the three of them sat enjoying the treats on the porch, John spoke, "Those were delicious cookies, Ma'am; thank you."

The old woman started her handwork as John continued, "My name is John, and this is my wife, Emily. We've been married about five years and Emily's soon to complete her education, so we are thinking about starting a family." He leaned back in his chair and continued, "With the world being in such a state of change, we want to make certain it's a wise decision to bring a child into all this chaos."

Emily dusted the crumbs from her cookie onto the napkin in her lap and placed it on the tray, then cleared her throat and said, "John and I know we will be good parents. Both of us have supportive families that will be marvelous grandparents as well as a source of support for our children and for us. I guess the biggest concern we have is how the rest of the world will affect our children — you know, we can't be with them 24/7, especially when they start school, and we know they will have friends they'll want to visit and spend time with."

She took a drink of her lemonade and continued, "John and I feel very lucky to have had parents that brought us up in church, stayed married, and lived in the same community our whole lives. We know the majority of the world has had different experiences. So, how do we know we can give our children what they need in order to grow up happy?"

A white chain emerged from the old woman's busily moving fingers as she began her story:

"It was a blustery, cold day in the lowlands of Ireland. A blanket of green covered the hills, divided into a mosaic pattern by stoned walls and ivy-veined bushes. Smoke rose from the thatched roof cottage as goats grazed the open field for early morning nourishments. A light was evident from a small window and voices of laughter could be heard inside the cottage. Birds chirped with delight as they chimed into the melody and added to the tones of life.

"To the left of the cottage was a small flower garden that offered a rainbow of color to the landscape, where hummingbirds and bees found nourishment and pollinated the flowers. Giggles could be heard as the front door opened and out ran three young children, followed by a very hairy dog, two cats, a man with a basket and a woman carrying a black bag.

"The 'group' moved to a rather large black vehicle as the woman climbed into the driver's side. 'You all take care of your dad today and I'll see you tonight,' the woman said as she turned the key and started the engine. 'Study hard, do your chores and be good to each other,' she said as the kids moved away from the car and waved goodbye. 'Don't work too hard, Mum, we love you. See you tonight!' shouted the tallest kid. The mom drove off as the kids chased the car waving their hands in the air.

"Then Dad yelled to the kids, 'You have fifteen minutes to play, then back to work.' The three younger children headed toward the back of the house where a brightly colored swing, slide and teeter-totter awaited their arrival. The dog chased the cats as the entire group assumed their early morning routine.

"Once inside, the dad moved to the kitchen table to inspect it for any crumbs or residue from breakfast, then examined the sink. Happy with what he saw, he disappeared into the next room and returned with his arms full of brightly colored baskets that he placed on a large kitchen table.

"After strategically placing the baskets an equal distance apart, he retrieved three glasses from the kitchen cabinet, filled each with water, and placed them to the right of the baskets. The dad opened the front door and yelled to the children, 'Come on in, play time is over.'

"Once the children entered their home, washed their hands, and smoothed their hair, they took their places at the table in front of the colorful baskets. Very methodically, the children took their places, reached for one another's hands, and listened as their dad spoke a few words of blessing for their lives, their health, and offered gratitude for the watchful eye of God. Almost in unison the three kids and their dad made the sign of the cross, and the children began unpacking school items from their baskets.

"It didn't take long for the middle child to decide he was bored with the assignment. Wearing a mischievous grin, he looked around at which of his sisters he could pester. *Well, Fionn's always good for a few laughs, and she looks awfully serious, so maybe I'll 'rattle her cage.'*

"Their dad was not in sight, so Ron took a small piece of paper from the corner of one that he was working on and rolled it into an ever-so-tiny ball that he secured with some of his spit. He watched for his dad, and when it was clear he was not within eyeshot of the room, he fired that spit ball at Fionn. Of course, Fionn let out a holler as if she'd been shot, and their dad walked briskly into the room.

"'What's up?' their dad asked as he hurried over to Fionn. 'Ron spit on me, how gross is that?' Their dad turned to Ron and asked 'Is this true?' Ron shot back, 'I did no such thing.' After a few moments of back and forth accusations and denials, their dad put his finger to his lips and simply said, 'No more talking. We will sit here until whomever did this takes responsibility for his or her actions.'

"By now the other sister, Geraldine, has stopped working on her assignments and observes the dialogue. She doesn't say anything because she knows the dispute is between her brother and sister, and therefore isn't any of her business. She trusts that her dad will get to the bottom of what really happened, so she goes back to her math assignment.

"Their dad, Fionn and Ron sit in silence for what seems like fifteen minutes when Ron finally says, 'OK, I did it. I'm sorry, Fionn; I didn't think it would bother you that much. I was just trying to have a little break from studies.' Fionn looks at her brother and says, 'It's gross to have someone's spit on you, but I forgive you. Next time you want a break, just say it and don't drag me into it.'

"Ron hangs his head and says, 'I am sorry, Fionn, and I promise to throw a big paper wad, without spit, the next time.' Fionn can't resist laughing as Ron lifts his eyes and smiles. Their dad tells Fionn to get back to her studies as he taps Ron on the shoulder. Ron gets up from the table and follows his dad outside; he knows he's earned a 'talking to.' Dad simply tells Ron the importance of telling the truth and taking responsibility for his actions.

"Ron and his dad go back into the house as Ron settles back into his studies. He looks over at Fionn and says, 'I know it's your night to bring in the wood; how about I do it instead?' Fionn looks up and says, 'Sounds good to me.' Then they all get back to the tasks at hand."

The old woman paused her storytelling and took a few deep breaths. Emily looked at John and reached for his hand. John squeezed her hand as he kept his eyes on a birdhouse just in front of the porch. He watched as a "mama" and "papa" bird flew back and forth retrieving worms from the soil for their babies. When either the mama or papa bird returned with a nice fat worm, little beaks emerged from within the nest of twigs and chirped with delight for what their mama or papa brought. John felt a tug at his heart as he observed this natural order of life occur without so much as a word being spoken. *But of course there will be no words; birds don't speak*, John smiled. *However, those little ones are certainly letting their mama and papa know they are happy! And, Mama and Papa are sure letting them know the importance of sharing; just look at them pull that worm away and offer it to another baby.*

Mesmerized by what he was observing, John allowed his heart to really connect to the family in front of him. Being the "dreamer" of the family, he stayed with his feelings and imagined what it would be like for Emily to be that mama bird. *She would be an amazing mama. Em's so practical, so organized, so ... opposite from me! I would be a great dad because I love the closeness of family, and gain much reward from giving to others. Em could pursue her medical dreams and I could actively be involved with the family.* He paused his thoughts as he looked over at Emily. *If I stay home and be a full time dad that sure will get the family talking!*

Emily was looking ahead at the family of birds as well, and tears rolled down her cheeks. When she felt John looking at her, she quickly wiped them away and smiled. *I love you so, John Wood; you would be such a great father. I don't know why I have even hesitated with starting a family.*

John seemed to know precisely what his wife was thinking, and, as he smiled at her, he leaned over and gave her a peck on her cheek. As they looked into one another's eyes they knew the decision was made. No words were spoken, and yet, communication between their hearts was very loud and clear.

The old woman tied a knot in the end of the tatted chain, placed her handwork in the black velvet bag and set it to the side of the porch swing. She held the chain in her fingers as she looked out toward the woods and spoke. "Life brings us opportunities to feel every emotion, every feeling; and, yet, we continue moving toward what our heart truly desires. One must be a fearless warrior to move forward even when our head tells us to be scared. Our head mind has many reasons to keep us from our heart's desires, and it is the faith and strength within our heart that moves us always toward what is true love."

She rose from the porch swing, turned to John and Emily and extended the tatted chain. "It is a lucky boy or girl that comes to teach you how to expand your heart even more. These are my words." And with that she moved to her garden.

Emily placed the tatted chain in her pocket, extended her hand to John and moved toward the porch steps. John paused, dropped a gift in the twig basket, and squeezed his wife's hand. "You know, Em, this has to be one of the best days of my life. Let's go home and make a baby!"

Emily giggled as her cheeks flushed from his comments. She smiled at her husband and said, "Why do we have to *wait* until we go home?"

They both laughed and turned back to take one more look at the old woman "playing" in her garden. After a moment of silence, they turned to the birdhouse, and, as though speaking from one mind, said, "*Thank you for your story.*"

As John and Emily began their walk along the path, Emily paused, looked at him and said, "How do you suppose the old woman knew I am studying to be a doctor? Or for that matter, that you are Irish?"

To which John replied, "Does that really matter? Let's not take the magic out of the moment!"

With that, they moved quickly along the path until they were certain they were out of sight of the old woman. All that could be heard were soft giggles and whispers as the movement of bushes and small saplings swayed to the rhythm of the *Love Birds*.

A Magnificent Oak

The old woman pointed a bony finger at a huge, magnificent oak tree just to the left of the porch where they sat. "See that old oak tree?" she said to the gentleman sitting beside her. "That tree is probably 200 years old. It's been standing there longer than this house has been here. Why, that old tree used to be surrounded by dozens of trees until the land was cleared to build this cabin. That tree has seen many storms, snowfalls, and steamy hot days. Truth be told, she's housed several generations of squirrels and birds, not to mention being a safe haven for critters running from predators.

"Yes, sirree, that tree's been holding her place in the Forest since she was an acorn fallen from her mama. She landed onto the ground of Earth Mother, fed from the rich soil, and was nourished by the rain and snow. The fallen leaves from the elders standing around her also enriched her growth. It took a community to help her become what she is today."

The air was humid and still, and the only sounds that could be heard were the families of birds that scampered about the Forest. Paul sat relaxed in the willow branch chair sipping the lemonade the old woman had brought to him. It was a typical summer day as the sun sent rays of warmth throughout the land. To the right of the cabin a patch of sunflowers stood tall with their faces lifted toward the sun.

The old woman's cat, Gracie, was curled into a ball, taking a nap beneath the cool shade of the porch swing as the old woman tatted away with her wooden shuttle and white thread. A delicate white chain began to emerge from her hands as she meticulously moved her hands to the rhythm of her creation.

Paul turned his eyes to the stately tree of which the old woman spoke and asked her, "How long do you suppose that old tree will continue to stand? It looks like a great deal of it is dead or dying."

The old woman never missed a beat with her tatting as she continued her story:

"There was a time that old tree was young and sturdy. It was surrounded by elder trees that served to protect it from the elements of nature, always teaching by example how to reach for the heavens. When the winds became fierce, the elder trees would stand securely in place and catch its fury to serve as a buffer for that tree until its roots were securely planted in Earth Mother and it could hold its own place.

"The young trees trust the wisdom of the surrounding elders to stand beside them until they are able to stand alone to face the elements. They must trust the elders that guided them along the way to assist them with knowing. Unlike some humans, the elders don't just talk to the tree and say, 'OK, you're on your own.' Instead, the elders in the Forest allow the young ones to experience life, as they stand close and lead through example. The elders patiently wait as the young ones grow and deepen their roots within their base foundation. They trust Creator to do the work as they maintain their balance by staying grounded in Earth Mother, while always reaching for the heavens.

"That oak tree is indeed growing old; its branches are fragile and are unable to bear the leaves it once did. It has many 'wounds' from woodpeckers burrowing through for a delicacy or two, and its branches are weak after years of providing a place for humans to sit and watch for deer. If you look real close, you will see a few planks of boards left from the tree house my children played in for many years. It has not been used for a very long time because my grandkids were only interested in playing in it for a few summers. Seems the younger generation has more 'modern day' devices to keep them busy than my children had, and that's as it is supposed to be, I guess.

"So, that old tree, like me, is tired. It has served the Forest well, and I haven't the heart to have it cut down. I figure I'll let Creator take care of that." The old woman paused her tatting as she affectionately looked at the old oak tree. "I suppose some day people will talk about me the way we are talking about that tree. But, you know, if they can say as many good things about me as I can say about that tree, well, I will feel I've done a good job on Earth Mother."

Paul shifted in his chair as he placed his glass back on the table between himself and the old woman. He watched her as she stared at the old tree. It was as if she was speaking about an old friend. *If the truth be told,* Paul speculated, *I'm sure they are old friends.*

Once again, the old woman returned to her story, only this time, she continued to stare at the old tree in front of her. "I remember the year the winter was very cold and the snow seemed to bring an endless blanket of white as it fell to the ground for five days. That old tree probably had about twenty squirrels and their families living in it that winter. It was darned near full from limb to limb with families. It was a real sight to see when the sun finally came out and all the families of squirrels poked their heads out to see who their neighbors were. Just like we humans, I believe they were getting cabin fever!"

The old woman returned her eyes to her tatting and held it up to see how it was taking shape. "I reckon life is like that old tree. Things are born, things die, and life goes on. But you know, I do believe that the world is a better place because every thing that has ever lived on it left something of itself behind. From the remains of the dying tree to the bones and ashes we leave on the ground of Earth Mother, the 'soil' in our life is enriched and feeds the next tree that comes after it."

She bit the end of the thread, tied a knot securely, and returned the wooden shuttle and thread into the black velvet bag. With a deep sigh, she slowly stood to her feet, turned to Paul and handed him the beautiful chain as she said, "You've added much to your family and community; the soil is richer because of you." After a short pause she concluded, "These are my words."

Paul received the chain and watched the old woman's eyes as she spoke. She had beautiful blue eyes that seemed to penetrate into his soul. The lines in her face expressed the wisdom she had learned from not only her personal experiences in life, but from years of listening to the hearts of others. Her cheeks had a hint of blush and her thick lips showed residue from the early morning application of lipstick. She was a pretty woman with a silver gray braid that hung down her back and white hair that caressed her face. Paul wondered, *Has she always known love so intimately?*

The old woman carefully covered the lemonade glasses and carried the tray into the house. Paul felt frozen in the moment as he glanced at the old oak tree. *Hmm, I remember the old tree at my grandparents' home. Haven't thought about that in a very long time; wonder if it's still standing?*

His eyes scanned the rest of the Forest that surrounded the cabin as he paid close attention to the burst of color that dotted the landscape. *Reckon life is like this scene: full of growth, colored by the events in life, and somehow orchestrated by a master musician. There are different tunes and different types of music, that require a variety of musical instruments to make good music. And each instrument needs a particular person with a passion for that unique instrument to be willing to spend time with it in order to diligently learn how to make it sound magnificent. Wow,* he scratched his head, *that's powerful stuff!*

He rose from his chair, took a big stretch and, for some reason, found it difficult to leave. *OK, we need to get going; can't stay here all day,* and yet, his feet felt attached to the floor of the porch.

After a couple of deep sighs Paul's feet moved. He walked over to the twig basket, dropped in a gift, and stepped off the porch. *OK, we're off the porch.* But he couldn't move — instead, he felt the instinct to turn in the opposite direction.

Hmm, he shrugged, *I do believe that tree is calling to me! What the heck?* After a few seconds, Paul found himself moving toward the tree. As he got closer to the tree he felt strong emotions. Again he thought, *What the heck!*

Paul heard a hum that pierced his heart as the tears he could not contain began to fall down his face. *I don't feel sad, so why the tears? So, what do I feel?* Paul asked.

Standing smack dab in front of the old oak tree, Paul stood as tears gently fell from his eyes. He felt his heart race as his breathing quickened and his mouth became dry. "Oh, my gosh," Paul whispered, "Oh, my gosh!"

It was a strange feeling Paul had never experienced. He felt no sadness, so his tears confused him. He was a strong man who handled everything in his life with confidence. Oh, sure, some things that happened were "foreign territory;" however, he always knew to find someone he trusted to help him figure things out. This was different, though, Paul felt no fear; rather, it was more an "uncertainty."

What's happening? Paul looked at the tree and without speaking asked, *What is it that you need?* He shook his head, *This is crazy!* He closed his eyes so as to not be distracted by what was around him.

Within seconds Paul heard a faint, yet strong voice. "Trust yourself, Paul," the voice said. "You have deep roots that provide you all the security you need."

Paul kept his eyes closed as he began to feel a sense of familiarity with the voice he heard. The feeling of uncertainty was now replaced with peacefulness. Paul opened his mouth ever so slightly and took in a deep breath through his nose as his chest rose. He noticed that he was now breathing, and realized that he had been almost holding his breath.

OK, I'm listening, Paul told the "voice."

"Remember what you were taught as a child, Paul, and those roots will bring forth the truths you once knew. Nothing has been lost; you have just forgotten to remember and call to you what you already know."

Paul continued to breathe to a rhythm that seemed to be in harmony with the tree. *Really?* he asked his mind. *I feel the tree breathing?* Suddenly his heart quickened and the thoughts dissolved.

"With your roots secured, always keep your heart focused upward for your guidance, and the balance needed to live in this world will be maintained," the voice continued. Paul felt only the presence of the "voice;" there was only Paul and the "voice."

As Paul stood tall and straight, he felt a gentle pulsating on the top of his head. The energy began to move down to his forehead, lips, and throat, until it paused at his heart. Within a few seconds, it continued down to his belly, pelvis, hips, thighs, and calves, and onto his feet. With a dense pull, he felt the energy move through the bottoms of his feet as it moved within the ground below where he stood.

It was a very strange feeling to Paul as he stood in front of the old oak tree and wondered, *Is this what it feels like to be a tree?* The energy continued to deepen within the very core of Earth Mother as he remembered sitting in church with his father and mother, feeling loved beyond words. *It was a safe place to be nestled between my folks,* he remembered. *I thought my folks were the most wonderful people on the planet — at least until I hit thirteen.*

From there, Paul had snippets of memories of Christmas carols, Easter egg hunts, Fourth of July fireworks, Halloween parties, Thanksgiving, graduation from high school, the passing of his grandparents, marrying Cassie, and the birth of their first child. It was a fast forwarding of events that made Paul wonder, *This must be what they talk about when someone has a near death experience. What an amazing life I've chosen!*

With that thought, Paul opened his eyes and looked directly in front of him at the old oak tree. There was an almost perfect heart shaped knothole directly across from his heart. *Is this a joke? Or, have I dreamed this all up? What sort of place is this?* he pondered, as he looked around and saw the cabin to the right behind where he stood.

"I am not believing this place!" Paul exclaimed as he glanced back at the tree and touched his hand to the knothole. *Jesus loves me, this I know,* ran through his head. He quickly removed his hand and the tune stopped. "Hmm," Paul sounded as he returned his hand to the knothole. *For the Bible tells me so,* continued once again until Paul once again removed his hand.

"That's it. I'm out of here." Paul said as he stepped back from the tree. "I have no idea what's going on here, but one thing is for certain: I got the message!" With that, Paul pulled the tatted chain from the pocket of his jeans and placed it under some leaves just in front of the old tree. "Thank you! Here's some magic back to you!" he said as he turned and walked the trail back to his car.

It's an amazing world we live in, Paul reflected. *I had no idea why I was coming to meet the old woman, and suddenly it is perfectly clear.* Paul stood by his car and looked back at the Forest for one last time. "I don't want to forget what happened here today. I do believe I was brought here to remember the truly important things in life. I have spent enough time making a living. Now it is time to really live!"

He looked up at the skies that were beginning to fill with clouds. "What a beautiful sky, so blue, so massive, so present." Paul sniffed the air, closed his eyes, and felt the strength that came from really taking the time to look up. "We have our work cut out for us when I get home. I am going to stop at Joe's Nursery on the way home and purchase a new tree for the yard. I'll let that tree help me remember today, and remind me to begin having more days like this one." As he turned the key to his car, he added, "I know what kind of tree I want, too — it's going to be *A Magnificent Oak.*"

The Web

The sun baked the landscape with an intensity that caused the flowers to turn their faces toward the ground. It was an extraordinarily hot day for mid-September, and with her straw hat secured beneath her chin, the old woman moved at a slow pace toward the front porch.

She stepped into the shade of the porch as she carefully removed her hat and gloves, and rolled up one sleeve of the thin cotton shirt, exposing an arm that glistened with perspiration. She carefully wiped her forehead with the other unrolled sleeve, and then rolled it up as well.

The old woman found her way to the porch and stood in front of a small table that housed a fabric covered tray. She removed the orange fabric, revealing an ice bucket, three glasses, and a pitcher of lemonade, just waiting for the old woman to quench her thirst.

"Sure am glad I brought out this lemonade," she said to her cat, Gracie. The cat didn't move a muscle, except to glance her eyes upward toward the old woman as if to say, "I understand precisely what you mean!"

With that, the old woman filled a glass with ice, poured a tall glass of lemonade and sat on the porch swing to survey the yard in front of her. *My goodness it is a hot day! I am grateful the warm temps are soon to be a faded memory!* She tipped the glass to her mouth and took a long swig of the refreshing drink.

As she felt her body begin to respond to the cold beverage, she pushed the swing with her foot and felt a breeze dry the moisture on her arms. "Gracie, you have the right idea; now is a good time to just sit still and take a nap." She looked down at Gracie, gave her a quick smile and looked back toward the Forest.

It appears our visitors will be here any minute, she thought as she watched two girls stroll slowly along the path to the cabin. "Looks like they know how to take care of themselves by not overexerting their bodies," she commented to Gracie. "Pretty smart girls!"

Within a few moments, the girls entered the clearing of the old woman's yard and carefully maneuvered their way along the stone path to the front porch. *The girls appear to be sisters, maybe seventeen and eighteen?* The old woman speculated. *This will be an interesting visit.*

The tallest of the girls spoke very clearly as she approached the old woman. "Good day, Ma'am. I'm Samantha, and this is my sister, Rochelle." She very cordially extended a hand to the old woman as she stepped onto the porch. "I am very grateful for the shade of your porch; thank you for seeing us today."

The shorter sister shot a broad smile to the old woman, then moved past her sister and also extended her hand. "Yes, thank you for seeing us today. I'm Rochelle and I'm most glad to be here today." She wiped her brow with her forearm. "My goodness, it's a hot day for September." The old woman methodically filled each glass with ice, then carefully poured lemonade into each glass as she pointed to the willow branch chairs to the left of the porch swing. "Please have a seat," she said as she motioned toward the chairs and handed each girl a tall glass of cold lemonade.

"Seems the heat has melted the ice a bit, but I am certain the lemonade will satisfy your thirst on this warm day," she said to the sisters.

Rochelle moved in front of Samantha, reached for the glass and quickly said, "Oh, thank you so much!" as she gulped down half the glass of lemonade.

Samantha accepted the glass and promptly said, "Please ignore my sister; she seems to have forgotten her manners." She looked over at her sister and shot her a look as if to say, *Where are your manners?*

The old woman settled back into the porch swing as she retrieved her handwork bag and commenced moving her fingers at warp speed. Gracie lifted her eyes to acknowledge the young girls, then quickly closed them in an attempt to return to her peaceful state.

"Well, Ma'am, we are here today to find out how to prepare for living on our own," Samantha said. "You see, our parents have decided to move out of state to seek work, and neither of us really wants to go."

Rochelle snuggled into her willow branch chair and wiggled her fanny a few times. Then a blissful look appeared on her face as she suddenly seemed to remember where she was at the moment. "I do love your place," she said to the old woman. "This is the sort of place I hope to have when I grow up."

Samantha continued, "As I was saying, our parents are moving, and my sister and I have decided to stay in our home town to complete our schooling."

She took a few more sips of her lemonade, puckered her face a bit and commented, "This sure is some great lemonade. It tastes so tart, yet sweet. I have a hunch you made this from scratch. I don't know of any ready-made drinks that taste this good!"

Rochelle sat quietly in her chair, enjoying the early fall mums whose buds were beginning to open. She looked around at the lush, full trees that were in the early stages of changing from summer greens, into the rich brown, orange, yellow, and red colors of fall.

Samantha broke the silence, "I am in my second year at the university in town and Rochelle is about to start her senior year in high school. It seems only logical to stay with what we know for now, and then decide later if we want to move to where our folks will be living.

A whisper of wind stirred the wind chimes and a deep, hollow sound echoed in the air. Rochelle looked at the chimes and commented, "That is a lovely sound. Most of the chimes I have heard are more high pitched. There is something very comforting in that sound; almost like it taps at my heart."

Rochelle felt the awkwardness of her words and quickly "corrected" herself. "I mean, I can feel that sound inside my chest." And she looked over at her sister. "I know, I can be overly dramatic about things, but you have to admit that sound is very … well, almost intoxicating!"

Samantha looked at her sister, then back toward the old woman and said, "Well, I guess you can tell my sister has a flair for the dramatic. She's always loved English literature and the arts, so it's little wonder she uses such 'artistic' words to describe her feelings." And with that, she watched the old woman rhythmically move her hands to the beat of the chimes.

As the three of them sat quietly taking in the peacefulness in the air, the world seemed momentarily suspended in time and space, and as though all that existed was in this very place in this precise moment.

The silence was broken when Samantha caught a glimpse of something sparkly to the left of the chimes. She strained to look more closely and said, "What is that shiny thing waving in the air?"

Rochelle turned to see what her sister was looking at, then she said in a rather 'smarty pants' manner, "What, Miss College Lady, you can't tell it's a spider web?"

Samantha darted a look back to her that would have killed if it had been a knife. "Oh, don't be so mean. I am sitting further from it than you are!"

Both girls now stared at the web in wonder. "Would you look at the size of that thing?" Rochelle said, "It must be fourteen inches in diameter!"

"Yes, indeed, and isn't it amazingly beautiful," Samantha commented as she stood up and walked to the web for a closer look. "Look at the details of that web!"

Rochelle stood up and joined her sister as both of them oohed and aahed at the intricacy of the details, the finely woven pattern in each section, and how perfectly designed it was, like a piece of fine art.

With no prelude, the old woman began her story:

"Grandmother Spider created the universe. She dreamed of a place that would be filled with beauty — a place where everyone found comfort and harmony in just being with one another.

"Grandmother would awaken each day to the early morning light of Grandfather Sun's face, and she would speak to him of her love for his gifts — for the plants, trees, critters, and all things in nature that he supported. She told Grandfather he brought great comfort to her world, and that even when he was hidden behind the cloud beings, it still brought her comfort to know he was present just behind their faces.

"Grandmother Spider felt such love for Grandfather Sun that she wanted to bring their worlds together. Somehow, she knew that if they loved one another respectfully, they could create something beautiful; something truly amazing that would bring joy to those that came into their presence. She simply knew that unconditional love and respect could, indeed, illuminate the world.

"And so, in the light of Grandfather's face, she began to weave a web of fine silver that mingled with the starlight of the night sky. Each day she would diligently weave her love for Grandfather into a web. As she did this, she thought only of her love for him and for those he sustained: the Standing Ones, the plants, the animals, the winged ones, and all the marvelous creations that shared space with her, and with Grandfather.

"At night Grandmother Spider would rest, as Grandmother Moon sent her moonbeams into the web so that the silver would become illuminated and glow when light was present. It was a time of beautiful lovemaking that created the dreams of all the inhabitants on the planet, so that something else could enter the world and receive the beauty of their hearts' song.

"From the love between Father Sky and Earth Mother, Grandfather Sun impregnated Grandmother Spider's web, and a new species was created. It was the great 'coming together' that birthed humanity."

Samantha and Rochelle looked in the old woman's direction, then back to the Spider web, and finally at each other. Then, as if on cue, both moved back to their respective seats and settled in for a story.

"A web is spun by all the dreams, fears, hopes and desires within our hearts. Whether we are paying attention to it or not, every thought, word and deed creates our personal webs. If a person is 'uptight' the web may become taut and susceptible to breakage; if it is too loose, it may leave a 'hole' through which our fears or dreams may seep. Our personal experiences create our web, and to ensure the web is secure and will sustain our dreams requires that we take great care in knowing precisely what we hope to bring into our lives.

"In order to take this action requires that one knows his or her personal truth; that is to say, what core values and heart-felt dreams they wish to see more of in life. For as we dream and weave our web, it expands out to those around us — whether we know them or not — and touches the lives of others. Those webs can trap us if we randomly move through our lives without paying attention to our thoughts, words and actions.

"It is the weaving of all humans, individually and collectively, that creates the community in which we live."

The old woman paused for a moment, then continued, "It is most interesting how nature — the plants, the animals, and all living things — clearly understands how this web is woven. If we humans would pay attention to them, we could learn a great deal about living in a beautifully woven web of peace and harmony. And, in those teachings we would find what most of us seek — the means by which to feel secure, safe and loved."

Samantha and Rochelle moved their eyes from the old woman toward each other and simultaneously took a deep breath. The wind chimes filled the air with a resounding tone that seemed to come from deep within the core of Earth Mother. The spider web gently stirred in the wind as a shimmering glow seemed to reflect the brilliance of Grandfather Sun. Yet another moment seemed to be suspended in time and space as the sisters stared at one another.

Samantha broke the silence by looking toward the old woman and simply exclaiming, "Oh, my goodness!"

Rochelle turned her head from the web and stared at her sister, then at the old woman, and said, "That is as poetic a thing as I have ever heard. What a metaphor for life!"

The old woman tied a knot at the end of the tatted chain and handed it to Samantha. "Weave your web with much love and care. Use smooth, round words, and remember that sometimes the best way to learn something is to 'talk less and listen more!'" With the tatted chain in her hand, she tapped Samantha on the forehead and said, "Use less of this," then tapped her heart, "and more of this!"

Samantha received the intricately tatted chain and examined it with both of her hands, then handed it to her sister and whispered, "I do believe this is the old woman's web."

Rochelle took the chain in her hands, held it to her heart and began to weep. As tears poured from her eyes, she sobbed, "I am going with Mom and Dad! I will miss you, Samantha, but I simply cannot leave home yet."

Samantha reached for her sister's hand and held it tightly as tears ran down her face as well. "I understand, Rochelle, I truly understand," was all she could verbalize at that moment.

The sisters sat beside each other holding hands, and allowed their tears to flow as the wind chimes continued to harmonize with their hearts' songs. The air had turned to a cool breeze that felt refreshing as emotions began to settle and the sisters released their hands to wipe their tears.

Gracie moved from underneath the porch swing and with an arched back stretched as though to reach for the heavens. Putting one paw in front of the other she moved toward the girls. When she arrived in front of Samantha, she began to purr and nestle her face on her leg until Samantha had to reach down and stroke her a few times. Once acknowledged, Gracie moved on to Rochelle as she repeated her "pet me" routine. After being recognized by Rochelle, Gracie promptly left the porch and moved toward the Forest.

After a few more moments of gathered emotions the sisters looked toward the old woman. She was tying a knot at the end of another beautiful chain as she rose from the porch swing and handed the second chain to Samantha.

"Whatever you do, do it with care, love, and an awareness that whatever action you take will add to the web of those around you. Remember to ask yourself, 'Is my action, necessary, truthful, and kind?' and then choose."

She turned toward Rochelle, patted her hand and said, "As long as you follow your heart, you will be happy. There is no room for self-doubt. If you choose something and it turns out not to serve your heart, then simply choose another direction. Above all, be gentle and kind with yourself and with others." With that, she turned and moved toward the garden as she said, "These are my words."

Samantha tucked her chain into her shirt pocket as she stood and gathered the drinking glasses, placed them on the tray and covered the tray with the orange fabric. She then carried the tray to the front door and set it beside the entryway.

Rochelle stood up, placed her chain in her pants pocket, then pulled a gift from her bag and placed it in the twig basket by the steps. As both girls stood together at the edge of the porch, they surveyed the yard, sniffed the air, listened to the chimes, and glanced at the silvery web gently swaying in the breeze.

With a deep sigh, Samantha stepped off the porch first, followed by Rochelle, and they slowly strolled the stone steps that led to the path to the Forest. In complete silence, they made the walk through the Forest last as long as they could. They paused from time to time to notice the dozens of spider webs of various sizes and shapes that hung from tree branches of all sizes, and that lay above the piles of leaves on the ground.

Without a word, the sisters looked at one another with puzzled faces as if to say, *Really, we didn't notice those spider webs before?* They turned toward the path ahead and Samantha broke the silence with, "I think it's time we notice *The Webs* in our lives!" To which Rochelle nodded her head, pulled the tatted chain from her pants pocket, showed it to Samantha, smiled and said, "I have my reminder!"

The King

Clouds blanketed the sky with gray as rain fell onto the plants in the old woman's garden. Cornstalks stood tall as their tan colored tassels reached toward the heavens, as if to say, "Thank you." Lush, rich green plants dotted with brilliant red tomatoes were tied to wooden stakes. Yellow squash brightened the large, green leafy vines that trailed along the dark brown soil, and delicate light green tops of carrots waved with the wind. It was an amazing reminder of how beautifully Earth Mother provides everything her inhabitants need, and she does so with color and elegance!

Just to the left of the garden was an old wooden shed that housed the various yard and garden tools needed to care for the garden. A faded blue tarp was draped over a neatly arranged stack of wood to protect it from the elements as it sat awaiting the cold months ahead. Everything appeared neat and tidy, ready for whatever presented itself.

Gentle rain fell upon the ground as Ruth stepped out of the Forest onto the clearing and paused to observe the quaint site. A chill caressed her body as a brisk, cool breeze sent a reminder to her that fall was just around the corner.

Oh, wow, that looks like something out of a storybook. What a tale of the woman who lives here this place reveals — I can hardly wait to meet her!

Ruth moved from under her umbrella to see if the rain had stopped. "It appears to have subsided," she said as she carefully shook the moisture from the umbrella and pulled it closed. She glanced up at the sky and continued, *Looks like more rain is coming; I think we're in for a gloomy day.* She quickly changed her thoughts. *Oh, well — at least the rain isn't pouring down.*

Ruth did her best to stay positive despite events that seemed to try her patience. After years of being an emergency room nurse, she had witnessed nearly every conceivable illness or injury known. Ruth had tended injuries that had been self-inflicted, accidental, or a result of someone else's cruel intentions; and, always, the broken hearts of family and friends that needed mending.

Ruth was not professionally trained to work directly with people's emotions; however, years of witnessing the reactions and actions of broken hearts had taught her a great deal about human emotions. She could size up a person by the way in which they confronted traumatic injuries. Some would fall apart and be of no use to the injured person, while others reacted stoically. There were those who incessantly asked senseless questions, while others remained silent throughout the whole ordeal. All of that had taught her to hold a space of neutrality in order to allow individuals to confront trauma in their own unique ways.

As Ruth stepped onto the porch, she carefully laid her umbrella against a support pole to keep the moisture run-off from creating a puddle on the porch. She then removed her raincoat and placed it neatly on a long nail she found poking out from the same pole. *There, that will keep her porch tidy and dry.*

Ruth clutched her bag close as she gently knocked on the front door. She smoothed her hair, straightened her blouse, and gathered her thoughts for the conversation. *Let's see ... I need to know if it's time for me to change careers,* she mused.

Within a few moments, she heard a soft voice say, "Come in." Ruth carefully opened the door, peeked inside and asked, "Did you say to come in?" The old woman who sat in front of a slow-burning fire simply replied, "Yes."

Ruth slipped out of her boots, stepped into the cabin, then moved to the chair next to the old woman. "You know, it isn't really cold outside, but that dampness surely does penetrate the bones. Your fire feels real good," she said as she sat in the chair next to the old woman.

"You have a lovely place here, and that yard is beautiful; I can tell it is tended with much love," Ruth said as she accepted a cup of cocoa offered by the old woman. "Well, thank you. It smells delicious," she continued as she carefully sipped from the cup.

The warmth from the fire penetrated Ruth's skin as the cocoa warmed her belly. *This is a most comfortable place*, Ruth thought as she watched the charred embers burn brightly beneath the slowly burning logs. *This is what peacefulness feels like! Much like the rainy, gray day outside, peace can be found in the warmth of a steady fire. I do remember that from living on our family farm. Didn't matter what was going on in the outside world*, she recalled, *we had a piece of heaven in our home. Oh, sure, we had problems like everyone else, but somehow they were confronted and dealt with in a peaceful manner.* At least that's how Ruth remembered her childhood years.

Ruth's father was the "country doctor," and anyone who needed anything could be certain a remedy would be found if they called Doc McMahon. It didn't matter what the concern; whether a health issue, a pregnant cow, or a kid that refused to go to school, Doc McMahon would do what he could to help, and everyone in the area knew this about him. A respect for what Doc did for others assured those in the community that they were in good hands. *I believe the word is "integrity."* Ruth realized not many people she knew bore that quality.

Ruth's thoughts were interrupted as the old woman offered her a plate filled with chocolate chip cookies. "Well, thank you. I do believe I'll have one of those; they look delicious," she said as she accepted one of the cookies. Chocolate oozed out and dripped on Ruth's lips as she took a bite of the cookie. She quickly located the chocolate with her tongue and licked it from her lips, and let out a groan. "Mmm, that is a delicious cookie. There are walnuts in the cookies, aren't there? What a treat!"

The old woman had put away her cup and saucer and pulled her tatting supplies from her black velvet bag. "Thank you," she replied, as she began tatting. Then she asked Ruth directly, "What is your question?"

Ruth cleared her throat, took another sip of her cocoa and said, "Well, I've been trying to formulate a single question since I know I can only ask one, and, believe it or not, it's been difficult to condense it into one." She placed her cup and saucer back on the tray.

"I have been a nurse for many years; my father was a doctor, so I've been exposed to the medical field my entire life. I love what I do, and feel very fortunate to have a job doing what I love; and yet, I feel in my core that I need to be doing something else. I wish I could explain why I feel this way because I cannot imagine *not* being a nurse; however, something in my very core keeps telling me there's something more."

The logs in the fireplace burned brightly filling the room with caressing warmth as Ruth's question slowly became clear. "I need to know what I can do to satisfy that inner nudge while continuing to do what I love."

Once she had spoken the words, Ruth felt content with the question. *That's it! That's exactly what I need to know!* She noticed the peacefulness within her core that had come from simply asking the question. *Hmm, most interesting*, she considered.

Stillness hung in the air as the old woman tatted, and Ruth sat silently, mesmerized by the fire in front of her. After a few moments the sound of rain broke the silence as it came down steadily and heavily on the tin roof of the cabin. Like a steady drumbeat, a rhythm emerged that seemed to harmonize with the flames from the fire. Ruth noticed the fire and water dancing together in such a synchronistic way that it seemed to orchestrate an audible melody.

The crackling fire, the sound of heavy rain, and the rhythm of the old woman's tatting conspired to create the perfect introduction as she began her story:

"Once upon a time, a long time ago, there was a King who ruled his kingdom with a gentle firmness. He was loved by most of the citizens in his kingdom because they knew he was dependable, reliable, and would listen to their concerns. It was a quaint kingdom nestled among the majestic old mountains in a country not far from here.

"Each day the King would arise and face the East, and ask for guidance, that he might rule the kingdom in such a way that every person would feel heard, loved and supported. He asked the East to help him see the opportunities around him and to be able to discern the highest and best for the country as a whole.

"The King turned next to the South and asked for guidance as to how to help each citizen remember to trust and have faith, and to forgive and be forgiven for things that had hurt their heart in any way. He also asked the South to help his citizens have more fun, and to laugh at some of the silliness that happens in everyday life. For the King knew that if the citizens took themselves too seriously, they would become hardened and cold, and therefore untrusting of those around them.

"The King would turn next to the West and ask for assistance to help still his mind enough to really hear what his heart was telling him. For the wise King knew that if *he* did not spend time in the silence, *his* head would constantly *tell him* what to do. The King had learned that, without the courage of the heart, things that really mattered would be ignored.

"The King would turn to the North and ask for the wisdom to guide his people. For the King knew the ancestors that walked before him waited to share these truths with those who were willing to open their hearts, and who were found to be trustworthy. So, the King would call to the seven generations before and seven generations after him to help him live his life as he asked others to live theirs. He knew that any man or woman who walked their talk would have the integrity to be given the truths from their ancestors.

"Finally, the King would raise his hands to the heavens and give thanks for the many blessings bestowed upon his country, and then he would lean over and touch the ground and say, 'As above, so below.' And with that he would drop to his knees and kiss Earth Mother."

The old woman held her hands up to examine the length of the tatted chain, then regained her rhythm and continued her handwork as she concluded her story. "It is a wise soul who knows how to begin and end his or her day by thanking the Creator for the divine guidance to live his or her life in service to others. Every day we are given the opportunity to remember who and whose we are, and those who guide his or her life by that knowing are the ones who satisfy the nudges in his or her belly that ask to be honored."

The old woman bit the thread to disconnect it from the spool, tied a knot in the end of the chain, carefully repacked her tatting tools into the black velvet bag and placed it beside her. She rose from her chair, covered the items on the tray with a piece of cloth, then moved toward Ruth. She reached for Ruth's left hand, gave her the chain, looked directly into her eyes and said, "There is a nudge in our bellies that lets us know when it's time to remember our connection to all that is true. That nudge will not let us go until we have taken the time to listen and acknowledge its presence. When that which we do is done in the spirit of love, realizing we are an extension of the divine, our bellies will be at peace."

The old woman wrapped her hands around Ruth's hands and gave them a squeeze as she said, "You are an instrument of God; allow Creator to work through you as the Divine worked through your father." She released Ruth's hands, picked up the tray and said, "These are my words," and disappeared into the next room.

Ruth sat for a moment clutching the delicate chain as she watched the fire dance in partnership with the logs. Her head was spinning from the story the old woman shared; and, as her heart pulsed with the fire, she felt a familiar flutter in her belly. *I believe I understand what you have been telling me,* she whispered within. *I love you and am grateful for your patience, love and guidance.*

Ruth took a few deep breaths, then stood and walked to the front door. With her right hand on the doorknob, she glanced at the tatted chain in her left, turned toward the kitchen and softly said, "Thank you for your story."

Ruth closed the door tightly behind her, stepped into her boots, and moved toward the porch steps where she retrieved her coat and umbrella. Slipping on her coat, she reached into the pocket, pulled out a gift and dropped it in a twig basket by the steps. *A very small price for the wisdom gleaned from your story. Thank you!* With that she began her journey back to her car.

The sky was still covered with gray clouds as Ruth carefully maneuvered her way along the rain-drenched path. "Grateful for these boots," she spoke out loud. "I am grateful to have exactly what I need, precisely when it is needed."

Ruth's thoughts moved from her head to her heart as she considered the King and his kingdom. "I wonder if any of the leaders in the world today pray every morning? I wonder if they ask God for guidance to do what is for the highest and best for their country?" She moved along the path, most grateful for the gentle rain and for the wisdom that had been given to her by her family. "They led by example and always considered how their actions would affect those around them."

Ruth stopped walking and stood quietly as she listened to the rain fall onto the leaves on the ground and in the trees. "Thank you, rain, for feeding sweet Mother, and for helping me realize that the tears I witnessed each day moistened and enriched my life. I do understand that it all works together, and that absolutely nothing happens by accident. I am grateful to be a person who can hold the neutral space when others are facing such traumatic situations. I now understand more clearly that you, Creator, God, are the great healer, and that my hands and heart are only instruments by which you can assist humans as they move through life."

A flash of lightning brightened the sky. *OK, I hear you! It is time for me to pick up the pace and get back to the car. I've done enough thinking for the time being.* Ruth pulled up the hood on her coat as she quickened her pace. *I am grateful to see the relationship between my head and my heart. Let's see: I believe the old woman said, "As above, so below." I like that!* She moved through the Forest at a rapid pace, careful to keep her balance as she completed her walk back to her car in record time.

Once inside her car, Ruth sat quietly as her heart began to return to its normal pace. She watched the rain gently fall as she looked at the tall trees in the Forest. *You know how to reach for the heavens and stay grounded in Earth Mother. I guess if you can do that, so can I.* Ruth looked at herself in her rearview mirror and continued, *I'm beginning to realize that I have spent more time thinking about my job than just enjoying my life.*

She settled back into her seat, *There are many creative and fun things that would be helpful for me to do. What did that King say ... that the South was where faith, trust, and the ability to play existed? And, didn't he also say it was where forgiveness was given and received? I like that. I really need to remember that because I tend to be serious most of the time. And, I realize I am very critical of myself, and it is time for that to change. If I can't love myself, how can anyone else love and forgive me?*

The windows began to fog, so Ruth turned on the car and put the defroster on full blast. *I need to see clearly what is in front of me. When things seem "muddled," I need to get quiet and listen to my heart, rather than "think about it." When guidance is given from my heart, I need to ask someone versed in the subject to help me figure things out.*

She felt strong emotions as those thoughts ran through her head. *Why do I think I need to do everything myself? Why cheat someone out of the joy of helping me? Heaven knows, I enjoy helping others, so why not allow them the same feelings?*

As quickly as the tears burned her eyes, Ruth dried them up with more realizations. *I will take these things into my heart and allow God to move me in the direction that will lead me to the person who can assist.*

Ruth felt rebalanced and ready for the drive home; she knew the answer to her question had led her back to her heart — to the place where her connections to her Creator is secure. She smiled, *The King has returned to his source; he knows precisely what he needs to do every single day so he can help his citizens find peace and harmony!*

Ruth took a very deep breath, inserted a favorite CD and said, "OK, enough of that; time to let the music take me somewhere I haven't been for a while: into the 'no thinking zone,' so that I can feel my heart!" As she pulled onto the road toward home, she felt something on her head and giggled. *There it is — my crown is back in place!* Then she exclaimed, "Off to my kingdom!"

Summer
Reflections

"Flowers know within their core that they are part of something greater than themselves — that they are the outward expression of their Creator's Love."

— These are her words.

HEAD TALK

What from this Summer season would you like to know more about?

Or, is there one thing you would like to *"think some more about?"*

What do YOU suppose you might discover in the Autumn season?

HEART TALK

Of the stories in this season, pause and consider what Truths were revealed.

What of these *Truths* apply to YOUR Life right now?

As you consider the Summer of YOUR Life, what "jumps out" as a theme?

What can you learn for your own life from the Teachings of the South?

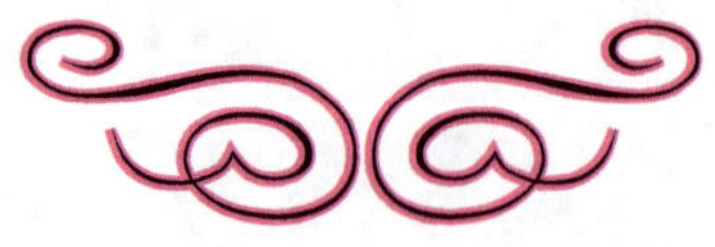

*Burnt oranges, dark browns and brilliant yellows splash the Forest with color
as Autumn heralds in a time to harvest the fruits of our labor.*

*Whether or not the crops were abundant, neighbors come together to share
and fellowship as communities rally together in Celebration!*

Being an adult brings many rich adventures! Finding a career that feeds our soul while providing adequate financial rewards to "feed" our family requires commitment, perseverance, and a willingness to "show up" in our life. Just as Autumn brings a cornucopia of the "fruits of one's labor," so our adult years require us to wear many hats! We are sons or daughters, perhaps a partner to someone we love, employee or employer for others, mother or father for our own offspring.

In the later days of this season of life, we begin to evaluate what we have accomplished. We will ask questions: Have we achieved our goals, been a decent person, loved enough, and changed the things in ourselves that needed attention? It is a time when we must look closely at what we have yet to complete during our lifetime, and a time to look closely at the questions we may have squirreled away until we had more time. For one thing is clearly apparent: the sand in our hourglass has reached a halfway point!

THE WEST

As we turn to face the West, Grandfather Sun leaves the sky so that Grandmother Moon can share her gifts with Earth's inhabitants. The feminine teachings of receptivity and intuition now take center stage. We are called from our busy minds to reconnect with home — to our Heart. It is the medicine of the Bear that shows us how to honor the quiet place within where we can hibernate for a while in order to gather the resources needed to carry us into the next and final phase of our Earth walk. The outward chatter and busyness of life begins to slow its pace so that our receptive side can listen. It is from the West that we can hear the whispers of our Creator.

"For it is only with the heart, one can see clearly,

what is essential is invisible to the eye."

— *The Little Prince* by Antoine de Saint-Exupery

Gramps and Grams

"Seven, eight, nine, ten; this must be the right spot," Hugh counted out loud. "Let's see, there is supposed to be a clearing on the right."

Scanning the lush green foliage, he downshifted his sporty black convertible. "Sure hope it's a well-kept clearing; I don't want this baby scratched!" he said as he surveyed the terrain.

He slowed to a near stop and carefully kept checking in his rearview mirror for approaching traffic. "There it is," he said, as he maneuvered his "pride and joy" into a secure spot. He turned off his car and reached for a basket sitting in the passenger's seat.

Sure is a beautiful basket. Maybe it's weird of me to notice such things, but Grams taught me to appreciate pretty things.

"Well, no matter; I'd like for someone to call me a 'sissy' for noticing beautiful things. Heaven knows I love beautiful women!"

As he exited the car and moved toward the Forest, he caught the whiff of a familiar scent. *That smells like Gramps' pipe; hmm, wonder what that means?* Then he remembered. *Gramps used to say, "There's a different world that exists within the Forest."* As he scanned for the path leading to the old woman's cabin, he recalled more of his teachings: *"Before you enter the Forest, you must first introduce yourself."*

Holding the basket in front of him, he said, "With respect for my gramps, I want to introduce myself." There was a cool breeze that wafted over him from the left of where he stood. He felt goose bumps run up his spine, and said, "I am Hugh, grandson of James Hugh Barry, from Decatur, Illinois."

He felt the hair on the back of his neck rise up to attention when a rustling sound came from the same place the cool breeze was felt. *I will not be afraid! The grandson of James Hugh Barry is fearless!* He hoped his thoughts would make it true! He focused his eyes in the direction of the sound, took a deep breath, turned, and moved toward the summons.

Gramps would say, "Listen with more than your ears, Hugh, and you will be given instructions," Hugh remembered. *I sure hope he knew what he was talking about!*

"Well, I'll be darned," Hugh, said out loud, "there's the path!" Of course, it was located precisely in the direction of the cool breeze and rustling sound, so Hugh stepped to the entrance and thought, *Let's see, Gramps also said to always "state your intentions, ask permission to walk onto the land and make no assumptions." I can't believe I remember that after all these years!*

Hugh took a few deep breaths, moved the basket to one side and said, "OK, so here goes nothing." He looked straight ahead and said, "I am here to visit the old woman who lives on this land." He noticed the squirrels darted from tree to ground at warp speed and heard the birds sing songs that only they understood.

He continued, "I request permission to walk the path to her home, to ask for her guidance about my life." After a moment of hesitation he cleared his throat and said, "Please let me know if this meets with your approval."

Geez, he scratched his head, *this feels weird! Sure hope I am saying this correctly.* Feeling a bit foolish, he waited for some outward "sign."

It was a beautiful day as the sun hung high in the deep blue skies. The birds continued bantering back and forth as chipmunks now shared the tree trunks with their squirrel friends. Hugh found himself carried back in time to the woods behind his gramps' and gram's farm:

Acres and acres of soybeans, corn and wheat blanketed the hills that offered a bountiful playground for two young lads filled with curiosity. Would the fields offer a sea of gold for two pirates seeking buried treasures, or a battlefield for two soldiers protecting their homelands? Hours and hours of endless adventures filled the days with merriment and the nights with giggles and whispered secrets.

"You've got to swear you'll never tell Gramps and Grams where we went today," Tommy said to his older brother, Hugh.

"Of course I won't! Do you think I want my hide tanned by either of them?"

"Oh, let's not be ridiculous, Hugh, you know neither one of them has ever touched us." Tommy replied.

"I know, Tommy, but the looks they give might as well be a wallop to the head!" Hugh commented.

"You are right about that, Hugh. It makes me feel like a schmuck to disappoint either one of them." Tommy replied.

"OK, so our lips are sealed?"

"Absolutely!"

And with that the two brothers set about gathering up their makeshift "weapons" and headed back to their gramps' and gram's farmhouse.

Hugh took a deep breath as he was brought back to the path in front of him. In the distance he heard a familiar sound that seemed to be calling to him. *That sounds like a hoot owl! Whatever is an owl doing awake in the middle of the day?* he wondered. The owl called to him in a well-patterned rhythm. Hugh shifted the basket to his left hand and realized he was receiving the "sign" he had requested.

Of course, it's just like Gramps said, you have to listen with more than your ears. He knew it was not a regular occurrence to have an owl hooting in mid-day; it was most certainly "out of the norm."

So, I have asked permission, stated my intentions, and received a sign, Hugh thought. *The third thing was to pay attention, so I'd better double check to be sure that what I took as a "sign" is correct.*

Hugh cleared his throat and said, "OK, Mr. Owl, are you telling me it is OK to enter the Forest and visit the old woman?" Feeling a bit silly, he continued, "My gramps said I was to make certain about what I heard, so please let me know if I am correctly reading the owl hooting as a 'sign.'"

The words were barely out of his mouth when Hugh felt another cool breeze move across his body. The rustling sound of someone walking on fallen branches was loud and clear, so Hugh turned to see what was coming. There was nothing visible, so Hugh again remembered his gramps' words, "Listen with more than your ears." He recalled the cool breeze on his skin, the goose bumps, and the hair that stood up on the back of his neck, and he knew that what he had interpreted as a "sign" was correct.

"Thank you," was all Hugh managed to say as he began his journey down the path to the old woman's cabin.

Hugh carefully walked the path with steady strides, admiring the various trees, wildflowers, and critters along the way. He paused a moment to look over to the left of the path at a particularly striking small purple plant. *Those must be Johnny Jump-Ups! Grams used to talk of how rare and beautiful those plants were. I wonder if I might be able to pick some of those for her on my way back to the car?* "Yep," he said, "I'm getting some of those for Grams. She will be so pleased, and even if she can't tell me that anymore, I'll know."

He made a mental note to himself to remember where they were as he continued along the path. As he approached the clearing, he was amazed by the richness of golds, burgundies, reds, and yellows that dotted the front porch of the cabin. *Wow, that woman has quite the green thumb. Here it is near the end of October and she still has magnificent mums.* He thought again of his grams and how she would love such a beautiful sight.

As he neared the steps to the cabin, the old woman emerged from the front door with a tray covered with orange fabric. *Hmm, those must be the biscuits I've heard so much about. Wonder if it's coffee or hot chocolate she'll serve?*

He stepped onto the porch as the old woman placed the tray gently on a wooden table that sat between the porch swing and one of her infamous willow branch chairs. She nodded to the young man, pointed toward the chair, and then removed the orange fabric. She handed the young man a cup of steaming hot chocolate, then poured a cup for herself and took a seat on the porch swing.

Hugh placed the basket he carried beside the chair and accepted the cup. "Thank you, it smells delicious. Just what a body needs on this cool fall day."

After a few moments of stillness, with only the sound of the chimes ringing from the breeze, Hugh began, "My gramps and grams raised me, and I suppose you could say they were my 'parents.' My younger brother and I spent more time with them than with our parents. We learned everything we know from our gramps and grams. They were honest, God-fearing folk that not only believed, but practiced the Golden Rule. My brother and I owe who we are today to our grandparents."

He paused a few moments to butter a hot biscuit, took a bite, and then placed it on a blue willow saucer. *Oh my gosh! These are beyond delicious! I thought only Grams could make biscuits like these.* While the biscuit seemed to melt in his mouth, he drank some hot chocolate to help them go down.

What a combination; buttermilk biscuits and hot chocolate. He felt tears fill his eyes as he smelled the fragrance his grams always wore. *Oh, I love you so, Grams,* burned in his heart as he remembered sitting on her porch hundreds of times.

He pulled himself together and said, "Thank you for this delicious treat. My grams is the only person I know that made such great biscuits and hot chocolate. Guess they took me back to another time and place when I would sit on my gramps' and gram's porch and enjoy such treats."

The old woman took out her handwork and began creating her trademark-tatted chain as the young man finished his biscuit. Hugh enjoyed the silence with only the sounds of nature for a few moments as he gathered his thoughts.

"My grandparents are the reason I'm here today. You see, it is my turn to care for them as they did for my brother and me. We — my brother and I — agreed a long time ago that when they got along in years we would take care of them. Since I work for myself I manage my business from home, which means I spend most of the time with gramps and grams. My brother certainly does his part in many other ways, so that makes it work for all of us."

Hugh paused for a moment to pour another cup of hot chocolate for himself, then turned to the old woman and said, "Can I pour you another cup?" The old woman shook her head as she continued her tatting and simply said, "Thank you, though."

Taking his full cup in both hands, he sat back in his chair, and continued, "What I am seeking is an understanding as to how to help my grandparents enjoy their last few years. They seem to just sit and tell the same stories over and over again. It is as though they have no other interests beyond what has happened in the past."

Sipping more hot chocolate, he continued, "My brother isn't quite as patient about listening to the stories as I am, but I must admit that it becomes very wearing. I am willing to hear the stories as many times as they want, but I don't know what else to do for them. Surely they are bored with the same stories day after day; however, nothing I try to bring up or suggest seems to be of interest to them. Every topic I bring up always returns to the same stories. I'm telling you, I could recite them word for word if you asked me."

Hugh leaned forward into his chair as he felt the discomfort that came from speaking about this. "Please know, I gladly listen to their stories; I just want to know what to do to make certain they are happy in every moment they are here on Earth. If you have any suggestions as to what I can do to ensure their happiness, I would be most grateful." With that he looked in the old woman's direction and watched her moving hands as a white chain emerged beneath them.

Without missing a beat in her work, she said:

"Stories carry truths from our hearts. They reflect the memories of what we hold near and dear from our life experiences. Many people complain about stories being repeated because they are uncomfortable hearing the same thing over and over. Many people are not interested in what happened in the past; they are only concerned with their own lives, what they know to be true, and what they feel is important. Stories are written in our hearts as we experience life, feel emotions, and move through events beyond our control. We develop certain beliefs about life, about ourselves and about the world, based upon our experiences, and it is from those events that we draw conclusions about ourselves and the world around us."

The old woman paused her handwork as she looked out at the flowers blowing from the North wind. "Every season of our life brings events from which we will interpret the meaning of why it occurred, why someone said something, what they might have done differently, how it will affect those around them, and the list of questions goes on. This is done to make sense out of life's experiences, and as a way to add value to our life."

She returned to her handwork and continued, "When people near the end of physical life, they often spend much time recalling their life experiences in an attempt to make peace with what life brought them. As people age, they often remember a period in their life when it was more joyful, more loving, or even very difficult, and they will ruminate about that event over and over again. To those that live with them it seems repetitious and boring and they will try to move them onto something else. What serves the elder most is for those that love them to listen, but not with just their ears. They need to listen with their hearts." She placed her handwork to her own heart before continuing. It was as though she was speaking from what she was experiencing firsthand.

"It would be most helpful if those listening could 'hear' the feelings — the hurt, joy, sorrow, pain, and love the story is telling. If the person could reflect that back to the elder, they would help that person acknowledge those feelings. Once a person knows someone 'hears' their feelings, they are more likely to release and move on from that place. Sometimes hearing your feelings spoken by someone else helps your heart to feel really 'seen.' For when we are really 'seen' is when we feel really loved."

She bit the thread, tied a knot in the end and handed the tatted chain to Hugh as she said, "It is a lucky gramps and grams that have such a person who loves them so unconditionally he will listen to their heart's stories as a way to help them release this life so they can go to their true home. What is important to remember is that it is only their bodies that die, and if one asks, their souls will continue to express their love for as long as they are needed. These are my words."

The old woman put her handwork in the black velvet bag, placed it on the porch swing, and moved toward her garden. Hugh sat mesmerized by her words as tears rolled down his cheeks. *I will allow these tears, Grams, for you have told me many times they will wash the windows to my soul.*

As he felt a deep purging of his own emotions that came from knowing he would soon have to let his grandparents go, he pulled a handkerchief from his pocket. *Whatever will I do without you two? However will I begin to give to others what you have given to Tom and me? What will I do with my life without you both?*

As Hugh sat very still feeling only the release of tears that he had held back for so long, a large gray cat appeared on the porch. It was a very old cat that looked exactly like the cat his grandparents had once had on their farm. *You look just like Friskie*, he paused, *but he's been gone about ten years.*

The cat snuggled up to Hugh's leg and began to purr. It was as though he knew that what Hugh needed was someone to love him, just like his grandparents had. Hugh reached down to pet the cat as he felt a calmness return. "Oh, my goodness, Mr. Cat, thank you so much for reminding me what I need to do next. You are a very wise one!"

With that he placed the dishes neatly on the tray and covered them again with the orange fabric. *That should make it easy for her to carry inside.* Then he gathered up the basket he brought and set it beside the old woman's gifting basket woven from twigs.

Walking along the path to his car, he stopped at the precise place where the purple Johnny Jump-ups stood, and he bent over to touch them. As he leaned over he felt a cool breeze come over him, and he knew; he was not to take the flowers, but merely to pay respect for their beauty. As he stood over them he said a silent prayer of gratitude for all the amazing love he had received from his grandparents throughout his life. He knew there was yet another action he needed to take before he proceeded, and so he dropped to his knees, right there on the path and closed his eyes. Smelling the scent of his gramps' tobacco from his pipe and his gram's favorite fragrance, he spoke his prayer out loud:

"It is my request, Gramps and Grams, that you continue to share your love with me after you leave your earthly bodies. I will pay attention to your smell so as to be certain you are near, as a way to show respect for what you have taught me. I will ask permission, state my request, and then pay attention."

With that, Hugh stood up from his prayer and felt a strength he had not felt for some time. He returned to his car, grateful to see that it was as he had left it. *I know it's only a car, but Gramps always said you should take care of everything you love, including your car.* He turned and thanked the spirits of the land for keeping him safe, for guiding his path to the old woman, and for once again reminding him how to be grateful for everything in his life.

As he turned the key in the ignition he began his journey home, knowing precisely what he had to do. It was time to help *Gramps and Grams* find their way home, knowing that everything they came here to do was done in an honorable and respectful way; and, if there were old hurts that needed mending, he would help them by listening with his heart.

Gutters

The peak stage of fall was in full array as the Standing Ones displayed warm hues of color. Various shades of orange, brown, green and burgundy filled the trees with the richness of autumn as Patty began her journey to the old woman's cabin. She had found the parking area with no problem, and welcomed the cool temperatures after a very long, hot summer. "Finally," she said, "It feels and looks like fall is officially here to stay."

She moved along the path to the cabin with a walking stick with which a very dear friend had gifted her. "You'd better have a stick with you," Billy had said, "or you may wish you had one if you come across one of those big, fat, black snakes."

Billy was her very best friend and she loved him very much. She smiled, thinking, *That Billy, always looking out for me. I'm grateful for his nurturing spirit; I just wish he were a bit more positive about life.*

She continued her thoughts as she reached the clearing to the cabin. *But, then again, if Billy didn't fret about things, I'd probably have my head in a cloud! I guess we make a good team since I seem to believe everything happens for a purpose.*

As she stepped onto the well-trodden path that led to the porch, she looked for movement on the land. *Everyone I've talked to said she'd be out in her yard.* She paused for a moment to scan the area for life. *Hmm, what a lovely place. I wonder if she's in the back working in her garden?*

She noticed the colorful mums that bordered the porch and the well-tended flower garden to the left of the cabin. *It's hard to believe an older woman keeps this place up so well. I wonder if someone comes and helps her out?*

About that time, she heard a humming sound coming from behind the cabin. *Guess she knows I'm here.* The old woman appeared from the right side of the cabin carrying two different rakes — one with long prongs, and one with short, sturdy ones.

Well, here goes nothing, ran through Patty's head, as she stood very still waiting for the old woman to notice her. *Breathe, Patty, and trust you will know exactly what to ask her.*

Patty felt a cool breeze blow from the North as she reached for the top button of her coat to hold back the cool air. *I'm grateful for this warm coat; Dad said to make certain I was prepared for all sorts of weather.* She moved her large shoulder bag from one shoulder to the other, and then greeted the old woman.

"Hello," was all she could muster up. *Guess I'm more nervous than I thought.* She cleared her throat. *Come on Patty; you can do better than that.*

She stepped toward the old woman and said, "May I help you with those rakes?" The old woman set the rakes to the right of the porch, walked onto the porch and said, "No, thank you, but have a seat," as she pointed to the willow branch chair next to the porch swing.

Patty waited until the old woman had made her way to the front door. Then she stepped onto the porch, placed her bag and walking stick behind the willow branch chair and simply said, "Thank you."

Patty took her place in the chair as she scanned the yard in front of her, admiring all the "treasures" the old woman cared for so sweetly. *You can tell she loves this place; you can feel it everywhere,* she paused. *Hmm, now isn't that interesting ... you can feel love just sitting here on her porch. I can hardly wait to hear what story she's going to tell me.*

Within a few moments the old woman emerged from the cabin with a tray piled high with "goodies" that were protected beneath an orange-colored fabric. Patty moved a few things on the small table that sat between the chair and the swing in order to make room for the tray. The old woman gingerly set them in place, removed the orange fabric, poured two cups of hot chocolate and handed one to Patty.

After a few moments of sipping hot chocolate and eating a freshly baked chocolate chip cookie, Patty felt the "buzz" of warmth brought on by eating such comfort food.

"Oh, Ma'am, thank you so much for the treats; they certainly have warmed my belly and my heart!" she said. "And, by the way, my name is Patty," she continued as she placed her cup, saucer and napkin back on the tray. "May I pour you another cup of hot chocolate?"

The old woman responded by dusting off her skirt, wiping her mouth and hands with the napkin, and placing it with her cup and saucer on the tray. She then picked up the black velvet bag that held her handwork and began tatting.

By now the air had warmed from the afternoon sun and Patty unbuttoned her coat to enjoy the breeze. "You have a beautiful place, and it is very clear the flowers love you as much as you love them."

Patty leaned back in her chair, took a few deep breaths and said, "I'm here to ask about faith. I know it is something often difficult to describe, but lately I've been wondering what faith is really all about. There are lots of books on the subject, lots of people talking and preaching about it, and yet, somehow I'm still not clear how you really know what faith is all about."

Patty sighed as she allowed her breathing to help her find the words her heart was searching to know. She looked over at the old woman, who seemed to be lost in the rhythmic movement of her hands. A white chain began to emerge as Patty continued, "I have a deep faith in a divine source, and I know there is more to life than what is here; and yet, with all the changes and upheavals I witness each day, I sometimes wonder: is anyone paying attention to us down here on Earth?"

Patty felt her heart pounding in her chest as she thought about the "crazy-making" going on in the world. *What am I doing here? Shouldn't I be talking to God instead of someone here on this planet? Maybe Dad is right; maybe I ask too many questions. What is it the scriptures say? "Come with the faith of a child." A child doesn't ask so many questions, but just trusts and lives in the moment. Little kids don't worry about anything but which cartoons to watch.*

As Patty continued the rants of questions in her head, the old woman began her story:

"A woman we will call Martha, decided to make some drastic changes in her life. She had lived in the same house for twenty-six years, worked in the same school system for fifteen years, and her three children were grown. She felt much unrest in her soul and knew something within her was calling for her to move, to shake up her life and to follow her heart to something 'else.' What that 'else' was did not seem clear to Martha; she just knew a voice in her head was calling to her, and she felt that voice was from God.

"So, Martha sold her home, moved out of state and began a new life, but it wasn't long before Martha knew she needed a more permanent home. She had spent three years living with other people, moving from one school system to another, and she was ready for some stability.

"Well, Martha heard the voice call to her again and tell her to move to another part of the state, find her own home and really 'settle' into a nest of her own. So, Martha spent several weekends with a realtor, looking at cabins in the mountains, and waiting to hear the voice tell her which home to buy. Before long, she found a cabin she knew was to be her new home, and set about making it her own."

The old woman paused for a moment and pulled more white thread from her black velvet bag. As the chain lengthened with her story, the old woman continued.

"Martha was a frugal woman; she repainted, mended, or simply decorated with fabric old items for reuse. She wasn't one to be extravagant, and never lived above her means. When she decided to follow the voice, she asked both herself and the voice how she was going to pay for the cabin. She was leaving the position she had and moving several hours away. While she had applied to several school systems, and had even applied for a couple of positions at the local community college, the truth was, she would be moving without a job. Oh, she figured she could do substitute teaching, but that certainly wasn't enough to pay all her living expenses.

"Nevertheless, Martha trusted that if the voice had told her to buy the house, she would be given precisely what she needed to sustain her. So, she applied for a loan without so much as meeting the mortgage company, and sure enough, they approved her loan. Martha could scarcely believe this, because while she did have some savings, it certainly was not enough to use as collateral for a home. But, Martha had learned that if the voice tells her something; it will somehow work out. So, without a job, without so much as meeting a loan officer, she was approved for the purchase of her home. Sure enough, she moved in and began to feel very pleased with her new home.

"After a couple of months Martha began to be concerned that she had still not obtained a full-time teaching position, nor had she even been called to substitute; so she went out on her porch and talked to the voice. 'You know I trust you, and I know you'll provide; but, you also know I don't expect you to give me something for nothing. So, let me know what I need to do next since I only have enough money to pay the bills for another month.' As she sat on the porch swing, she heard the voice say, 'Go clean your gutters.'

"Now, it was fall, and sure enough, the leaves were abundant in her gutters, so she said, 'Are you sure?' When she heard only silence, and she knew she had heard the message clearly, she got up and went to a neighbor to borrow a tall ladder. Martha finished the front gutters of the cabin, and then climbed up the ladder to complete the back one. She decided it might be handy to pull her hose up there to wash them out real good. Well, wouldn't you know, she finished the cleaning, and then pulled the hose to begin washing them out, and sure enough, her ladder fell over. There she was, stuck on top of her cabin with only a water hose."

The old woman paused again, this time to adjust herself on the swing. She proceeded with tatting the chain and continued.

"Martha realized that she was in a predicament! She looked at the gorgeous blue sky, very grateful that it was clear and with no chance of rain, and decided it best to just sit there and enjoy the beauty. After a few minutes her thoughts began to engage. *Let's see, my son who jumps out of planes says that when you land from a jump, it is important to bend your knees, then roll. I can do this; which side of the house is closest to the ground?* Just before she decided to jump, she told the voice, 'OK, you got me up here; you need to catch me so I don't get hurt. You know I don't have medical insurance, so I can't get hurt.'

"About that time she noticed a man come out of the cabin next to hers, closest to the side of her own cabin from which she planned to jump. Now, Martha had never met this neighbor; she pretty much kept to herself, just like her neighbor, I suppose. So, she gave a holler to him and said, 'Hey, neighbor.'

"The guy looked up at her on the roof and said, 'Need some help?'

Are you kidding me? she almost blurted out. She knew that would be a smart-aleck answer, so she said, 'Yes, please, my ladder fell over.'

"So, the neighbor came over, put the ladder back in place, and Martha climbed down from the roof. When she got off the ladder she thanked the man and told him that he had come at exactly the right time.

"The man wasn't one to be real friendly; he had a stern look on his face. He handed her his business card and said, 'If you need anything else, just let me know.' Martha noticed that while his words were cordial, his face had a scowl. She took his card and noticed that he worked at a juvenile center, so she asked him what he did, and he described his job. The man asked her what she does for a living, and Martha explained that she was still looking for a job, but that she had been a counselor in public education for many years.

"Well, wouldn't you know it; the neighbor man said, 'The school system in the next county over is looking for a school counselor.' Martha smiled real big, knowing the man probably did not understand her reaction, but she simply said, 'Thank you very much.'

"It was a Friday afternoon about 2:00, and Martha knew that schools generally closed by 3:00, so she went directly into the cabin, found the phone number for the high school, and called. The lady who answered the phone explained the position had not been 'officially' posted, but that if Martha wanted to submit an application she needed to contact the central office and speak with a man named Joe Farr. Martha thanked her and immediately made a call to the central office. The receptionist told her that if she wanted to pick up an application they would be open for another thirty minutes.

"So, Martha washed her armpits, threw on a clean shirt and headed to the central office. She entered the office and identified herself as the lady who had just called about the high school counseling position, and the receptionist handed her an application. Martha thanked her and the receptionist said, 'We haven't posted the position; how did you find out about the opening?' As the woman spoke, Martha noticed a man standing close to the receptionist desk. He wore blue jeans, a tee shirt and a John Deere hat. He just stood there and watched the two of them. She answered the lady by simply saying, 'I heard about it from my neighbor.'

"As Martha turned to leave the man moved closer to her and said, 'I don't mean to eavesdrop, but did you say you are applying for the school counselor's position?' Martha smiled and said, 'Yes, I've been a counselor for ten years.' The man asked, 'Do you have your school counselors license right now?' Martha replied, 'Yes, I do.' The man extended his hand and said, 'I'm Joe Farr, and I'm very glad to meet you. Bring that application in on Monday and we'll talk.'

"Martha shook his hand, and with a smile that looked like the cat that ate the canary, she thanked him for his consideration, and then told him to have a good weekend. She walked to her car, feeling as though her feet were not touching the ground. She simply put her car in gear, headed back to the cabin and said out loud, 'I will never doubt you again. Thank you so very much for always providing.'"

The old woman tied a knot at the end of a long beautiful chain of tatting, put her handwork back in her bag, and handed Patty the chain and said, "'Faith is the substance of things hoped for, the evidence of things not seen.' These are my words."

The old woman stood for a moment to feel the porch beneath her feet. She then covered the tray with the orange fabric and carried it into her cabin. Patty sat there completely speechless. She could hardly believe what she had just heard. *Is that story really true? How is it possible?* She felt a cool breeze bring her back to her senses. "Of course it's true, you silly," she said. "You've seen such things happen; it has just been a long time since you were quiet long enough to listen."

Patty rose to her feet, looked around to see if she had left everything as she found it, then retrieved a gift from her bag and placed it in the twig gift basket. She turned and gathered her walking stick, and then headed back down the path that led to her car.

As she walked through the Forest she smelled the scent of burning wood. *Mmm, smells like someone has a campfire burning. Golly, it's been a long time since I hung out around a fire. S'mores ... I would love to have some of those delicious treats. Doesn't matter if you try to make them in the microwave, there's nothing like having them fresh from a real fire!*

As she meandered through the woods she felt a sense of lightness, a resurgence of something she had not felt for a very long time. *When did I become so practical? I've always been the one that dreams, that follows her heart; and yet, here I am stuck doing what is "right" or best for me. I have quit listening to my heart.*

She paused for a moment to smell the scent of fall hanging in the air. *Crumbled up leaves, the ground beginning to nestle in for the winter, frost in the morning, squirrels gathering for the long season ahead. I will use this winter to reconnect and listen with more than my mind; rather, I will listen with my heart, with my gut, with the openness to know the path will be made clear. I know this; how did I? ...* She paused that thought and said out loud, "It doesn't matter 'how' I got this way; what matters is what I will do about it." As she arrived at her car, she turned one last time to look at the amazing beauty of the Standing Ones display this time of year. "You are beautiful beings; thank you for sharing with me how to simply trust the natural order of things, I don't need to clean my *Gutters* to allow my faith to direct my path."

She touched her heart, then bent down to touch the ground and said, "Thank you ... with all my heart, thank you!" A very cool breeze blew crisply across her face as she said one more time, "Thank you. My heart is full."

She settled into the driver's seat of the car, turned the key and said, "Oh, Billy, just wait until you hear this story; even you will be a believer!"

Meddling

It was a crisp, cool morning as dew blanketed the ground just off the paved road. "I guess this is my place to park," said the young woman as she maneuvered her car to the side of the road.

Let's see, Dad said to watch for a clearing just after a sharp left turn. She scanned the area and noticed a clearing, *This must be it. I sure hope the ground is steady so I don't get stuck!*

As she put her car into park, she reached for the bag she brought, filled with an assortment of "goodies." "We'll see which of these wants to stay with this lady. I'd better take the whole bag so I'm certain the 'right' thing gets to her."

Her ears were filled with a hum in the air as she opened the car door and stepped onto the wet ground. *Good thing I wore boots this morning,* she told herself. *The walk just might be a bit soggy.* She stood up straight and sniffed the air. *How I love that smell. The scent of freshness, newness, the beginnings of something different ... just what my soul needs.*

Stepping onto the path, Lisa asked, *What do I want to ask this lady? I've tried not to the think about that too much, but it's time to decide what assistance I need from her.* As she stepped lightly onto the path she heard the sound of "slush," made from the mixture of moisture and mud beneath her boots. *That's a funny sound, that "squishy" noise; it's sort of like the sound the pigs made on the farm we visited when I was a kid,* ran through her head as she felt the heaviness of her legs from walking through the thick mud. *I remember wondering, "However do they live in this mess?"*

As she rounded the final turn on the path she noticed smoke rolling upward from behind the cabin. *Guess the old woman is up and burning brush already. I've heard she's a hard worker. But, then, seems everyone worked hard "back in the day." Wonder what today's youth would do if they had to work that hard?*

Lisa gathered her bag close and moved the final steps to the clearing as she paused for a few moments. *OK, it's now or never; what am I to ask this woman?* Then, without a moment's hesitation, she knew. "Got it! Let's get this done!"

Lisa was a thirty-something-year-old working woman who had spent most of her life keeping track of other people's investments. She started out when she was only fourteen, helping her mother figure out how to raise four children on a minimum wage job. After twenty years of marriage, her mother found herself leaving her routine duties in the home to venture into an arena she knew nothing about: the work force. Even with her experience as a mother, managing a home, tending the needs of her children and making certain her husband was properly cared for, she found herself needing to develop new skills that could produce a paycheck to support the family.

While it seemed a daunting task, Lisa's mother confronted the challenge and employed Lisa as "chief money manager." Fortunately for both of them Lisa was a perfect fit. She diligently took her mother's paycheck each week, divided up what needed to be set aside for each of the various bills, and placed a specific amount of funds in separate envelopes. Some weeks, money had to be moved from one envelope to another, especially if the "freebies" from working at the grocery store were not available that week.

Then, of course, the medicine required by her father for his recovery from a serious car accident often required moving resources from one envelope to the other. While her father was a sturdy man and not one to complain, he did have times when his body simply would not cooperate with his will to be free of pain. At those times he needed medication in order to get his rest, so as not to experience the emotional "hangover" that often came from feeling helpless and useless to his family. It was one thing to feel pain, but quite another to feel himself a burden.

As Lisa stood at the clearing remembering her family, she smiled at the simplicity of the cabin in front of her. *I am grateful for the ability to know what a blessing it is to live simply, without frills, and just to be able to find a way to use everything available to meet one's needs.* She smoothed the hair from her face, took a deep breath and said, "OK, let's get this checked off my list," and she moved toward the front porch.

Stepping onto the porch, Lisa noticed the old woman dusting off her skirt and brushing debris from her hair as she rounded the corner to the porch. The old woman looked about seventy, give or take a few years, with a long gray braid hanging down her back. She was a pretty woman with clear skin, rosy cheeks and a hint of pink lipstick. *Hmm,* she observed, *she must care about how she looks to be wearing lipstick. Guess that's her generation, 'cause Grandma wears lipstick at all times.*

She had to giggle as she thought of her grandma. Always wearing red lipstick, rouge on her cheeks and never leaving the house without her shawl. It didn't matter what the temperature was, Grandma had to have her shawl; she carried it like a warrior carries a shield. *Perhaps it is her "shield of courage,"* she mused. *It's that, or she is some sort of caped super hero!* She chuckled at the thought of her grandma living a life no one knew about.

"Hello, my name is Lisa," she said as she extended her hand to the old woman. The old woman merely nodded and pointed to the willow branch chair as she said, "Have a seat."

Lisa watched the old woman enter the cabin and close the door behind her. *Guess she's going in for the biscuits and hot chocolate.* She stood for a few moments scanning the yard in front of her. Moisture from the rain the day before hung heavy on the bushes that bordered the side of the cabin as she walked to the edge to view them more closely. *I do believe that one is what they call a "burning bush." They are my favorite fall bush, so full of fire, so rich with warmth; it's a marvel to watch the bright green leaves turn such a brilliant color.*

Lisa was deep in thought as she turned and saw the old woman placing a tray on the table between the swing and willow branch chair. "May I help you?" she offered the old woman.

Without a word, the old woman poured two cups of hot chocolate. Then she removed an orange fabric from the tray, revealing steaming hot biscuits, butter, what appeared to be strawberry preserves, and two saucers. Lisa took her place on the willow branch chair and accepted a cup of the hot brew.

As she blew into the cup, she watched as the old woman placed a buttered biscuit on a saucer, sat on the swing and began "chowing down." *I'll bet she is hungry as hard as she works! Might as well show respect by eating one of those huge biscuits. Would you look at those biscuits!* With that, Lisa smothered a biscuit in butter and joined the old woman in devouring a warm biscuit.

After both had enjoyed refueling their tummies, Lisa wiped her mouth with the napkin, placed it on the saucer, and returned both items to the wooden tray. She carefully picked up her cup of hot chocolate as she watched the old woman retrieve her handwork from a black velvet bag and begin twirling white thread through her fingers.

Grandma does a lot of handwork, but I'll be darned if I know what the old woman is doing. It's not crocheting, and certainly not knitting. Whatever is it she's doing? Lisa wondered. *Guess I'll just ask!*

"If I may ask, what sort of handwork are you doing?"

The old woman kept moving her fingers as a white chain began to emerge just beneath her hands.

"Tatting," was all she said. Lisa took a few more sips of her hot chocolate, poured herself some more, and began her question.

"First, thank you for taking the time to sit with me today. I know you must be swamped with household and yard duties if you live here by yourself. And, the biscuits and hot chocolate are absolutely delicious. Thank you so much for being so thoughtful."

She paused for a few moments to watch the squirrels that scurried all around the yard in front of her. *Gee, there must be a half dozen of those critters — they must be on "food patrol" for the winter.* They were busy gathering walnuts from the huge tree just to the left of the yard, along with hickory nuts from the smaller tree just to the right of the walnut tree. She watched as they seemed to move at warp speed. Scampering from one tree to the next, there seemed to be no particular order to what they were doing. It was as though each squirrel knew what needed to be done and simply took action with what was in front of them.

Lisa was lost in her thoughts of the squirrels when she remembered she was there to speak to the old woman. She continued, "I'm wondering if you can assist me with understanding how to be of service to people, without caring what they do with the advice/information that I give them?"

"You see, people come to me when they have money concerns, whether about money they want to invest, or money they need. People have all sorts of reasons for seeking my help, but it all revolves around money. Whether too little or too much, people seem to not know what to do with either concern."

Lisa watched for a moment as two squirrels fussed over a walnut. One dropped it, the other picked it up; then the one that dropped it came back to "reclaim his prize," but the other one seemed to be of the view, "Finders keepers, losers weepers," since he didn't seem to want to let it go so easily.

She returned to what she was saying. "I have always been good with money management; I learned very early in life how to divide up what we had and make it work, regardless of how much money I was given. What I have discovered over the years is, not everyone learns that skill.

Sometimes people grow up apparently never having to be concerned about money, since they did not take into consideration that they might not always have what they have at the moment. Those sorts of people spend money like it is water, and give little regard to appreciating what it takes to earn the money."

Lisa moved in her chair as she glanced over at the old woman. *Wonder if she's listening? Well, makes no mind, I'll find out when I finish my question, which I need to get busy doing.*

"And, then there are the sorts of people who have money they are afraid of losing, so they come to me to find ways to 'hide' it in order to make certain no one gets it from them. Those sorts of people hang onto money like it is a precious commodity they must cling to. Why, I've seen people who don't speak to their families because of money issues. It's a very sad state of affairs; nonetheless, I listen to their concerns, offer suggestions, and then take action according to what the client decides."

By now the half dozen or so squirrels were in a frenzy over their tasks. One darted past the other as two others joined together to survey the hickory nut tree.

Lisa continued, "Don't get me wrong; I enjoy my job, overall. I feel what I offer my clients makes for a better quality of life for them; that is, if they will follow my suggestions. I mean, everyone has a choice as to what they want to do; however, if they are to be satisfied with that choice, they have to do their 'homework,' so to speak. That's where I come in. All they need to do is tell me what their dreams are for their future and I find ways to help them obtain those dreams."

She finished her hot chocolate and poured yet another cup, then offered more to the old woman. When the old woman didn't pause her tatting, Lisa placed the china pot onto the wooden tray and sat back to enjoy her third cup.

"Don't mean to be overindulgent, but this is the best hot chocolate I've ever tasted," she said, as she closed her eyes to take her first drink of the third cup.

After pausing to enjoy swallowing the rich cocoa taste, she continued, "I guess my problem is, when people choose to not follow what I've done the research to recommend and then come back to me with the same problem, I feel very frustrated. I mean, if they had followed my recommendations they would have been closer to their goals. It really makes no sense to me, why these people pay me money to help them find solutions, then ignore the recommendations and come back for more advice. I have actually turned people away because they didn't follow my instructions. I would prefer to work with people who follow through with what they say they are going to do."

She paused for a few moments, looked at the old woman and asked, "Is that wrong of me? Am I expecting too much of them to keep their commitment? Or, should I just take their concerns back, start again and readjust what needs to be addressed? The last thing I want is to not be respectful to those that come to me."

Then Lisa felt the question take shape as she concluded, "So, my question is, what is the best way to respect both my client and myself, when dealing with people who do not follow through with what they say they are going to do?"

She felt pleased with the question that had emerged. She was not one for vagueness; she respected clarity and diligently worked to be clear in all her dealings. She settled back in her chair, very willing to wait for the old woman to begin her story whenever *she* was ready to reply. *I'm not rushing this woman; I know how much I appreciate people allowing me to just ponder something for a few moments until my thoughts are in order.*

It did not take long before the old woman began her story:

"People go about rushing here, rushing there, making appointments, changing their minds, rescheduling, then deciding things need to be a different way. It seems the world has become one in which the only thing that is a constant is change. And, there is nothing wrong with change if we are aiming to make things better in our world, in our lives, and in our communities.

"The problem seems to arise when people make changes based only upon how it affects them. When people think only of themselves, they cause a ripple in the pond of life that affects everyone around them. It wasn't too long ago when everyone realized that whatever they did had a direct influence on their families, their friends, and their communities. People used to think about these things, and when they needed to change they spoke with their neighbors, their families, and the elders in the community, and asked for some direction.

"The truth is, those that are the elders in the community know about change and how it affects others. Most have experienced many changes in their lives, and they saw how their actions influenced others.

"Back then, people valued each other, and they considered their resources as well. Most people knew that to have something was a gift, and to not treat it like a gift was to disrespect both the gift and the giver. It was a given that whatever they had in their possession was their responsibility to care for respectfully, with love, and with regard for what had been given. It mattered how others felt about what had been given to them.

"Nowadays, it seems we only think about ourselves, about how we are affected by what we want, what we can achieve, what we can acquire, and by what we can accumulate. Imagine how the world would be if everyone grabbed what they wanted without consideration for others in their families or communities, and hid away their 'treasures' so no one else could take them. It would be a very sad world."

The old woman stopped her tatting and looked out at the squirrels doing their winter work. "Can you imagine if the squirrels took everything they could find, even if it was more than they needed? Why, there would be chaos if they took all they could without regard for their friends. Imagine how you would feel when the winter comes with the coldness and snow, and you knew your friend in the next tree had a family that was hungry.

Why, there's not an animal put on Earth Mother that doesn't care about its friends. Oh, they may have competitions to see who can get the most, but when all is said and done, they share what they have stored."

She returned to her tatting and continued her story. "There is a fine line between judging others for their actions, and noticing what their actions say about them. If we are to be loving toward our families and friends, we will honor what we observe and take action for ourselves based upon how we feel inside our hearts. Sometimes it is best to leave people to their choices, even if it means they experience discomfort or uneasiness. Only the Creator can really know what is in someone's heart, so we can't really make sound observations about what they are doing, because we are not Creator. We can only look at our own hearts and ask if what we are feeling is based upon respect for those we know. If we are certain the actions we see are harmful or do not honor the words that have been said, then we need to demonstrate what that honoring looks like by keeping our word to them.

"Sometimes that is difficult because we want everyone to like us; but the truth is, some people just like being angry or unhappy, so we must respect them by allowing them to feel what they choose to feel, and not try to change their minds. If we try to make other people do what we feel is best, we are meddling in Creator's business with them."

The old woman stopped her hands, lifted them in the air to see how long the chain was, and then said, "Love is something we show by our actions, rather than by our words. Keep love in your actions and you add to the sweetness of community among the squirrels, you help the birds migrate South in the winter, and you help your own life to be full and complete."

She bit the end of the chain, knotted it, handed it to Lisa and said, "These are my words."

Lisa watched the old woman neatly tuck away her handwork, gather the items onto the wooden tray and enter her cabin. Without speaking a word, Lisa held the tatted chain in her hands and made a promise to herself. *Never again will I question my decisions. I will honor my word as a way of honoring my clients.* She sat very still on the willow branch chair and carefully considered the old woman's words.

Lisa had tried her very best to pay attention to details her whole life. As a young girl, her mother and father depended on her in order for all the bills and expenses to be covered. She considered for a moment the enormity of such a responsibility for a girl of only fourteen; and, yet, she felt a sense of pride in what she had learned so early. While the circumstances by which she became the financial planner for her family were indeed unpleasant and even downright scary at times, she knew the reason she was so very good at her job was because she had learned the importance of good money management very early.

"I suppose it was my destiny," she said. *Many people have been grateful for how I've assisted them with getting their finances in order.* With that she picked up her bag, dug through it for the perfect gift, then stepped to the twig basket and dropped it in as she stepped off the porch. *I think she'll enjoy that gift. It always makes me happy to have something practical that is also pretty.*

As she began her trek back through the Forest, she turned one last time and spoke to the squirrels that seemed to be watching her. "Oh, I guess I didn't properly thank *you* all for teaching me about sharing. Thank you so much." With that she dug into her purse and pulled out some peanuts she had hidden away just in case she got the munchies. She opened the bag and placed them in a pile on the ground. "There's your gift, my friends."

Dusting off her hands, she picked up her purse and the bag of goodies and headed back to the car. As she walked along the path she noticed the trail had become dry from the air, and her boots now became a soft brown from the dried mud. She stopped for a few moments, moved to the side of the trail and ever so gently wiped her boots in the tall grass. *That should help clean off some of the mud. By the time I get back to the car they will be clean as a whistle.*

As she continued along the trail she slowed her pace to enjoy the scent of the dirt and trees. *Such a refreshing smell,* she lifted her nose and sniffed the air. *It certainly makes me feel more grounded.*

It didn't take long before Lisa found the clearing where her car was parked. She paused for a few moments to consider the words given by the old woman. *How did she say it? "If we go around trying to make people do what we feel is best, we are meddling in Creator's business with them."* She spoke out loud, "Well, this lady has no intentions of meddling in Creator's business."

She settled herself into her car and said, "If a client comes back to me for help and has not followed the course of action we developed the first time they came, I'm going to just be honest and tell them that, if they can't keep their commitment to follow through with our plan, they will need to find someone else to work with. In the past I would have felt that a bit harsh. And, yet, my gut let me know that was part of the reason they were in the situation they were; they couldn't keep their word. So, I'm committed to helping them learn how to do that by keeping *my* word that the plan we developed was the best course of action to meet their needs and goals."

Just as she finished her words a very large blackbird swooped down onto the hood of her car. "OK, Mr. Blackbird, I take it you are in support of my decision."

With that, the blackbird spread his wings and flew off. "Such an amazing place this Forest is, and the old woman holds many truths she shares so freely. Thank you, Creator, for reminding me how to share my truths and keep my word. You have my promise that I won't be *Meddling* in your business again!"

Best Friends

Carefully scanning the grassy areas, Beth spotted the gravel parking area; it was precisely as her mother described. She eased the truck onto the pullover, checked her rearview mirrors to make certain she was a good distance from the road and put the truck in park. She surveyed the cab seats to make certain she had everything she needed. *Let's see, bag, umbrella and walking stick.* "I think I'm ready!"

Beth then scanned the area and found a place where grass was matted down. "Looks like this is the path to follow." As she proceeded on her journey she heard a faint sound in the distance; she stopped to listen carefully and see if she could identify the noise. *Nope, not sure what that is,* ran through her head as she stood perfectly still and listened intently. *Sounds like music of some sort; is someone singing?*

Her mother had told her of the many stories about this magical Forest, which held the old woman's cabin. Beth stood as still as possible, and all she could hear was her own breathing. *Hmm,* she pondered, *maybe it was my imagination playing tricks on me.*

As she began her journey along the path she remembered how, as a very young girl, she had felt more comfortable outdoors rather than "stuck inside." *It always felt so confining; so "stuck in a box with walls."* "I'm grateful for the wide open spaces, without the limitations of being inside!

Sorta like wearing your clothes when you're in the shower," Beth said softly.

As a young girl, Beth had spent most of her time with her "secret friend" — at least that was what she called him. To Beth he was no secret; he was as real as her brother. Her friend was with her at all times, and the comfort of knowing that made her feel very happy and safe. *Gosh, Peter, I haven't talked to you in a very long time.* "Are you still around?" she asked.

As her thoughts rambled through her head, she felt an urge to begin humming an old gospel hymn tune from her childhood. The tune ran rampant through her head as she heard a voice singing along:

> *No, never alon-n-n-e, no, never alone.*
> *He promised never to lea-ea-ea-ve,*
> *Never to leave me alone.*
> *No, never alon-n-n-e, no, never alone.*
> *He promised never to leave-ea-ea-ve,*
> *Never to leave me alone.*

Wow, it's been a hundred years since I heard that song, Beth remembered. *Well, maybe not a hundred years, but it's been a very long time!* She recalled the time she and her cousin were to sing this hymn at a church gathering. She was so nervous that when she began to sing, nothing came out — absolutely nothing! There she stood, beside her cousin who was singing away, and all she could do was lip sync the words. She remembered her cousin glaring at her as if to say, "What are you doing? Sing, stupid!" *Thinking about it now, it seems rather humorous.* At the time, however, her cousin was fit to be tied, and rightly so. "That had to be such an embarrassing moment for her!" Beth exclaimed out loud.

She returned to thoughts of her "secret friend," and recalled the hours and hours the two of them would sing, dance, roll in the grass, and giggle at the toads in the creek behind her house. They spent every day together doing something "adventurous." The truth was, Peter was the risk-taker; Beth just came along for the ride. She knew if Peter put some hair-brained idea in front of her, it would undoubtedly be fun. Despite her hesitations, Beth knew she could trust Peter to make certain she was safe, and she had a sore belly from the laughs that would ensue.

"Guess it makes sense that you're here today, Peter; we are on yet another adventure," Beth said as she stopped dead in her tracks, "Where have you been, Peter? I have missed you tremendously."

As she stood in the stillness with only the moist dew glistening on the ground cover, she felt a stirring within her stomach. "Peter, is that you?"

Once again, a faint sound could be heard in the distance. *Peter, I need to know if you are here, or if I'm just imagining you?* A lump arose in her throat and tears began to burn her eyes as Beth remembered what it felt like to have Peter around. *Silly goose, if it's you, let me know ... you remember our secret code; show me so I know it's you.*

Without so much as a moment passing, a huge hawk appeared directly overhead. The large wings made a fanning sound as he perched himself on an oak tree just ahead on the path. Beth began to breathe heavily as her stomach once again flipped and her heart nearly sprung from her chest.

Beth said, "Oh, Peter, it *is* you! I have missed you so very much!"

The hawk looked directly into Beth's eyes as she stood very still and, through tear-filled eyes, greeted her old friend. "Peter, where have you been? Why have you been gone so long?" As though she expected an answer, she stood there, shivering.

"Say, Peter, do you happen to have a spare jacket? Guess I didn't expect the morning to get cooler rather then warmer." She crossed her arms and rubbed them briskly with her hands, "Oh, I really don't mind, Peter, I'm just so glad you have come back; and, I did enjoy your singing! I never know what form you are going to take. Guess this time you decided to be a hawk."

The hawk sat pristinely on the wide branch of an old oak tree and stared back at Beth. He seemed to be watching over her like he had done most of her life. Within a few moments a warm breeze came rushing through the trees as Beth's mouth widened into a smile. "Why, thank you, Peter!"

Beth broke her gaze with the hawk as the scent of baked biscuits filled the air. "Well, I'm very glad you are back, and you have a lot of explaining to do, but for right now we need to get about the business I'm here for." Her stomach now growled from the delicious aroma that seemed to be leading her back to her task.

"What's the saying? 'Follow your nose?' Come on, Peter, I think you'll have fun with this adventure." As she continued on the trail she said out loud, "How about that, *I'm* finding us an adventure this time; this has to be a first!"

As the clearing became visible, Beth readjusted her bag strap and looked ahead at the small cabin snuggly nestled among the tall trees. *How I love the Standing Ones; how much fun we've had playing in and around them. Can you remember the first tree we shimmied up, Peter?*

As though expecting Beth, the old woman was sitting quietly on the porch swing. Beside her was a wooden tray with an orange fabric that covered the delicious scent. Beth approached the porch and greeted the old woman with a simple "Hello."

The old woman took the cover off the tray and poured a cup of hot chocolate, then handed it to Beth and nodded toward the willow branch chair. Beth placed her bag beside the chair, accepted the hot brew, then took a seat.

"Hi, I'm Beth, and thank you very much for the treats," she said as she took a whiff of the chocolate and blew on the hot brew. "Mmm, that smells delicious," was all she could say before she took a sip.

The old woman filled a cup for herself, then buttered a hot biscuit as she nodded to Beth to help herself. Beth gingerly put her cup on the wooden table, took a hot biscuit and smothered it with butter. *I don't care how many calories are in this thing; I'm eating it!*

As the two ladies feasted on the warm biscuits and hot chocolate, the large-winged hawk that had greeted her on the path landed on a stately walnut tree directly in front of the porch. Beth had to giggle. *Too bad you don't eat human food; you'd love these, Peter.*

The old woman placed her napkin on the cup and saucer, took out her handwork, and began moving her fingers in a rhythmic, almost majestic manner. Beth could not take her eyes off the hawk as she filled her belly with yet another warm biscuit, this time smothered with strawberry preserves. *I do believe I've died and gone to heaven,* she thought as she slowly chewed the last bite of the tasty morsel.

"Thank you for that absolutely delightful treat. I'm generally not good with idle talk, so I'll get to why I'm here." Beth put away her napkin and saucer, poured another cup of hot chocolate, then began her story.

"When I was a very young child I had an imaginary friend." She paused for a moment, wrinkled up her nose and said, "Well, I guess some would say he was imaginary. To me he was very real. It wasn't until I started elementary school that I realized not everyone had such friends. Most of my classmates looked at me weird when I talked about my 'friend;' they quickly let me know that was strange, and that it was time for me to 'grow up' and stop being a child who still believed in such things."

The old woman hadn't made so much as a peep, so Beth glanced over to see if she was listening. To Beth's surprise, the old woman and the hawk seemed to be having a staring match. She watched as the two peered intently at each other, and it was clear they were communicating with one another. *Hmm...No one had acknowledged her friend's presence before.*

With only the silence between them, Beth watched Peter turn his head to the right, with only his left eye visible. *Oh, my goodness, Peter; I do believe you are flirting with the old woman! I thought I was the only one you communicated with.* As if she realized what a ridiculous thought she had just had, Beth let a giggle slip out.

The old woman stared at the hawk and moved her head to the left, allowing only her right eye to be visible to the hawk. After a few turns of the head by both the old woman and the hawk, their communication seemed to be complete, and the old woman returned to her handwork as the hawk flew further up the walnut tree.

"Well," said Beth, "it seems you have met my dear friend." The old woman never broke stride with the rhythmic weaving of her thread, letting Beth know she had nothing to say.

Beth felt a stirring within; a stirring so strong she could hardly sit still in her chair. She adjusted herself in the chair, smoothed her skirt and began again, "I came here today to ask about my friend; to find out if what I felt so real as a child was, indeed, imaginary, or if it was a gift. Truth is, Peter takes different forms, too. He's not always a hawk; sometimes he's a real human." She sighed as a smile widened on her face, "Strange as it seems, I have my answer."

Reaching for the pot holding the hot chocolate, she offered it to the old woman. After the old woman shook her head, Beth poured herself another cup. "Thank you for helping me *know* the truth. There was never a doubt in my mind; however, from sixth grade on I quit talking to Peter. Of course, he would show up from time to time in various places I visited, but I never allowed communication to begin again. After all, how many adults do you see talking to creatures in the wild?"

The warmth of the hot chocolate brought a comfort she had not felt in a very long time, but Beth found herself feeling sad. *Peter, I am sorry for ignoring you, for allowing those silly kids to keep me from being with you.* Tears burned her eyes as her heart felt something it had avoided for years — it was Love! *Oh, Peter, please forgive me for not believing!*

As Beth moved through the emotions that stirred from her memories, the old woman began a story:

"Many years ago, before humankind decided it was the most important species on the planet, there were communities of people who lived in relationship with all of life. These communities relied on everything that lived to share their gifts with one another, or to provide a service. They looked around at the various creatures and asked what strengths they had, and embraced the talents of each.

"For example, the horse had great strength; it carried the gift of speed and self-reliance that comes from moving forward in life. So, the horse came into the community; it leaned its head to the ground and allowed the two-leggeds, now called humans, to mount its back, and carried them wherever they needed to go. It didn't take long for the humans to realize that they could use the horse to carry items, and to pull goods they needed to transport to the next community of humans. They moved South in winter, and in the summer they migrated back to the North.

"And so, the humans developed a relationship with the horse, caring for its needs so as to honor the gifts it brought to the community.

"The same form of communication developed between the humans and the deer, the elk, and those creatures that offered their bodies to feed and clothe the community. The humans did not need to kill all creatures; some of the creatures they found had already died from another, more powerful creature.

"The humans soon found that if they dried the skins from these creatures in the sun, they made good blankets and robes in the winter, and their antlers could be used for spearing fish from the waters, cooking a rabbit over a fire, or worn for special ceremonies. There were many ways in which the community used the resources put in front of them to survive the elements of nature and to continue the chain of life for both humans and the creatures of the land.

"What is most interesting is, there were no words used between humans and creatures, and yet they communicated with one another. The deer allowed humans to kill them for food because they felt the love and gratitude from the humans for providing their bodies as food for the community. Likewise, the humans knew the creatures were giving themselves in order to feed those in the community. It was a mutual love and respect that kept the community growing and thriving.

"Even when humans took plants from the wild and prayed over them they received health and healings from each one that was honored with respect and love. The plants felt this love and continued to grow and multiply in order to be used not only by humans, but by any creature that needed to be fed.

"It was a peaceful time on the planet, as everything that lived felt loved, respected and valued for the gifts they offered to the community. There is much we can learn from those that walked before us, and it was not only the humans that offered teachings about peacemaking. To remember these truths is to remember your purpose for coming to this planet. It is a true love measured by the natural gifts of every creature, and for this no words are needed because it is felt within each creature's heart."

The old woman bit the end of the tatted chain, knotted it, handed it to Beth and said, "It is a wise soul who knows how to giggle and play with all of God's creatures. These are my words."

With tears running down her cheeks, Beth accepted the gift. "Thank you for sharing the truth. My heart is full," was all she could say.

Moving to her garden, the old woman held her hand out to the hawk, touched her heart, bent to the ground and touched it as she mumbled some soft words Beth did not recognize. The hawk seemed to understand perfectly what the old woman was doing, because he extended both wings in the air and flapped them gently three times before settling back on the tree branch. It was as though old friends acknowledged one another's presence.

Beth gathered her bag, dropped a gift into the twig basket and moved toward the path that led to her parking place. She kept her eyes on Peter as she wiped the tears from her cheeks. *Peter, please never leave me, I promise to always acknowledge your presence. I love you, and I want you to teach me how to love unconditionally, to stay committed and to keep my word. You have done all you promised to do even when I chose to ignore you. Thank you for being my friend!*

The huge hawk kept his eyes on Beth as she faced the Forest in front of her. As she disappeared into the thick of the woods, he lifted his wings, unhooked his talons and took flight toward his beloved friend. As he soared above the treetops Beth could hear him "cawing" to her. She stopped just shy of the truck, looked up and said, "I love you, Peter; let's always be, *Best Friends!*"

The Father

His son said to him, "Everybody knows you don't deal well with stress." The Father felt shocked as his mind jolted to attention. "I don't deal with stress well?" he asked, pointing his finger to his chest, "Really, you think I don't deal well with stress well?" The words were felt deep within the Father's core, as he wondered, Did I hear that correctly? Really?

His shock and surprise were clearly visible on his face, because his son looked across the table and said, "Yes, uh, well, uh..." The son stopped short of any other words as his eyes widened and his face revealed concern that he had said something wrong.

The Father saw his son's concern and said, "It's OK if you think that, Josh. I am just surprised, that's all."

It was an awkward moment as everyone at the table became quiet, waiting to see what would happen next. Josh glanced across the table to his brother, Troy, for some reassurance, or at the very least, some moral support, and said, "Maybe I'm not saying that right?"

The Father saw an all too familiar look on his son's face that he had seen many times over the years: the concern that he had said something "wrong." So the Father repeated, "It's OK, Josh, you are entitled to what you feel. It really is OK." He continued, "So, what were you going to tell us about?" The Father hoped to bring the focus back to his son's story, rather than the awkwardness of the son's words.

With that, the son continued his story and the tension of the moment became a memory. The Father was most grateful for that since he cared very much how his son felt. He knew his son well enough to know his words were meant with no judgment of the Father's behavior; rather, they were simply observations the son had made. The very last thing the Father wanted was to create a situation in which Josh would "revisit" an old pattern his son had worked very hard to eliminate.

After everyone had left and the dishes were cleaned up and put away, the Father recalled the incident and found his son's words a bit disconcerting. Could his son really think he did not handle stress well? The Father had spent his whole life assisting others with problems and concerns in their lives. His entire professional life was one of helping others identify their problems, set goals, and discover ways to achieve whatever they chose. How could his son think he didn't handle stress well?

As was always the remedy for his thought process, the Father wrapped himself snuggly in warm clothes and headed outdoors for a brisk walk. The cold, North wind blew sharply as he wrapped his scarf tightly around his neck. It feels good to have the freshness of fall on my skin after a very long, hot summer, he reflected as he picked up the pace. It really doesn't matter that Josh feels I don't handle stress well; I mean, does any young person really understand what their parent does at work?

He approached a favorite old barn located along his usual walking path, and hurried toward it to escape the strong winds for a few minutes. Once inside the barn, he sat down on one of the farm implements housed within and pondered the situation. Josh has heard me speak of my clients, and he knows I just came from my mother's and all the responsibilities that went along with her care. Hmm, he thought, as he looked about the rickety old barn. The tin roof clinked and clattered as the wind continued heralding in the icy blast from the North.

Why does this even bother me? he wondered as he briskly rubbed his hands together. That's probably a better question. I mean, it isn't as if my kids don't know that when something's wrong, or when they are confronting a difficult situation; I'm the one they call to help them out. *His thoughts continued to ruminate through his head,* Hmm ...

The Father drew his gloves from his coat pocket, slipped them on his hands and headed back to his house. *It doesn't matter; just shake this off, you silly goose! I believe this is something you used to do all the time — be concerned what others thought — and that isn't important to you anymore, remember?* He tried to convince himself.

The walk back home took much less time as the sharp North winds pushed him quickly along the path. The Father noticed the various hues of gray and black as blue peeked through the gaps in the clouds. *What a beautiful sight! How people can see the skies and not know without a shadow of doubt that there is a Creator, is beyond me!*

As he rounded the corner to his house and approached the back porch, he thought, *Nothing like a good, brisk walk to put everything into perspective and blow the "stinkin' thinkin'" right off ya!*

The Father released the memory as he took a breath and smelled the freshness of the air. The sun was high in the sky and birds of every size and shape dotted the blue skies. He closed his eyes and took another big sniff, allowing the scent of pine to fill his whole being. *What a refreshing scent! Reminds me of Christmas, gifts, colored lights, caroling and freshly baked cookies.* Then he released his breath, *Ahh, life is good!* Frozen in the moment of time, the Father kept his eyes closed and allowed the warmth of the day to surround him like a lover's embrace.

What an amazing life we are offered. Thank you, Creator, for all that you give us! The Father stood just outside the clearing to the old woman's cabin as he refreshed his thoughts with the simple, yet exquisite surroundings in which he stood. He opened his eyes, took a deep sigh, *OK, let's see what happens.* And with that, he proceeded to the porch of the cabin.

The Father stepped onto the porch as the old woman walked out carrying a fabric-covered tray. He took off his hat, ran his hand through his hair and said, "Good Day, Ma'am, it's a pleasure to meet you." After placing his hat on the edge of the willow branch chair, he extended his hands and said, "Let me help you with that."

The old woman allowed the Father to take the tray and removed the black velvet bag from the table between the chair and porch swing, leaving a clear space for him to rest the tray. The Father placed the tray on the table and waited for the old woman to take a seat on the porch swing before he sat down in the willow branch chair.

"It's a mighty fine place you have here. I thank you for your time today."

The old woman removed the fabric, poured two cups of coffee and uncovered a wicker basket that revealed warm chocolate chip cookies. *Mmm*, the Father breathed in the scent as his stomach gurgled with glee! *Maybe I did smell this a while ago!*

"Help yourself," she said, as she extended a cup to the Father.

"Why, I'll do that," he said, as he received the cup, placed it on the arm of the chair and quickly retrieved a cookie from the basket. "Mmm, those smell great," was all he could say, as he took a large bite and chocolate oozed out the corner of his mouth. "Wow, these are as good as they smell!" he said as he washed it down with a sip of the coffee and licked the chocolate from his lips. "I didn't know I'd be treated to such a delectable snack. Mighty nice of you to be so thoughtful!"

The two sat in silence for what seemed like ten minutes, until the old woman stood up and walked to the edge of the porch. She stood facing the sun as it began to move toward the West.

With her eyes closed, she took three deep breaths, and then began her story:

"Stress is a word that is used a lot these days. Doesn't matter where you go, people are talking about how stressed they are. Too much work, not enough work, too many things to do, not enough to do. Seems no matter what a person feels they need, if they don't have enough of it, or if they have too much of it, they're stressed."

She opened her eyes, returned to the porch swing, took out her tatting shuttle and thread, and began "curling thread." There was silence once again as the Father sat still, watching her move her fingers with a rhythm and fluidity that was almost intoxicating as she continued her story.

"I believe people just like to talk. They like to hear themselves say things, even if what they are saying doesn't make a lot of sense. People open their mouths and begin talking before they even have their thoughts clearly arranged in their heads. It's little wonder they are 'stressed;' they've overworked their jaws! How can their heads figure out answers when their mouths are moving at warp speed? The truth is, most of the people they are talking to don't really hear their words; they, too, are busy thinking about how they are going to respond to the 'talking head' in front of them."

The Father had to chuckle at that comment. He reached over for his coffee cup, leaned back in his chair and settled in for a good "listening" session.

"Yes, sir, people got lots of ideas, lots of things rolling around in their brains even when they're asleep. It's little wonder they are tired all the time. It is also not surprising they feel 'stressed;' they have overworked their brains *and* their jaws.

"What people need to remember is that life was meant to be simple. No need to fret about what's going to happen tomorrow; it won't get here until then, so why think about it today? Doing that makes you lose sight of what is happening right in front of you at this very moment."

The old woman paused a few moments and looked out at the woods in front of her. "See those squirrels chasing each other up that walnut tree? The only thing they're 'stressed' about is how they can catch up with their friend. Those squirrels spend time just having fun. They gather nuts and goodies when the season presents those gifts, but until then, they just play and chase each other around.

"The problem with people today is, they don't take the time to just have fun. When they do get together they are busy talking about their problems or about other people. They don't realize how much singing, telling stories or playing games can lighten their burdens. Don't get me wrong; there's a time for talking to people you trust about what lies heavy on your heart, but first you need to take the time to just sit quietly and *listen*, rather than think.

"The good Lord made us to love and support each other and, more importantly, to have a relationship with our Creator. It doesn't matter what 'religion' a person follows; if they don't know their Creator as their best friend, they're going to carry burdens. Other humans are good to talk to about concerns, but they are just as encumbered with the things that bother them. The sooner humans realize that the Creator is their best source of support the sooner they will realize there's no need for 'stress.'"

The old woman bit the end of the thread and tied a knot in the end, "Every situation has an answer, and there *is* a way to resolve every single concern," she said as she gathered her tatting supplies, placed them back in the black velvet bag and set it beside her on the swing.

She continued, "The real problem with people today is that they fail to talk to the one that created them, and then be still long enough to hear an answer. The good Lord loves us in heavenly ways — ways we cannot always understand while on Earth Mother because we're inundated with our 'talking heads.' It is time for humans to use their ears to hear solutions, and then they just might find they don't have so much stress. They just might realize that life was meant to be simple, and that they can return to that place at any moment. Yes, sir, if people could just take their situation to God, *be still and listen*, and then take the action they are given, they'd have more time to be like those squirrels and just play!"

She rose from her swing, stood in front of the Father, bent over and handed him the white tatted chain. "You see, when people have learned to enjoy the moment, they keep their lives very simple. People who have not learned this often see 'simple' people as those that cannot handle stress." She touched his heart with the tatted chain and continued, "You have a great heart. Keep listening to your Creator, and your years on Earth Mother will be long." The old woman gathered the items onto the tray, covered it with the cloth, turned to him and said, "These are my words." Then she turned and entered into the cabin.

The Father felt warmth in his heart. It had been a very long time since anyone had acknowledged his heart. *Oh, I don't need any recognition; I know people respect me, but it sure is nice to have someone I just met really see me.* The Father stood up and stretched, then tucked the white chain in his pocket.

He grabbed his hat from the edge of the willow branch chair and placed it on his head. *Pretty amazing how that woman pays attention to God.* He dropped a gift in the twig basket as he stepped off the porch and headed toward the trail.

As he neared the Forest he heard a hawk "caw." He stopped and looked about until the hawk was just over his head. Leaning back to see the hawk, he stared at the magnificent bird and felt the warmth of a whisper. *What was that?* he wondered. *Feels like a breath in my ear.* Standing very still, he felt the warmth again, only this time he heard soft words. *I love you; I'm sorry.* The Father felt his heart begin to pound as a strong tug of emotions overcame his being.

"Maria?" he whispered. "Is that you, Maria?"

The fresh scent of pine again filled the air, as the Father waited for an answer to his question. The hawk circled above, cawing to the Father, whose mouth was now dry and his palms sweaty. "I'm listening, Maria," was all he could say.

As the hawk disappeared beyond the treetops, the Father somehow knew there would be no more words, so he began his trek back to his car. As he moved along the path he watched and listened, as his heart seemed to call to Maria, *Oh, how I wish you were here. How I wish I would have told you what a treasure you were to me.*

Meandering through the Forest, the Father arrived at his car, took out his keys and opened the door. As he reached for his seat belt, he noticed something pink sticking out from between the seats.

What is that? Could it be ... ? "Oh my goodness! IT IS!" he exclaimed as he pulled the pink hankie from between the seats. He took it in his hands and immediately buried his face in it. *Oh, my goodness, Maria,* he exclaimed as he inhaled her scent on the hankie.

As the Father stood frozen in time he felt his heart open wide. He wept with tears of both sorrow and joy, held the hankie again to his face and allowed his heart to really feel her absence. The blending of grief and love allowed the Father to release the pain of his loss, regrets about his choices, and once again to embrace the memory of love and remember how it feels to forgive and to be forgiven.

As the Father gathered his wits about him, he looked back to the path and thanked Creator for this magical place. *Maria, I know our life together is over ... I have accepted that. I guess my heart just needed to open a bit wider.* The Father knew Maria was now the wife of another man, and it had been over ten years, after all, since they were married. Yet, even though he had developed a life without her, the sadness of losing their relationship seemed to sneak up on him from time to time. The Father knew he would always hold a place in his heart for the mother of his children. They shared two amazing children that would forever keep their hearts somewhat connected, and for that he was eternally grateful.

Nestled inside the car, the Father realized the "talking head" was having its way with him, so he recalled the old woman's words: "Yes, sir, if people could just take their situation to God, *be still and listen,* and then take the action they are given, they'd have more time to be like those squirrels and just play!"

He closed his eyes for a moment and said a silent prayer to his Creator. Within a few moments, the Father opened his eyes and looked in the seat beside him. "Yep, there it is," he said as he picked up the new

CD he had just purchased "for some strange reason." *I knew there was a reason I bought you*, he thought as he slipped it into the CD player.

"OK, Maria, let's have some fun and sing some of our old favorite songs." With that, he drove away, grateful that he had learned to keep his life simple. He knew he was a "better man" for having made the trip; and, that the best gift he had ever received, Maria had given him — the gift of being a Father.

As he drove the road home listening to his new CD, he felt the warmth of memories and felt the joy that only his favorite music could bring to him. *What a gift!* he smiled. *What a way to sing away the thoughts that can clutter my mind!* And then the Father's thoughts meandered back to the situation with Josh. He pushed the pause button on the CD player and thought, *I realize why Josh thinks I don't handle stress well! The truth is, he never sees what I do that relieves my stress.*

Traffic began to pick up as he entered the city and his thoughts continued. *All I show others is the "composed" side of me — the problem-solver, the motivator, the grand cheerleader!* He felt a tinge of guilt, then quickly said, "I can fix this! It is time for my family and friends to see my silly side. The boys knew that side of me when they were young; however, they rarely see that now that they are older." *Maybe it is because we are all so busy ...* Then he quickly stopped his thoughts. "Hogwash! No excuses, no explanations! It is time for this to change!"

A smile widened on his face as he pulled his car into the driveway. "We haven't played games in years! And when was the last time I challenged you to a good game of horseshoes? Or put on the 'jams' and played some head bangin' 'air guitar?'"

The Father pulled into his garage, gathered his things and walked to the front door as something brownish-red caught his eye. He turned and noticed a squirrel that had scampered up the tree in his front yard. "Hey, little buddy, it is good to see you having fun! Guess it's time the humans that live here learn to adopt some of your ways." He continued, "Bet you didn't know you could teach us how to relieve stress!"

With that *The Father* entered his home, knowing everything in his life was about to become different. He was about to once again teach his children how to reduce stress in life, how to have fun, how to be like ... squirrels!

The "Container"

Butterflies fluttered in her stomach as Katie approached the front door. *For heaven's sake! Be still!* she told her tummy. *You agreed to be here, now be calm!*

She took a deep breath to "regroup" herself, then gently tapped on the door. A hammered copper hummingbird figure hung in the center of the door. *My, my, I did not anticipate feeling so nervous,* she thought as she brushed her hair to one side and stared at the copper fixture. *That's a lovely piece of copper work; wonder if someone gifted her with that? How lovely!* She adjusted her cap, raised her hand to knock a second time, and with her hand in mid air, something to the right caught her eye. She turned and saw the old woman, dressed in blue jeans, well-worn black moccasins and a bold green corduroy jacket. The old woman removed her work gloves, brushed dried leaves from her clothing and stepped onto the porch.

Katie turned, removed her cap, and extended a hand to greet the old woman. "Hello, I'm Katie, and I am most grateful to finally meet you." She cleared her throat and, with a poised and confident voice, continued, "I have heard many good things about you." Inwardly, Katie felt quite nervous, and she could not really explain why she felt that way. *For heaven's sake, Katie, pull yourself together!*

The old woman nodded, pointed to the willow branch chair, and simply said, "Have a seat, Katie." Katie felt a bit awkward, as she had been taught to wait until the elder in the room was seated before taking a seat herself; however, she did as the old woman instructed and moved toward the willow branch chair.

The old woman walked toward the porch swing. *Looks like she's going to sit on the swing, so I guess it's OK to sit down.* Then, *Stay focused!* Katie reminded herself. *Do not get distracted by protocol!* She paused for a moment to regroup and continued. *They said she doesn't like idle talk, so just pay attention; you'll know when to ask the question.* She stood waiting for the old woman's next move.

As the thick early morning clouds parted, the mid-morning air began to warm Earth Mother. Blue skies cleared the way for Grandfather Sun to bring warmth and life to the activities of the day. The Standing Ones stirred from the breeze as they stretched toward the heavens, and Katie felt the wonder of the land.

"Why, you can almost hear the trees yawning and stretching from the sun's warmth," Katie said aloud to the old woman, as she placed her bag beside the chair and took a seat.

The old woman had a sweet, subtle smile as she placed her work gloves onto the swing, and reached toward the table to remove the fabric, revealing the items beneath. An elegant china tea set, complete with shiny silver spoons and ecru-colored, lace-trimmed napkins, was carefully positioned on a wooden tray. *That seems out of place for this quaint cabin.* Katie observed. *That china looks fit for royalty!*

She watched the old woman place her rough, leathered hands over a napkin-lined basket as she closed her eyes and mumbled a few words. *I think she's praying.* She watched the old woman open the napkin, revealing beautifully peaked, brown muffins that filled the air with the scent of cinnamon.

Wow, those look almost too pretty to eat! Katie thought as her stomached growled. Her tummy seemed to say, "Are you kidding? They look good enough to eat right now!"

Katie remembered being a young girl in 4-H and entering her muffins in the competition. *I remember our Home Ec teacher telling us good muffins would have a "nice peak," with small air holes within the body of the muffin. Goodness, I haven't thought about that in eons!*

The old woman poured a cup of tea, extended it to Katie, then poured a cup for herself. After she carefully placed her cup on the edge of the table, the old woman placed a muffin on a dainty saucer and offered it to her.

Katie's mouth watered as she gingerly set the cup of tea on her side of the table, accepted the muffin and said, "Thank you! They look *and* smell delicious!" She then took a lace-trimmed napkin, placed it on her lap, and waited for the old woman to take the first bite. She was most grateful when the old woman almost immediately began to eat the muffin, and Katie promptly followed her lead. *Mmm,* Katie softly moaned as she looked at the muffin. *Those are so good, and sure enough, there are those tiny holes!*

A whisper of the wind moved through her heart as she sat in the silence of the wordless stillness. Blackbirds "cawed" to each other, and in the distance a faint sound of a bobwhite could be heard. The trees swayed in the cool fall breeze and dried leaves resounded a rustling noise as they swirled in spiral shapes thorough the yard in front of the porch. Katie drank the warm tea, very grateful for its presence in her belly, which was now very content.

The old woman placed her cup and saucer on the table, removed her tatting tools from the black velvet bag and began to do her magic with the thread. Katie watched the old woman. *Now might be the best time to ask my question before I forget it.* With only the sounds of nature filling the air, she felt content to just sit on the porch and watch the old woman curl the thread into a beautifully crafted chain. She closed her eyes for a moment, breathed in the air, and recalled her question.

"I am here today to ask for a teaching about emotions. Most of my life I have listened to people talk about the stories of their lives. As long as I can remember, I've listened to the hearts of people as they work through the challenges, struggles and confusions that life can bring. Someone I love very much once said I seemed detached and 'unemotional.' It made me stop and think. I do have lots of feelings about life. I feel very deeply about the feelings and emotions of those around me. Fact of the matter is, I don't even need to know the person. I can watch the news, or read a story that will often bring tears."

Katie paused for a moment; she could feel the onset of tears begin in her heart, move upward, and create a lump in her throat. Simply thinking about the sorrow and pain of others stirred her soul to the point that she felt her nose get red and her eyes burn with emotion.

"I do know I don't show my deepest emotions to many. Mostly, I keep them to myself. I take my tears to bed, or bake up some cookies for others; I write, and I exercise. But mostly, I take my feelings into the silence and pray about them. I respect that people have their word for the divine, so I'll use what I know. I take my feelings to God."

Katie felt a wave of softness replace her tears as the warmth of tenderness filled her heart from just speaking of her connection to the divine. "I am grateful for my relationship to God; and, I feel God is in all things, not just in a church or in the Bible. What I know is, God is present in all beings on this planet. That brings great comfort to my human heart. When I can remove myself from the strong emotional energy that people often carry, all I need do is call to God for assistance."

The sun disappeared behind the thickening clouds that returned, as the once cool breeze now became cold. Katie buttoned her coat, poured herself another cup of tea, took a sip, and warmth returned to her belly.

"The air has become cold; may I pour you another cup?" she asked the old woman. The old woman nodded "yes" as she paused her tatting, placed it in her lap and zipped up her corduroy jacket. She then held her cup as Katie poured steaming hot tea from the teapot.

"Looks like the tea is still very warm; this is a very nice teapot you have," Katie said as she once again warmed her own cup before returning the teapot to the tray. After a few moments Katie continued.

"I understand why people may think I'm unemotional, but you know, I have figured out that when I ask God to assist, the divine always steps in and answers. For me, that answer comes with a warmth in my belly that moves into my heart. It is a peacefulness that fills my body with a calm abiding that only God can bring."

Katie looked over at the old woman who had returned to her tatting. A white chain extended beneath her hands and Katie was amazed by how dainty and delicate the chain appeared. "I must say, that chain is beautiful. I cannot imagine how you take that thread and make something look so intricate. You have quite a gift," Katie told the old woman as she took another sip of her warm tea.

"I was not going to talk so much — I was told to keep things short and to the point — but words have been something I have never lacked." Katie smiled as she continued, "That's something I can agree with others about; I do talk a lot! But, you know, I love telling stories, and, I believe everyone has one. Sometimes people just need to see that what unfolds during their life *is* the story they will leave when they are done here on Earth."

The old woman bit the thread to detach the chain from the ball of thread and tied a knot in the end as Katie said, "I guess I want to make certain I'm not kidding myself that I am handling my emotions. I have a very big heart that feels very deeply. I just choose to not show people that side — at least at the time of *their* great emotional release. Seems to me if *they* are letting go of their feelings, they certainly do not need *me* to become emotional. If I did, it wouldn't help them unwind their emotions; instead, it would put the focus on *me*, and that would take away from what *they* need to work through." Katie placed her teacup on the table as she concluded, "At least, that's how I see it!"

The old woman placed her tatting tools back in the black velvet bag, set them to the side of the swing, and stood up. Katie rose from her chair as the old woman moved directly in front of her, extended the chain to her and said, "You are a container, Miss Katie; that is a gift to this world. There are many people who never learn how to give their own problems to the Creator, let alone anyone else's concerns. Stay close to your God; let that relationship carry you through your life and you will add beauty to those around you."

The old woman placed her aging hands on Katie's hands and said, "People's emotions can block their dreams. A container takes the concerns of others and offers them to the universe, so they can be transformed into something that can help those people become what their hearts dream of being. Keep your container clean, and all of your life will be a sacred gift to the world. Our Creator works through those willing to be such a container."

She patted Katie's hands and concluded, "You are a beautiful container. These are my words." With that, the old woman gathered the items back onto the tray, replaced the fabric cover, turned, and carried the tray into the cabin.

Katie sat in the stillness of the moment with only the sounds of her heart beating, as the rhythm of the wind swirled a spiral dance with the once alive leaves that now let go of their home. Layers and layers of the leaves rested on the ground where they would serve as a blanket to protect and enrich the land during winter's fury. Katie closed her eyes and smelled the scent of pine in the air as her skin felt the crispness of fall. All of Katie's senses were alive as she stood in the presence of all that is divine — in the very moment of NOW!

A container! A smile appeared on her face. *I like that! Makes me feel like what I do has purpose!* Katie opened her eyes as she recanted the old woman's words, "People's emotions can block their dreams." *She is absolutely correct! That is precisely why I have been given the gift to detach from my emotions and not get caught up in the emotions of others.* "I understand — I understand," she spoke softly to her heart. "Thank you for the clarity; thank you for bringing me here."

Katie looked down at the tatted chain she clutched in her hands. She sighed deeply as she exhaled a breath that released the doubts, questions, and apprehensions she held in her mind about what others had said. "No place for those obstacles!"

She took another deep breath from her belly to her chest, then slowly exhaled the breath out loud. When the breath was completely emptied from her body, she said, "There! The container is clean again!"

Katie retrieved her bag from beside the willow branch chair, pulled out a brightly colored package and placed it in the twig basket by the porch steps. After taking her first step off the porch she paused, turned around, and stepped back onto the porch.

She paused for a moment, then reached into her bag to fumble for her wallet, *I believe something else wants to be gifted.* She paused for a moment, then reached into her bag to fumble for her wallet. She retrieved some money, lifted the brightly colored package and placed the cash underneath. "A very small token for your generous spirit," she whispered as she glanced toward the front door.

Katie walked the path to her car with a light step; she felt as though the weight she had carried to the cabin had been lifted. *Guess my container was pretty full! Looks like I'm going home a whole lot lighter!*

As she settled back into her car, she said, "Home; what a marvelous place to be! From this moment forward I am keeping my home uncluttered and simple; just like *I* need to be!" She glanced back at the Forest through her rearview mirror and said to the trees, "*The Container!* That is what *you* are, for you hold within your clearing a very special lady!" She felt tears moisten her eyes as she took a deep breath and blessed the Forest with a simple, "Thank You!"

The Trout

"I wish to tell you a Love story," the old woman told the gentleman sitting to her left, as she tatted away with her thread and wooden shuttle.

The gentleman drank the last of his coffee and poured himself another cup as he replied, "Then it's a Love story I will hear! But first, may I pour you some more coffee?" And he pointed the pot toward the old woman's cup.

"No, thank you," she replied, and she began her story:

"Kenny knew the girl of his heart was already in his life by the age of sixteen. As life would have it, however, the girl did not necessarily share his 'knowing.' Oh, she thought he was a delightful and very cute boy, but she also knew every girl thought the same thing. So, Rachel kept Kenny at bay with all sorts of excuses, but she was kind enough to not be so forthcoming in her words as to tell him she had no intention of being yet another girl waiting to be his 'chosen one.'

"Rachel was a spirited young girl who knew her heart well, and to be second to someone else was not on her list of desires. She knew her already insecure personality would never tolerate such feelings. So, Rachel learned to protect her heart early in life, and as her life unfolded she began to lay a foundation of brick and mortar that would eventually become high and thick walls.

"Over the course of the next thirty years Kenny and Rachel led somewhat similar lives. Each had chosen marriage partners and careers, and each had three children, two girls and one boy, in that precise order. Each of their lives was filled with activities to ensure their children a solid home foundation. However, Kenny lived in a huge city, filled with lots of travel and financial successes, while Rachel fed her heart living in the country, and her career choice provided a modest means.

"It was a good life for both of them since each had a deep love for family with a desire to provide stability for their children. And yet, both knew something within their hearts was 'unfulfilled.'

"Rachel's life took some major turns when her children were grown and had moved out on their own to begin their adult lives. Her marriage had been over for a dozen or so years, and as the loneliness of an empty nest tugged at her heart, she knew it was time to face the unknown that lay ahead of her. How she was going to do this, she had no idea; however, she did know how to listen to the still, quiet voice within her heart that told her to 'move on.' What that meant she also had no idea; and yet, she knew when the time came, she would be given specific directions.

"Kenny's children were still teenagers, his career was blossoming, and yet something within his soul yearned for more. He was not certain what that was, but he was willing to follow the path before him.

"One day, Kenny discovered through mutual friends that Rachel lived just outside a major city he would be visiting on a business trip. He called Rachel and they made arrangements to meet for dinner.

"For Rachel it was an 'odd' meeting, as she felt his eyes on her in a way that was most uncomfortable. She wasn't quite certain what it meant, but she had been single long enough to know it spelled trouble. As the evening came to a conclusion Kenny said to her, 'Stay with me,' to which Rachel responded, 'What!? Kenny, I have not seen you in nearly thirty years, and you are married, for heaven's sake!'

"Kenny's reply was short, 'My wife has nothing to do with this.' This was not the man she had known some thirty years earlier. She wondered how he could have become so 'out of integrity.' She felt completely disillusioned by her old friend and left for home.

"Apparently, Kenny felt the meeting was delightful. A sense of knowing, of familiarity, of a comfort he had long missed was once again in his life. While his intentions were purely heart-felt gratitude for seeing her again, Rachel's now very high walls were riddled with suspicion and mistrust, and the chip on her shoulder grew larger!

"So, Kenny left enthralled with the mystery of it all and Rachel retreated back into her usual indignant 'who do you think you are?' attitude! It was not a pretty picture; rather, it was filled with unsettled emotions.

"A few months later Kenny returned to the area in which she lived, so he contacted her to ask if they might meet again. Rachel agreed to see him; however, she knew she would need to be very clear with him about the boundaries in their relationship if they were to remain friends.

"When Kenny returned, Rachel decided a safe thing to do would be to take him to visit her sister, who had also been an old friend of Kenny's. It was at that point that events took a major turn."

The old woman put down her tatting, lifted her cup to the gentleman and said, "I will take some of that coffee now." The gentleman quickly obliged and poured himself another cup as well. As they sipped coffee and watched the fire slowly burn in the fireplace, the gentleman said, "So, do Kenny and Rachel end up together?"

The old woman merely smiled, sipped her coffee, set it on the table, and resumed her tatting and continued. "As Kenny and Rachel were driving to her sister's house, Kenny busily chatted about everything from the weather, to his family, and to what she had been doing for the past thirty years. Then, out of nowhere, he reached for her hand.

"Of course, indignant Rachel pulled her hand away and gave him a puzzled look. She was perplexed by his behavior and prayed for the kindest words to respond to him. While she 'normally' would be quite clear about her feelings regarding someone's actions, she somehow sensed his intentions were very genuine, and respectful rather than arrogant. While this perplexed her, it also put her in quite a quandary as to what actions to take!

"Once they arrived at her sister's house, she felt relief as Kenny became fully engaged in conversation with her sister's life story. That is, until the conversation came back to Rachel. She was the only one who had grandchildren at that time, so they inquired as to how her grandson was doing."

"So, Rachel began to tell about how her grandson had a thing for people's hands. She described how her grandson would take a person's hand and place it between both of his. She turned to Kenny and said, 'May I borrow your hand?' to which Kenny quickly offered his left hand.

"Rachel took his hand, sandwiched it between both of her hands, and without any warning she felt an electrical spark. It was so intense it nearly took her breath away. She regrouped as quickly as possible, promptly concluded her story and released Kenny's hand.

"Kenny and her sister continued their conversation while Rachel was numb with emotions. She could not understand what had just happened. She felt as though an electrical charge had transformed her heart. The reverberation ran from her toes to the top of her head as she felt a sensation she had never known. *What was that?* she questioned her heightened senses. *What just happened?*

The old woman paused for a moment, lifted the tatted chain to examine its length, then promptly returned to her story. "Keep in mind, Rachel had been single for more than thirteen years. She was no fool when it came to being around men, and she had mastered the fine art of self-control. But this was something she had never experienced.

"After they said their good-byes, they drove back toward Rachel's home, and once again Kenny chatted away while Rachel sat in silence. She just stared at him like it was the first time she had ever seen him. A million questions whirled through her head as she tried to understand what had just happened. And, when no logical conclusions were available, Rachel reached for his hand. Of course, Kenny quickly responded by staring back at her with pure delight.

"When they arrived back at Rachel's Kenny approached her with caution. He stared into her eyes and told her he really wanted to see her again. This time when Rachel really looked deeply into Kenny deep blue eyes, she saw a different man standing in front of her and her heart could barely contain itself. She finally mustered up enough 'common sense' to say, 'I'll have to think about that, Kenny; you are married and that has always been sacred ground to me.' Yet, she knew that while her words said one thing, her heart told her quite another version of what was going on. It was a predicament she had never confronted."

The gentleman stirred in his chair, leaned forward and stared at the fire. "Oh, my goodness, this is simply too much! Please tell me, do they end up together?"

The old woman tied a knot in the tatted chain, stood up and handed it to the gentleman. "You are a fisherman, is that correct?"

The gentleman received the tatted chain and said, "Why, yes, how did you know? And how is that pertinent to this story?"

"I will be back in a moment," she said as she turned and left the room.

The gentleman was now preoccupied with trying to figure out how the story was going to end, and how in the world fishing had anything to do with the story! As his mind wandered all over the place, he caught sight of a picture hanging on the wall to the right of the fireplace. It was a colorful picture of blue skies, billowy clouds and what appeared to be a sailboat gliding on the water. Two people sat in the sailboat, but the gentleman could not quite make out the details. He stood up and walked to the picture.

Yep, the gentleman observed, *it's two people sitting on a sailboat. What a lovely picture, simple and serene.* As he examined the picture more closely, he noticed a title near the bottom: "The Trout."

Hmm, that's an interesting title for a sailboat picture. His brow wrinkled as he wondered, *Why that title? One doesn't generally think of fishing with sailboats.* Then he heard the old woman stir in the next room, and as he turned, she came through the doorway with a tray.

He quickly hurried over to her and said, "Oh, let me help you with that."

The old woman allowed the gentleman to take the tray as she sat back down in her chair in front of the fire. The gentleman gingerly set the tray on the table between them as the old woman removed the cover, revealing a plate of sandwiches and assorted crackers and cheese.

As the two of them settled back into their chairs, each filled a blue willow saucer with generous portions of sandwiches, crackers and cheese. "Well, you didn't need to go to so much trouble, but I am most grateful," the gentleman said as he devoured his first half sandwich. "Reckon you heard my stomach telling me to feed it! Now, where were we?"

The old woman finished half of her sandwich, wiped her mouth and said, "If you don't mind, I'll eat and tell the story." The gentleman nodded his head as he devoured the second half of the sandwich and mumbled, "Oh, sure ... please do!"

"Rachel decided to move beyond her 'moral judgments' and follow the direction put in front of her — that powerful electrical charge was simply too strong to ignore. So, she agreed to fly to another big city where he worked and see what might unfold. Of course, this was not an easy decision for Rachel, because everything she knew her entire life went against the flow of this choice.

"Now all of this occurred before everyone had a cell phone, so when Rachel's plane departure was delayed, she had no way to contact Kenny to let him know. She relied solely on whatever divine intervention was leading her. When she landed some two hours later than she was supposed to arrive, she found an empty airport, and no Kenny, and she immediately felt God had punished her for her choice. Yet, something inside her told her to 'be still,' and to call some hotels.

"Rachel thought, *I am in a major city! How in the devil will I find him?* And then an inner knowing directed her to a pay phone. On the second call, when she asked the receptionist if a Kenny Jones was staying at their hotel, Kenny answered the phone within minutes. Rachel simply said, 'Come and get me; I'm at the airport,' to which Kenny responded, 'I'll be right there.'"

The gentleman cleaned up his plate, poured himself another cup of coffee, looked at the old woman and said, "This story can't be real! ... can it?" The old woman merely continued.

"Kenny and Rachel met only another half dozen times over the next two years, and yet it was their regular conversations about each other's lives that deepened their relationship. That is, until Rachel came to a point in her life when it became unbearable to know he went home to someone else. She had now spent fifteen years alone, her children were gone, and she wanted more from Kenny than he could offer her. It was yet another quandary that seemed to have become commonplace for Rachel, and with that the relationship ended."

"Oh, no, please do not tell me that!" the gentleman exclaimed as he sat up straight in his chair. "I thought this was a Love story, and I always want Love stories to have happy endings!" He stood in front of the fire, grabbed the poker and stirred the embers, "Please tell me there is more to this story! Oh, there simply must be more."

As the fire began to build, the gentleman sat back in his chair and looked toward the old woman, who stared at "The Trout" picture on the wall.

"It was a horrible time for Rachel as she struggled to find new footing. She had become dependent upon their regular conversation, their laughs, jokes, and the genuine sharing of each other's lives. She attempted to fill the hole in her heart by throwing herself into deep soul-searching for a new way of being in life. It was not so much that she couldn't live without Kenny; she knew she could do anything she set her mind to do. It was just an absence of such profound depth that it took complete abstinence from any conversations with or about him.

"It was another eight years before Rachel was willing to do more than have an occasional phone call with Kenny. She had embarked on another segment of her life that required her full attention. During that time she had spent considerable time with a couple of very good gentlemen; however, something held her back that made no sense to her, but then she told herself, that this was clearly an affair of the heart.

"Rachel's parents lived in the same state as Kenny and, on one of her visits to them, he called and asked if he could take her to dinner. That opened the door. Rachel felt enough time had lapsed that she could see him as an old friend and nothing more. She did, after all, care very much that his life was going well for him.

"They met at her parents home and went to dinner, and when she looked into his deep blue eyes she felt lost in time. Everything she had left behind felt as if it were directly in front of her as she looked into his eyes. He spoke of how he had missed her, how life was different, and how things might be possible for them now. He asked her if, he were free, would she be with him, to which Rachel said, 'I will not be the reason you leave your wife.'

"While she wanted to believe everything he said, her practical side cautioned, 'Don't be a fool!' and so she struggled between her inner voice — her heart — and her practical head."

The old woman stopped for a moment and stared at the fire that was slowly burning, and for a brief moment it seemed as though she was lost in her memories. The gentleman looked closely at her fair skin, rosy cheeks and silver white hair that hung in a braid. *She must have been a beautiful woman when she was young. I would imagine she broke many a man's heart.*

Within a few moments, she continued, "Nothing came of things at that time, either; while Kenny said he was ready, he really wasn't. As I have said before, he was a man of commitment to his family; he understood that anything that fed his heart might, indeed, disrupt the hearts and lives of those he loved. And so, another eight years passed."

The gentleman said, "Good grief, you have got to be kidding me! Two people love each other so deeply and it's now some sixteen years later? Whatever happened next?" He leaned back in his chair, crossed his legs at the ankles and found a comfortable position in which he could clearly see the old woman.

The old woman glanced over at "The Trout" picture and continued, "Kenny had a heart attack just prior to his seventieth birthday, and he told a mutual friend of theirs to let Rachel know. Of course, Rachel contacted him immediately. As they spoke of life, and what was unfolding in their families, Rachel said to Kenny, 'A heart attack, huh?' Kenny said, 'Yes, a heart attack. My heart is broken, Rachel.'

"From that moment on they stayed in contact; oh, nothing of significance, just a monthly 'check-in' to see how life was going. Rachel, of course, felt very in control of her emotions. It had been sixteen years since they were intimately connected, so the routine chats felt comfortable and safe. That is, until some six months later."

The gentleman readjusted himself in the chair as he took a couple of deep breaths. *I cannot believe this story is true?* He leaned back in the chair and stared at the fire as the old woman continued.

"Rachel was once again visiting her parents' home when Kenny called and asked if he could take her to dinner again. She agreed to meet him if their mutual friend was also invited. Kenny was willing to play by whatever rules Rachel wished; he simply wanted to see her again.

"Rachel's stomach flip-flopped as the three of them ate lunch, though she did her best to assure herself that once the evening ended and Kenny went home she could regroup and refocus with some distance between them. That is, until he dropped off their friend and they were alone. Rachel looked into his eyes, and once again it was as though time had not passed; those years were gone and she was back in his arms.

"It was an hour of deep remembering that left both of them wondering, 'What if?' Nonetheless, while no physical intimacy was exchanged during that encounter, Rachel knew this was something she could no longer ignore. As she lay in Kenny's arms, she confessed to him she had not been with another man since they had last shared love with each other some sixteen years prior.

"Tears were plentiful as Rachel and Kenny parted ways. The last thing she heard from him was, 'You tear me up, Rachel. What am I do with you?' All Rachel could do was cry. They were tears of ignored love, from emotions stowed away out of respect for the marriage vows Kenny and his wife had made to each other. And yet, she knew the ache in her heart could not be satisfied with words filled with moral justifications. What she felt was deeper than her mind could explain.

"The next three days were peppered with tears as she did her best to busy herself, in hopes that her emotions would calm the pain that lingered in her heart. She returned home with memories of the warmth of his embrace. She did her best to regroup her emotions. That lasted maybe three weeks."

The old woman stood up from her chair, moved to the picture on the wall and touched it fondly with her leathered hands. The few moments of silence caressed the gentleman's heart as he imagined in his mind what the rest of the story would look like.

As the old woman returned to her chair, she continued, "Kenny began to communicate with Rachel via text message and pictures of places he had visited. He knew of her love for the mountains, the countryside, and all things simple. It was clear he saw her everywhere he went. Rachel could not deny that her heart was not only speaking to her; it was crying out for attention. It seemed no matter what happened in her life Kenny always seemed to know when she needed to hear from him. It was an uncanny precedence that could not be rationalized, intellectualized or understood. It was a connection that was beyond human emotion. It was as though their souls were one.

"The next drastic change occurred when Rachel attended her grandson's graduation. As she sat in the auditorium and watched her son and his wife, who had endured deep wounds during their twenty years, sit together as their oldest graduated, tears burned in Rachel's eyes. *They have managed to find each other and stay together through all of their hurts, and they have focused on their love for their family to keep them together. I wonder what that feels like?* Rachel knew she had kept her heart at bay; she had given to others, but had closed her heart to receiving love from a man.

"She left the graduation in tears, went home, threw herself on her bed and bawled. Of course, as was often the case, she received a text message from Kenny; it was a picture he shared of yet another amazing place in nature. That was it — that was all she could take. The floodgates had blown open, so she called him and agreed to meet him. She had no idea what would come of it, only that to deny her feelings was to ignore the very core of her existence. As logical as her mind was, and as in control of her emotions as she had always been, the walls that protected her heart crumbled down before her.

"Rachel sat at the airport waiting for her flight to go visit Kenny and opened up her new journal to record her feelings. Wouldn't you know it, at the top of the page was a Rumi saying that read: *'There is a candle in your heart, ready to be kindled. There is a void in your soul, ready to be filled. You feel it, don't you?'*

"Rachel was dumbfounded! Her mouth went dry, a lump arose in her throat and she could barely contain her emotions. She felt these truths reverberate throughout her body, *This is beyond anything I can control!* She then read another verse that nearly took her breath away. She stared at the words and felt herself merge in time and space, in some dimension beyond anything she could intellectually understand.

"Rachel wrote the verse at the bottom of the page, tore off the strip of paper, and tucked it into her purse to give to Kenny. She knew he, too, would be blown away by the words that just *happened* to appear at that precise moment in time.

"Rachel met Kenny for lunch and her stomach flipped around in her belly like a fish on a hook. While Kenny chatted away about his life Rachel knew it was just his way of dealing with the strong emotions they both felt. Tears moistened their eyes during that lunch as they made every attempt to keep the conversation on 'surface' topics.

"Both of them now had white hair, the youthful firmness of their bodies had disappeared, and lines from their years of experience creased their faces. Yet, as Rachel sat across from Kenny, it was as though time had folded and some fifty years had disappeared. She was still very determined to honor the sacredness of his marriage commitment, and yet she hungered to hold him as close as she possibly could."

The old woman paused her story, rose from her chair and moved into the next room. The gentleman took the opportunity to stoke the fire and place some additional logs on the hot embers, so that when the old woman emerged from the kitchen with a blue willow plate heaped with sugar cookies, the room was warm and toasty.

The old woman placed the plate on the table between them, poured another half cup of coffee, and began to eat one of the cookies. It didn't take any encouragement from the old woman for the gentleman to secure a couple on a napkin, pour himself a fresh cup and commence satisfying his taste buds.

"Mmm, Mmm, these are delicious!" the gentleman said with a satisfied look on his face as his tongue retrieved the crumbs from his lips. "A Love story and sweet sugar cookies," he moaned. "It doesn't get better than this! Please continue!"

The old woman nibbled on a cookie, sipped her coffee and proceeded with her story. "To add another quirk to this story, Rachel's daughter lived in the same state Kenny was visiting. Now, Rachel's daughter knew all about her mother's 'dance' with Kenny over the years and she had no judgments, for she knew her mother had never loved another man like she loved him.

"Arrangements were made for the three of them to have dinner the next evening. Since it was the middle of a work week for her daughter, they secured a place for both of them to stay for the evening that was close to where they would go for dinner. Her daughter figured her mother could take her to work the next day, and then have the car to meet Kenny for lunch one last time before she had to return home.

"The next morning as Rachel drove her daughter to work, her daughter suddenly realized that her leftover trout from the night before was still in the refrigerator in the room where they had stayed. Since the room was a place of retreat for one of her colleagues, she obviously did not want fish to be left for several days! Since Rachel would be returning to that area to meet Kenny for lunch, she offered to pick up the leftovers for her daughter.

"During the return trip, Rachel realized that she now had a room for the day. Without a moment's hesitation, she knew in her heart that it was time for her to step again into the flow of life and to follow the stream before her, just as she had done some sixteen years earlier."

The old woman poured herself another cup of coffee and tipped the pot toward the gentleman, who promptly extended his cup for a refill. Warmth filled the air, and with only the sound of popping and crackling from the fireplace, they sat in perfect stillness.

The gentleman looked over at "The Trout" picture thinking, *I wonder if this is that old woman's life story.*

The old woman sat perfectly still as a bright orange yellow sunbeam streamed through her living room window. The beam of light seemed to fill the air with a glow as she broke the silence to continue her story.

"That afternoon, Rachel and Kenny finally had the opportunity to discover what unfolds when love is honored, without restrictions, without judgments, and with the natural flow of two hearts remembering. Rachel knew why she had not been with another man; her heart had never left Kenny's heart.

"Many tears were shed as Rachel and Kenny recommitted to the dance between them. Kenny looked at Rachel and said, 'You look exactly like you did at fourteen.' Rachel laughed through her tears and said, 'I can tell you don't have your glasses on!' Kenny merely said, 'I knew then, Rachel; I knew then.'

"While neither had any idea where or how things would unfold, one thing was perfectly clear: their hearts would forever be intertwined. Rachel cried many tears over the next few weeks, not because of sadness, but because she realized she had pushed away the very thing she had wanted her whole life. Her tears showed her the harsh ways she had judged him earlier as 'only thinking of himself,' when in reality she knew it must have been very difficult for him to keep his life in order, knowing he loved his wife and what his heart also felt for her. She cried for forgiveness for all the judgments she had made and for the harsh words she had used; and, she cried because she now had the opportunity to give back to him what he so deserved.

"Rachel cried for all those who hunger for love, who, like her, use societal norms to keep relationships 'in order' and to do what is 'right.' She cried because she felt so fortunate to have another chance to really allow her heart to receive the love she desired; the love she had given so many people over the years, but that she had not allowed to flow back to her.

"Rachel cried because she realized that following the flow of life and trusting the divine unfolding, as silly as it may have seemed, was symbolically shown to her by the trout dinner that had been left behind. She knew that she did not have the answers to the 'what ifs' in her life; however, what she *did* know was how amazing and wonderful it was to be held in the arms of someone who loved and knew her so deeply.

"She cried because she had another chance to go with the natural flow of life; and, with all the confidence of the universe, she knew she was loved beyond time and space. She had found in the eyes of her beloved Kenny, her real self, the one that loved unconditionally and without limits."

"It was then Rachel remembered the Rumi verse she had written down and given to Kenny, *'Lovers don't finally meet somewhere, They're in each other all along!'* And with that, Rachel made peace with her heart."

The old woman wiped her eyes, "Rachel became stronger through her tears, as we all can, *if* we allow them to flow, and *if* we are brave enough to move with the currents of life and follow our hearts down the stream. She knew her Kenny had always wanted a sailboat, and so she put that on her list of things they would do together."

The old woman looked at the gentleman and said, "As a fisherman, you know it takes patience and silence to gain the trust of the fish that chooses to become your evening meal. You know that logic only works if you move with the current of life, enjoy the serenity of the moment, and show up on the water." With that she stood, arranged the dishes on the tray and carried it toward the kitchen.

"Wait!" exclaimed the gentleman. "I need to know if Kenny and Rachel live happily ever after, so to speak. I mean, did he leave his wife and marry Rachel? I really must know how this ends."

The old woman turned toward the gentleman and said, "Happy endings are based on personal interpretations of 'happy.' You may complete the story in the way that pleases you. All I can report is that Kenny and Rachel discovered what love truly 'looks' and feels like when you have an open heart. There are many people in relationships who rarely catch a glimpse of that truth." With that, she looked toward the gentleman and said, "These are my words."

The gentleman sat perfectly still, allowing the story he had just heard to sink in. There were no words, only the sounds of the fire and a muffled clatter from the kitchen. He took several deep breaths as he felt his feet on the floor. He scanned his body and felt the heat move upward through his legs until it reached his heart. *Oh, my God,* ran through his head, *oh, my God!* He gently shook his head from side to side as he closed his eyes and took another couple of belly breaths.

As he slowly opened his eyes, a tear slid down his cheek to his mouth. He could taste the salt from the tears that had spilled from his eyes. *Such a love; will I ever feel such a love? And, if I do, will I accept it, over my basic values of what is "right?"*

He stretched his legs, turned each foot to pop his ankles, and lifted himself from the chair. *Oh, dear Lord, please help me accept such love!* As tears moved slowly down his cheeks, he walked toward the fire, stoked it, added more wood, and turned toward the front door.

He dug in his pockets and dropped a gift in the twig basket, slipped on his hat, coat and boots, and reached for the door. He turned one last time and looked toward the kitchen. *I know she knows such love. No one could tell such a story without knowing those feelings so intimately!* He opened the door and spoke softly, "Thank you for the food, the fire and the story. My hope is renewed!"

As the gentleman arrived back to his car, he noticed that a light dusting of late fall snow had begun to blanket the ground. He raised his face to the heavens and allowed the snow to moisten his skin. Through a cracked voice he said, "Please, God, allow me to know such love. I promise to move with the downstream of life and honor such a powerful feeling. I know, Creator, that such feelings are from you. They *are* you; they are you, made real on this Earth! Thank you, thank you, thank you!

With that the gentleman headed toward home, knowing the next fishing trip he took, he would be watching for trout. He would sail along with the current of life and wait for *The Trout* to show up in his life!

Autumn Reflections

"... There's a time for talking to people you trust about what lies heavy in your heart, but first you need to take the time to just sit quietly and listen, rather than think!"

— These are her words.

HEAD TALK

What from this Autumn season would you like to know more about?

Or, is there one thing you would like to *"think some more about?"*

What do YOU suppose you might discover in the Winter season?

HEART TALK

Of the stories in this season, pause and consider what Truths were revealed.

What of these *Truths* apply to YOUR Life right now?

As you consider the Autumn of YOUR Life, what "jumps out" as a theme?

What can you learn for your own life from the Teachings of the West?

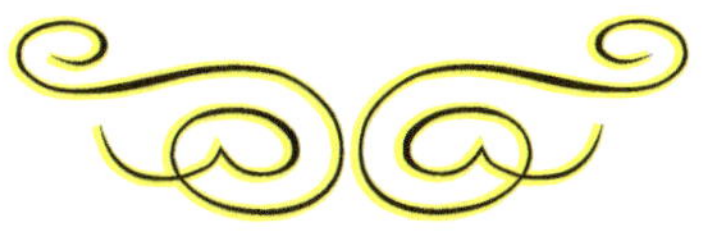

Within the warmth of our homes we discover the meaning of the "place within."

Memories flood our heart as our Soul beckons our attention.
The quiet space of winter feeds our hungry heart, waiting to tell us its dream!

The Winter of our life provides an outward expression of what we have spent our life working on, both professionally and personally. As we move into the later years, we often find the gift of non-attachment, especially to what others say about us. What a relief this is after the years we have spent carefully designing our life to meet the needs of "others," in order to have what we desire. The often daunting task of allowing our busyness to shape shift to a steady pace often takes time; however, with that time we will discover that our experiences have actually helped us develop wisdom.

Our winter years give us the opportunity to share what we have learned with those who follow us. If we truly want to leave this world a better place we will heal the places within our own heart that have been "overlooked," and allow our authentic self to leave that piece of ourselves to our community. We will then return home, leaving behind the best part of ourselves — Our Love!

THE NORTH

As we face North, we see our ancestors waiting for us! North is the place of the Wisdom Keepers, those that remember the ways of the Heart. In the North we find our True Source, the place where all that is pure resides. It is our quiet place, our essential core. The white ones of the North remind us that all is in perfect order and under the watchful eye of our Creator. White Buffalo shows us the abundant gifts waiting for those willing to pray each day to re-member. Buffalo teaches us how to be good stewards of all that we have so that we might serve our community.

"There are places in the Heart
that only Silence can describe …
These are my words."

— The old woman with the tatted chains!

Red Boots

now blanketed the countryside as the woman pulled her car onto a clearing just to the left of the path leading to the old woman's cabin. As she surveyed the snow-covered terrain, she wondered, *Why am I doing this? I'm over forty, have lived a very full life, and certainly have many very interesting experiences under my belt. What does this old woman who lives in the quiet, passive Forest know that I don't?*

She scanned the white, virgin snow dotted only with paw prints of various sizes and shapes and thought, *This must be the path to her cabin.* As she climbed out of the car, *It is certainly obvious that no human has stepped on this trail.* She looked down at her black leather boots with four-inch heels, and wondered why she chose to wear those; she had paid over $700 for these boots and here she was, about to tromp through more than six inches of snow. She wrapped her wool scarf around her neck and tucked it inside her fox coat as she stepped onto tracks that appeared deep enough to hopefully protect her "prized" boots.

Staring at the path directly in front of her, she took about six steps when she felt someone or something grab at her. She nearly jumped out of her skin as her heart began pounding in her chest. She stopped dead in her tracks and let out a scream. She remembered, *I have faced the streets of New York, San Francisco and Chicago; I can confront what is behind me.* With that, she reached in her pocket ever so slowly for the can of mace, and when it was securely in her hand, she quickly turned and began spraying a skinny tree branch heavily laden with snow. Feeling very foolish, she took a deep breath, put the mace back in her pocket and stood in the silence of the Forest. To the left of her she could see a squirrel on a nearby tree staring at her. As their eyes locked, she began to giggle and said out loud, "I must look like a foolish human to you!" The squirrel kept eye contact with the middle-aged woman, rapidly whipped its tail in the air, turned, and scampered up the tree. With that, the woman gathered her senses, turned back to the path ahead and continued her walk. This time, she paid close attention for branches along the path in front of her.

After a few steps, she looked beyond the path and could see smoke in the air; she breathed a sigh of relief and made a wish that it was coming from the old woman's cabin. Sure enough, after a couple more turns the cabin became visible, and the middle-aged woman picked up her pace as she closed in on the clearing. She could hardly believe it, but the old woman was chopping wood to the left of the cabin. As she watched the old woman, *How could that old woman do that without hurting herself? Good grief, someone needs to bring this woman some wood so she doesn't have to do it herself.*

The old woman put down her small hatchet, dusted the wood chippings from the front of her coat, turned to the woodpile, picked up an armful of wood and walked up the steps to her front door. The middle-aged woman hurried to the front door and opened it for her, and the old woman made a soft mumble that sounded like, "Thank you." With that, the two women now stood inside a very warm and cozy living room where small flames burned in the fireplace. The old woman took her stack of wood and placed them off to the side of the fire. As she began placing each piece of wood in the fire, she asked, "What is your question?" The middle-aged woman said, "I have many questions; however, I know I can only ask one, so first, may I sit down?" The old woman took the next piece of wood and pointed toward a chair sitting to the right of the fire, then placed the wood into the fire.

After a few moments the fire was roaring and the middle-aged woman took off her fox coat, placed it on the chair and sat down. It was then that she noticed the snow from her boots on the floor, and looking over at the old woman's feet, she noticed that she apparently had slipped off her boots prior to coming to the fire, and that the snow on the floor was from her own boots. She stood up and said, "I seem to have forgotten my manners and brought snow into your home; may I have something to clean up this mess?" The old woman rose from her knees, went into the next room, brought back a very worn towel and handed it to the middle-aged woman. With that, the middle-aged woman cleaned the snow from her tracks, wiped off her boots and placed them next to the old woman's boots near the door. She brought the towel back to the fireplace and placed it on the edge to the right of the fire.

The old woman rose from her task, took the towel in the next room and returned with a pair of socks, which she handed to the middle-aged woman. The woman thanked her and said, "My name is Mary. Thank you for the socks and I apologize for the mess." The old woman took a chair to the left of the fire, picked up a pouch that was sitting in the seat, and took out her handwork.

A few moments of silence followed as Mary looked around the cabin; she was grateful for the warmth now coming from the fire. As her eyes continued scanning the cabin, she wondered how the woman kept herself "entertained" with no TV visible. She considered, *Maybe it is in her bedroom?* She then quickly dismissed that idea with, *Nah, that is not possible; the old woman is probably so tired at the end of the day that she is asleep as soon as her head hits the pillow.*

She watched the old woman "curlin' thread" and finally said, "I want to know why I feel bored, and like there is something missing in my life. I have everything anyone could want — lots of friends, beautiful clothes, a very expensive car, I travel wherever I want, give to charities, and I like my job; it pays quite well. So, why do I have this 'empty' feeling like something is missing? If you could help me understand that, I would be most grateful."

The old woman gracefully and rhythmically moved her hands with the delicate thread, allowing the silence to be "heard." Mary felt very uncomfortable, and wondered if the woman had heard her request; she was very old, perhaps her hearing wasn't so good. After what felt like an eternity, Mary said, "Did you hear my question?" The old woman continued in the silence and finally said, "What do you hear, Mary?"

Mary anxiously responded, "I don't hear anything; am I supposed to hear something?" The old woman then said, "What do you smell?" To which Mary said, "I can smell the fire burning ... and I can hear it burning as well." She was very pleased with herself; she knew her answers were "correct."

The old woman said, "Where is your fire, Mary?"

This completely confused Mary. What did the old woman mean? Was she going to tell a story or make riddles all day? It was becoming quite irritating. She had traveled all this distance, tromped through what seemed like knee-deep snow, and probably ruined her $700 boots, only to have this old woman make riddles instead of conversation. She squirmed in her chair and felt her frustration level rising as the old woman put down her handwork, placed it in the chair, and left for the next room.

Oh great, Mary thought, *now I've made her mad. This was a mistake, I knew this woman couldn't help me; what does she know? She lives among trees, critters, has no TV, no car - whatever does she know about life? Does she have an occupation? Has she traveled to Europe, and mingled with the elite and powerful people in this world? Does this old woman know how to invest in stocks and bonds? Well, that is a stupid question; of course, she doesn't. Look how she lives. Anyone with money would have this place modernized, decorated with more color, and for God's sake at the very least have a furnace! What planet is this woman from? What has she done that gives her any sort of wisdom? Has she read Shakespeare or Hamlet? When was the last time she* heard a newscast? Does she know we are in two wars, and that we have major economic troubles? Does she know we have elected a black president, and that a woman ran for president? And what is she doing out in the wilderness at her age? There is not a hospital within 100 miles of this God-forsaken place.*

She felt her blood boil and her pulse rise as she continued, *And what about family? Does the woman have one, or is she so selfish she wants nothing to do with anyone? It is obvious this old woman needs to get caught up with this century ... I wonder if she even knows women have the right to vote?* She stood up and continued musing. *I need to just leave here; that old woman is probably asleep in her bed because she's so tired from chopping that wood.* She looked down at her feet. *I wonder if she washed these socks after wearing them. Where are my boots? I need my boots, so I can get out of here before it gets dark and I have to tromp through that snow to find my way back to my car. And speaking of my car, I hope no mountain man decided to make it his new "snow mobile."* She was fuming as she looked at her watch and noticed that it was only noon. *How is it only noon? It feels like I've been here for hours.*

Just then the old woman came into room with a silver tray, and two amazingly beautiful bone china teacups and saucers with a matching teapot. There was a lace tray cover upon which sat two silver spoons, a silver creamer and sugar bowl. Beside the teapot was a saucer filled with homemade chocolate chip cookies. They looked delicious, and she felt her stomach growl from the smell of these delicious morsels. Maybe she was hungry; maybe that was why she was so grumpy. At least, that was what she would like to think was the reason for her "outburst." Feeling a bit embarrassed for her thoughts, she was grateful the old woman had not heard her ranting.

The old woman sat the tray on a small end table made from an exquisite piece of walnut. Mary loved beautiful furniture, and she certainly knew the difference between handcrafted and factory made items. *And that lace! It had to be handmade from Ireland: the delicate and intricate patterning was not found anywhere in the world but in Ireland. Look at that china, and those dainty spoons are most commonly used in Europe; perhaps she has a friend that sent them to her.* Mary just knew somehow, that the woman had not brought them back from her own travels. The china was no doubt straight from England. *Where did these come from?*

As the old woman poured hot tea from the pot, Mary settled herself into her chair. She knew how to be polite, so she offered to help the old woman, to which the old woman merely extended the cup and saucer to Mary and moved the table so that it was easily accessible for both ladies. After placing a beautiful lace napkin on her lap, the old woman poured herself a cup of hot tea, and placed a chocolate chip cookie on the edge of the saucer.

A few moments of silence followed with only the sound of the fire burning; then she placed her cup back on the table and picked up a small very worn black leather book from the basket sitting beside her chair. She reached for the pink ribbon that marked a place in the book and began to read the following:

> *And since you know you cannot see yourself,*
> *so well as by reflection, I, your glass,*
> *Will modestly discern to yourself,*
> *That of yourself which you yet know not of.*

Mary stared at the old woman and thought, *oh my goodness; she reads minds! And she does know Shakespeare! I have made a complete fool of myself!* The old woman placed the book to her heart and closed her eyes; a few moments later she returned the book to the basket beside her chair.

The old woman poured Mary and herself another cup of tea and handed Mary the saucer with the delicious chunks of chocolate cookies, as she spoke, "Where are your red boots, Mary?" Mary thought that an odd question and responded, "I have black boots and they are over by your door; again, I apologize for tracking in the snow." She spilled tea from her cup, placed it on the saucer, and was too embarrassed to accept a cookie, so she shook her head and said, "No, thank you."

Keeping the saucer extended, the old woman said, "I know what color the boots are that you wore when you arrived; I am asking about your red boots." Mary accepted the cookie this time, and, trying not to scarf the whole thing down, took a small bite and placed it on the saucer beside her teacup. "I guess I do not understand what you mean; I do not own red boots."

The old woman looked directly at her and said, "Oh yes you do; you just haven't put them on for a long time." She looked away and watched the fire burn as she continued eating her cookie. The chocolate oozed from the cookie and left a small trail on her lip, which her tongue quickly found. She took her beautiful lace napkin and blotted her lip. Mary's head kicked into gear, *That chocolate might stain the napkin; I hope you have a good stain remover or it will be ruined.* She then focused back on the statement and said, "What do you mean, I have red boots? I think I would know if I owned a pair or not, and how do you know if I do?"

Without hesitation, the old woman said, "Everyone has red boots; we come into this world with them, but we just get too busy to recognize them. And, chocolate comes out of this fabric; I eat a lot of these cookies!" Very embarrassed, and feeling "put in her place," Mary wiped her lips with her lace napkin and said, "I get it; you are talking about something besides red boots; that is a metaphor for something else. Am I right?"

The old woman smiled and looked back to the fire, "It is interesting to watch people sashay around life; it seems to be more important to spend time acquiring 'things,' keeping track of what they have, checking things off their 'list,' than merely enjoying their red boots."

She continued, "Yep, everyone has red boots; something that makes their heart feel both excited and 'at peace.' Some people's red boots look very worn because they have carried the person through many adventures, many experiences, and have witnessed their unfolding into the sacred human being they truly are. Red boots help to free a person, and when all is said and done, they assist that soul with walking back home — exactly where they came from.

"Red boots are the vehicle by which we find our authentic self, for they help us to not care what others think about us, what we've accomplished, what we have acquired or what we have achieved — that is, by 'earthly' standards. There is not a soul in this world that has not struggled to find their red boots; and, once they do, they find peace. With that, they ask themselves, 'What was I waiting for, and why didn't I find them earlier?' Yes Ma'am, there is not a soul in this world who doesn't want to find their red boots."

Mary sat perfectly still in her chair; she felt a bit woozy and like she was being carried into another world, another dimension, one in which she remembered.

I know this place, she remembered, it feels very familiar. And then she smelled the scent of clean laundry, and she remembered helping her mom fold sheets from the clothesline; how she had enjoyed doing this small task with her mom. She then heard the sound of giggles as she and her sister told "ghost stories" to each other in the makeshift tent suspended from her mom's clothesline by two blankets held together with wooden pins. She remembered seeing the wooden pins with "gnaw marks" and her mom telling her those were the marks she left when she was teething as a baby.

The vision continued as Mary felt the warmth of summer, coolness of Popsicles, taste of burnt marshmallows and those delicious graham cracker, chocolate and marshmallow treats melted over the campfire her dad built. How she loved her dad, and so wanted to marry someone just like him when she got older. He smelled like Old Spice aftershave, wore brightly colored plaid flannel shirts, and was forever tracking mud in on her mom's floor as she would yell, "How many times do I have to tell you to take off those boots before you come into the house?"

She loved her family, and while she argued with her younger sister, she did admire her determination to be just like her "big sister." It did not matter what anyone at school said about her; at least one person in the world admired her and wanted to grow up and be just like her. It was so annoying to always have her under my feet, always wanting to wear my clothes and flirt with my boyfriends; but she did love me unconditionally. How merciless I was to Sally; I never did acknowledge what a sweet spirit she was. I was too focused upon "me."

I remember in grade school someone dared me to sneak up on some boys that were hanging out at a "fort" they had made. Everyone, especially girls, was strictly forbidden to come near the timber-built fort the boys had spent weeks constructing. There were all sorts of signs stating, "No girls allowed," "Enter at your own risk." "Trespassers will be dealt with!" Looking back, it was very funny, although at the time it was quite scary, because we did not know what they would do to trespassers. Nonetheless, it was a red flag to me, and they might as well have double-dog-dared me to NOT try!

One evening about dusk, several of us from school set into the woods to see what this "fort" really looked like. There must have been eight of us — five girls, two boys and myself. Of course, I was the only one who volunteered to get inside that fort; the others were there to "watch," and they knew from witnessing my many adventures that I would do it. They just wanted to make certain I really did get inside the fort — that I really would do what I said I would do. Interestingly, they even doubted that! Well, I showed them I meant business by agreeing to let them accompany me to within eyeshot of the fort. They agreed to stay a good distance away so the boys did not hear intruders approaching. It was all part of the "grand scheme," and so the adventure began that cool late summer night.

Sally had threatened to tell Mom and Dad if I did not let her go with us, and she promised to stay back with the others as I went the final distance to the fort; so, I agreed to let her go. If my mom had known she would have killed me; she thought girls were meant only to be "girly." Sally fit that bill better than I, so I felt no remorse that mom did not have the "girly" girl she wanted in me. Dad understood me; he wouldn't have really cared, except that Mom would be mad at him for "encouraging me" (as if I needed any encouragement!). Nonetheless, I let Sally go with us to ensure the success of my "mission."

I told Mom and Dad that Sally and I were going to the house of a friend of mine for the evening and that we would be playing outside, and not to worry (that was before cell phones.) I assured her we would be home before our bedtime, and that I would make certain Sally was "looked after." With a pink Barbie tote of Sally's I packed all the necessary items for the excursion: flashlight, matches, green paint for my face, a black stocking cap of Dad's, my navy blue sweatshirt, and, of course, some water in case I got thirsty. My three months of Girl Scout training taught me to always be prepared, and water was a must for any outdoor excursion.

We met just outside the woods at the clearing near the boys' fort, as planned. The fort was located just East of the city park, so it really was not in some wilderness area in which we could get lost. Nonetheless, as the eight of us gathered, Sally finally spoke up and said, "Are you sure you want to do this? You could get hurt, or who knows what they could do. I heard they tied some kid to a tree and left him there all night one time. They didn't go back and untie him until nearly noon the next day." I remember looking at her and saying something like, "Don't start that Sally. We all agreed to do this and not back out at the last minute." With tears in her eyes, Sally agreed to be still and we began our journey into the woods.

Not five minutes into the woods, one of the boys started to hiccup; darned if he could quit, and the others began to laugh. I did not think any of it was funny, so I gave the boy a drink of my water and told him to hold his breath and count to ten before swallowing the water. He did that several times until the hiccups subsided. About the time we were going to continue our hike, one of the girls had to pee, so I directed her to find a place and make it quick. She argued that she would get poison ivy if she peed in the woods, and finally, I told her to just leave. Of course, she was afraid to go alone and no one else wanted to leave, so I accompanied her back to the clearing where she could leave and go home. Before she left, I made her cross her heart and promise to not tell anyone else what we were doing. She nodded as she crossed her heart and off she went.

I turned to head back to where we were and three other kids met me on the path. "What are you doing?" I asked, and they mumbled something about hearing some sort of creepy noise when we left. Feeling very frustrated and that we were wasting time, I turned to the group and said, "OK, who's going to go and not be afraid, 'cause I'm not going to keep doing this. It is getting dark and I promised to be home by bedtime." Sally started to cry, then quickly pressed her lips together and said, "I'll go, I'll stay with you," to which another boy said he would go, and then another girl agreed; and so we headed back into the woods.

Within ten minutes we could see the lights from the window and the cracks in the walls of this infamous fort. It was quite a sight to see the boards nailed neatly together, complete with an open space for a glassless window. We could see a boy's face staring out toward where we approached; obviously, they meant what they said about this being a "privately secured" fort since they had someone standing guard.

We laid flat on the ground beneath a tall oak tree that was big enough to hide one person if they were standing. Sally and the other girl and boy lay perfectly still on the ground. The sun was beginning to set, so I knew I needed to make haste so that all was completed in time for Sally and me to be home on time. I remember smelling the dirt beneath me as I lay there frozen to the ground.

Sally finally said, "Are you going to go, or have you chickened out?" That gave me the boost to get my wits about me and tackle the task in front of me. That was all I needed — someone to even begin to presume that I was not brave enough to take action.

I shot her a dirty look, to which she stuck her tongue out at me, and I was out of the shoot. I crawled on the ground like a snake as I forced my very apprehensive body into action. With the stocking cap solidly on my head, my green painted face exposed, and flashlight stuck down my pants, I continued on. Slithering along the ground, I was within a couple of feet of the fort when I could hear the voices of the boys inside. They were chatting about silly things: football games, baseball trading cards, and, of course, the sixth grade girl with "humongous boobs," as I was now securely perched beneath the window.

My heart was thumping and I felt the dryness of my throat; no doubt about it, I was scared. Whatever would these boys do to me? Would they tie me to a tree and leave me to the creatures of the night? Perhaps they would make me wash and polish all their bikes for a month as penance for invading the private space of their fort. Whatever the consequence would be, it could not be any worse than not completing the task and facing the kids in school the next day.

I had witnesses watching my actions; there was no way to make up my own version of the event.

I brought myself back to my senses by reminding myself that those witnesses could also be my saving grace. These boys were really decent kids; they were not about to do something to me with other people present; they knew their parents would administer consequences on them that would have far more "impact" than what they could do to me.

Armed with that information, I looked back at my two friends and Sally, and proceeded to crawl to the doorway. I had made it past the "guard" in the window, and I was home free! Within two minutes I was off my belly and charging through the door to the fort. Four boys were sitting on the floor looking at a full-page picture of a completely naked woman when I surprised them with a "Hello boys!" In that moment every fear I'd had about performing this task was completely dissolved. Victory! I had faced my fears and completed my mission. Success was mine! As I stood there in front of the shocked faces of those young boys, I looked down and saw red boots! I had red boots on my feet.

Mary felt her feet proudly displaying her red boots, as she took a breath and felt the chair supporting her weight. With the next deep breath, she heard the crackling of the fire, smelled wood burning and tasted the chocolate still on her lips. Her eyes focused upon the old woman sitting directly in front of her; she was biting the white thread in two as Mary watched her tie a knot in the completed chain for tatting.

The old woman said nothing, but simply put her handwork into the pouch, leaned forward and handed Mary the beautiful tatted chain. As Mary looked down at her feet, they sported the warm socks the woman had given her when she first arrived. She felt the softness of the yarn on her feet as her eyes moved to survey her surroundings.

Where am I? More importantly, where have I been, and what just happened? It was as though time had been suspended and that somehow she had been transported back in time, and then back to the present. She glanced at her watch and it was 12:30. How could it only be thirty minutes since she had taken a bite of that delicious chocolate chip cookie?

The old woman gathered the teacups and saucers, placed the empty saucer where the chocolate chip cookies had been onto the silver tray, rose from her chair and turned toward the room in which she had retrieved them. Feeling completely relaxed, Mary took the lace napkin from her lap and placed it upon the small walnut table between their chairs.

Rising from the chair, she moved to the door, slipped off the socks and placed her feet into her boots. As she gathered her coat and scarf, she took a gift from her pocket and dropped it into a twig basket that sat on a beautiful pedestal table by the door. *What a beautiful table. The last time I saw one like that was in a castle just outside France. That couldn't possibly be ...* and she stopped, because she had learned that anything was possible with this old woman. *"Old woman" — I really do not like referring to her in that way; it seems rather disrespectful. From what I have experienced today, this woman deserves all sorts of respect!*

Mary placed her hand upon the door knob, turned toward what she thought must be the kitchen and loudly said to the old woman, "Thank you greatly," and with that she opened the door and walked out. As she stepped off the porch, she turned and saw the old woman fussing with something in her kitchen. The room was quaint, like the rest of the cabin, and suddenly she felt something very warm and familiar in her heart. Her grandmother had always been so important to her, and it had been years since she had thought of her. A tender moment of love swept through her being as warmth permeated her skin. She had to giggle, *This must be how it feels to be a chocolate chip cookie being baked.*

As she moved toward the path that led to her car, she moved swiftly and lightly, without any hesitation, any fear, or any moment of doubt. She held her shoulders back, and, wrapped in the warmth of remembering, she was fearless; there was nothing she could not do. She made a mental note to herself to book a flight home to see her family. As she reached the car, she turned the key, started the car to let it warm up, and pulled her cell phone from her pocket. She quickly pushed the button, heard a ring, and then a familiar voice said, "Hello?" As a tear slid down her cheek, she pushed through the lump in her throat and said, "Hi, Sally. When can we get together?"

Sally answered, "As soon as you can get here. What's up?" Mary responded, "I simply must tell you about my new find." To which Sally said, "Oh, another fashion find? Are you in Paris?" Choking back tears, Mary replied, "No, I've been to the boys' fort in the woods; just wait until you hear about my *Red Boots!*"

The Fire Within

It was a blistery cold morning; even the critters of the Forest were sheltered within their nests, holes, and underground burrows. Grandfather Sun was just barely visible on the horizon as the young man parked his four-wheel drive truck in front of the path to the old woman's cabin. His trusty dog sat beside him as he turned off his truck and slipped on his gloves. He said, "OK, Shiloh, are you staying or coming?" to which the dog moved only her eyes in the man's direction. "I guess that means you're staying," and he threw a blanket over the critter. He poured some water from his bottle into a dish sitting on the floor board, slipped out of the truck, pushed the lock button and pulled his stocking cap down snuggly over his ears.

This weather was perfect for trapping, and, being an outdoorsman, he was layered from head to toe. *This is my kind of morning,* he sighed, *there is nothing like a crisp winter's morning to get the old blood flowing.*

As he began the journey to the old woman's cabin, he noticed all the beauty that surrounded the Forest. *I'll bet this place is full of good hunting,* he surveyed the surroundings, *and I'll bet she has lots of poachers.*

In the blink of an eye he was standing at the steps to the old woman's cabin. He sniffed the air as his stomach began to growl. "Mmm, smells like fresh coffee," he said, as he saw the old woman through the window, coming toward the door. She opened the door and said, "Bring some wood in with you." The young man had spied the woodpile to the right of the cabin as he approached the cabin, so he knew precisely where to go. His arms filled with wood, he stepped onto the porch and the door of the cabin opened. He knocked the snow off his boots and entered the cabin. Once inside, he eyed the wood box to the left of the fireplace and carefully placed the pieces of wood into the box. "Wow, that was perfect," he said, as the pile he brought in filled the wooden box perfectly!

He walked back to the door, removed his boots and placed his coat and hat on pegs next to the door. As he began rubbing his hands together, he said, "It's a cold one out there this morning!" He turned to face the fire and noticed two chairs sitting in front of the fire. The old woman was nowhere to be seen, though he could hear someone stirring in the next room. As he began placing wood on the fire, the old woman entered with a silver tray. She placed the tray on a small walnut table that she moved between the two chairs.

Mmm, that's the coffee I smelled outside. He dusted off his hands over the fire and took the empty chair opposite the old woman. Steam rose from the hot coffee as she poured it into two sturdy mugs. He extended a hand to receive the welcomed warmth and said, "Just what a person needs on such a cold morning," he tipped the mug to this mouth.

They sat in silence for a few moments until the young man began, "I have come to ask about how to deal with my anger. I am not often angry, but when I am, it is pretty ugly." He reached for one of the large biscuits that sat on the tray and continued, "I am not one for talking to someone I don't know; I never have been, and probably never will be. Yet, here I am, sitting with you."

The biscuit nearly melted in his mouth as he took a bite and said, "Mmm, these are delicious; I can tell they are homemade! Why, only my granny made biscuits like this. We'd put some of her strawberry preserves on them and feel like we had died and gone to heaven." Then he leaned back in his chair to savor the moment.

The old woman placed her mug back on the tray and picked up her handwork to begin her ritual of tatting a chain. The young man continued, "At any rate, I am a happy person most of the time, and feel that life has been pretty good to me. And, I am not bragging, but I am pretty good to other people. It is just that from time to time I get so angry my blood boils, and I can't say that I understand exactly what happens that makes me feel that way. I have a good life, good parents, and a good job; it just makes no sense at all. My family seems to think I have anger issues, although they love me despite my outbursts. The fact is, my family prays for me a great deal; at least, that's what they tell me all the time. And, I'm certain it is true, because I have made it through some pretty scary things."

He reached for yet another biscuit as he continued, "Fact is, my dog is my best friend; I like people, but I just feel more comfortable being myself with my dog. I have had a lot of girlfriends in my life, but no one that I stuck with. My mother says I have commitment issues. I think she just wants more grandbabies and figures that, if I feel guilty, I'll settle down and give her one or two."

He gulped down the rest of his coffee, placed the mug on the tray and said, "So, I guess I would like to know if there is anything I can do to get rid of this anger?" The old woman never looked up, but continued moving her hands and tatting the string, as a beautiful chain began to emerge from between them. The young man looked around at the cabin and noticed there were no pictures of people, only landscapes or animals. "Do you have any family? I notice there are no pictures of people in your home?"

The old woman ignored his question and began her story:

"Once upon a time there were two people who loved each other very deeply. The man was a faithful one with a work ethic any employer would love. He loved his family and provided for them in the best way he could. He was a simple man, who asked little of anyone, and gave much to others. He was a great outdoorsman who enjoyed fishing, hunting, and just 'hanging out' in the Forest. We'll call this man 'Jim.'

"Jim began working for the local sawmill when he was sixteen, doing everything from sweeping floors, carrying timber and scrubbing toilets, to just about anything that was asked of him. He enjoyed working and earning his own money.

"After twenty years of doing whatever job needed to be done, Jim had become part owner of the sawmill. He was known for 'practicing what he preached,' so people in his community sought him out when things needed to be done. They knew he was good to his word, so if he said he would do something, it would be done precisely as he promised, and in a timely manner. Yep, the sawmill was the place to work, for Jim was as loyal an employer as he had been an employee!

"Jim's wife was also known as a good woman; she was devoted to family and took great care providing for their needs. Her name was Sarah, and just like the woman in the Bible, she had great faith. The 'fruits' of their union brought three children, two sons and one daughter, each as uniquely different as the other; and, yet, their hearts were always connected through their love of family. It was a sweet family, though certainly not without its life experiences."

The old woman placed her handwork to the side of the chair, rose, and moved to the fireplace. As she placed more wood on the fire, she continued, "There was a fire in Jim, something he could not put his finger on; yet, he knew something deep within him was burning. Over the forty years he had lived, he had felt this fire, and had engaged in various activities as a way to 'touch' that fire, to feel that burning that tempted fate. He enjoyed the thrill of stretching himself to see how far he could go without really harming himself; that was what 'fed' that fire at that time! He loved feeling the adrenalin rush of putting himself at death's door."

She placed the wood in the fireplace in such a way that a blaze roared and heat filled the room. She continued, "Sarah was not certain what to make of it all. She supported her husband and most certainly did not want to be a 'nagging' wife; so, she simply observed Jim as he embarked upon these risky ventures. He gave her and the family all they needed; how could she say anything about what he did for adventure? Still, she felt 'left out,' even though she did not need that thrill, and she did fear that something could happen to Jim. She loved him deeply and could not bear to think that something might happen to him; and, yet something inside her felt that it was inevitable. She would think, *You can only tempt fate so many times. It is like playing Russian roulette; something is bound to happen.* Still, she never shared those words directly with Jim. She did not begin to know what to do with the fear she felt inside."

The old woman stood in silence in front of the fire for a few moments, and he noticed she was turning a thin gold band on her left ring finger, as though she was remembering something in her own life. He watched as she stared at the fire and wondered, *Is she talking about her own life?* He looked at the corduroy skirt she wore and noticed a tiny yellow lace edge hanging out of a pocket on the side. *My grandmother used to carry hankies; I'll bet that's what she has in her pocket.* He noticed the long gray braid that hung down her back over a purple sweater he was certain she had knit.

She just stood there looking at the fire for what felt like ten minutes. He dared not interrupt her thoughts, although he was curious as to what they were. The old woman pulled the yellow edge from her pocket, moved it to her face, then placed it back in her pocket. After just a few moments, she turned from the fire, moved to her chair, sat down and picked up her handwork. *Yep*, he smiled, *it was a hankie.* The old woman continued.

"Sarah envied that fire in her husband's heart and wished she could kindle something within herself so that she, too, could feel the excitement she saw in her husband's face when he returned from participating in those adventurous deeds. She had never been one to do 'risky' things; it made no sense to her, even though she seemed to be attracted to others who had that fire within." She moved her hands gracefully as the tatted chain became longer, and he could see that it looked like the yellow edge on the hankie she had in her pocket.

"Pretty soon, Sarah decided that it was time for her to work outside the home. She had given up a regular job to stay home with her children, and, while she loved the opportunity to do that, it felt like time for something 'more' to be added into her life. Perhaps she could find her 'fire' by doing something with other adults.

"So, Sarah approached Jim about the prospect and, being the compassionate man he was, he said to her, 'Don't know why you don't like just being here; you do a great job. But, if you feel you need something else, then do what you wish.' Being a fair man, Jim knew he could not ask Sarah not to follow her heart; she stood by him with his endeavors, and it only seemed right that he do the same for her, even though he was skeptical. He liked Sarah being home; he wanted his family to have a good, solid base, and it was very convenient for him to know his children were with a parent at all times. But, like I said, he was a fair man, so he said he would support her."

The old woman paused her handwork, poured more coffee for herself and pointed the pot toward the young man's mug. He picked up his mug and extended it toward her.

"How can I pass up that delicious coffee? I think I'll have another one of those biscuits too!" As they sat in the moment drinking coffee, the old woman continued.

"It was not long before Sarah and Jim began having problems. He had a feeling in his gut that something was 'not right.' Sarah had started dressing differently, going places without the kids, and the intimacy between them had changed. As you can probably figure out, the kids began to notice the changes, and their actions brought more upheaval in an already tense home environment. It did not take long for Jim's fears to be confirmed: Sarah had been seeing someone else.

"While he did not know exactly how far things had gone, it was fuel for the fire within, and he became enraged. He said many hurtful things to Sarah; things that pierced her heart deeply, although nothing he said could have been any more hurtful or negative than she had already said to herself. And so the chasm between them became even wider.

"It was not long before Jim moved out and the rumors spread like wildfire. Jim began doing things completely outside his nature as he allowed the fire within to rage. But, after about six months, Jim realized the rage he felt inside had not been quenched by his actions. It was the first time that Jim realized the fire was really his own insecurity; that he was not a lovable person, and that people had been 'nice' to him only because of what he could do for them.

"He began to recognize a familiar feeling he had felt in his own family. His father and mother were both jealous, insecure people, and their lack of trust and suspicion was evident. Whether Jim liked it or not, he realized he had taken on those insecurities himself and with those feelings came a burning within to know what being loved really felt like. He realized that being loved had many 'colors' and the one he held in his heart was based on the belief that you cannot trust anyone. With that new awareness, Jim began the journey toward healing that old wound. He did this by talking to Sarah about his insecurities.

"Sarah was most receptive; she knew she had not spoken to Jim about her own feelings, hopes and dreams. She felt somehow 'less' than Jim for not having desires for such thrill-seeking adventures, or for having goals or aspirations outside the family. It was watching her husband seek thrills outside the family that had made her curious about why she did not have such aspirations. Sarah did know one thing for certain: her actions took her further from her fire than she had ever been. She felt shame and remorse for her actions and asked Jim to forgive her.

"So, Jim and Sarah began to talk more deeply and intimately than ever before about things that had not been discussed in their relationship. After several months of trying life apart from one another, they came to realize that the love they shared was still burning. Despite any attempts to justify, explain or rationalize one another's behaviors, the simple truth was that they loved each other. What would become of their relationship, or how they would move past the events that had occurred, they had no idea; they only knew whatever they needed to do they would do, in order to help each other find their fire within, and still keep their integrity, love and commitment to themselves, to each other and to their family. In reality, Sarah's fire within was, indeed, being fed by the love she shared with her family; Jim's fire within was an attempt to fill the insecurity he held as protection for his heart. Once each realized this, they began to move toward one another, rather than apart."

The old woman bit the thread at the end of the chain, tied a knot on the end and, without making eye contact, she said, "There is a fire within for each of us; the secret is to recognize it, discern what it takes to feed it, and above all, to find ways to support ourselves and those in our lives as they fuel their own fires. That fire is what keeps us feeling alive, and it opens our hearts to all of life's experiences. If we fear that fire, we will do all we can to protect our hearts by keeping our distance from others. It begins by trusting ourselves enough to acknowledge that fire and to know how to feed it. If we are afraid of our fire, we will become angry, for not feeling loved is the biggest fear we all have; and when that happens, we will put ourselves through all sorts of gyrations to replace it with something else. It is a tricky place to be, and yet, to ignore that fire is to live a life without love. 'That is no fun at all.'"

The old woman rose from her chair, moved toward the young man and continued, "Life was meant to be shared, and if we fuel our fire with love, it allows others to fuel theirs; imagine the warmth that would then spread in our communities. If we feed our fire, it fuels more love; if we run from it, it becomes an elusive search filled with thrill-seeking actions to find it. It is a cycle in which each person must consciously choose to take action. Love is what fuels the world with hope, faith, and the assurance that there is a purpose for being in this life." She handed the chain to the young man and concluded with, "The choice is yours; these are my words."

The young man accepted the gift as he watched the old woman pick up the silver tray and move to the other room. He wondered, *Is my hidden anger really my need to feel loved? I never considered that I felt unloved, although I have always known I was afraid that I would really fall in love with someone and they might find out I am not so perfect and leave me.* "Better to leave them than to have them leave you" — *that's always been my motto.*

He stood up from his chair, walked to the fire and placed a few logs on it; he figured the least he could do was to keep the fire blazing in her fireplace, although he was certain she was very capable of doing that with the fire she held within her. *That is one smart lady,*" he reflected as he moved toward the door. *I'll bet she misses her "Jim."*

Once at the door, he slipped on his boots, cap and coat, then dropped a gift into her basket and pulled on his gloves. *Shiloh is going to be very glad to see me,* he thought as he opened the door and quickly moved along the path to his truck.

"Frozen wonder," he said, "that's what this place is; an amazing place to find peace. It is time for me to leave my 'frozen heart' and fuel my fire with some good lovin'. That Betty Jane has been very patient over the years, and she has always said she was waiting for me to 'quit running' from my heart. I guess she knew what this old woman knows, and I guess she has been waiting to share her fire within with me."

As he opened the truck door, Shiloh was still huddled under the blanket he had left over her. He poured out the water he had left for his dog, cranked over the engine and put the heater on, full blast. He patted the top of the blanket and said, "Thanks for keeping my *Fire Within* fed until I realized how to share it with another human. You have been a very good teacher, Shiloh!"

The Hammer

Bruce began his journey through the Forest with great vigor. *What a glorious day to be tramping through the woods,* rambled through his head. *Can't imagine a better place to live than among all these beautiful trees! Wonder how long the old woman's lived here? She must be a sturdy woman to be living so far from the city.*

He paused for a few moments to "sniff the air," and noticed a giant woodpecker drilling away on an old oak tree. "That's a nice piece of wood you're pecking on, buddy; hope you realize what a fetching price that tree would bring in the city." Keeping his eyes on the bird he continued, "Don't suppose it matters to you about such things. I mean, only we humans look at something and think about the money we can make from it!" Rubbing the back of his neck, Bruce said, "My neck is a bit stiff, so I'll be letting you get back to your work."

As though understanding the man's words the woodpecker paused a moment, looked down at him, then turned and proceeded with the task in front of him. *Atta boy, do your thing!* He turned his eyes toward the path in front of him and rubbed his neck once again. *Darn ol' neck; guess all my hammering through wood is taking its toll on this ol' body. Wonder if the woodpecker has any aches and pains?*

Stepping into the clearing that surrounded the cabin, Bruce stopped in his tracks. *Dang, am I sure I want to do this? I mean, at my age, I should know what I want and be able to make decisions without asking someone else for advice.* In a moment he was transported back to six months earlier when his world had turned upside down:

"I need my space; I need to know I can support myself," she had said. "I'm really sorry, but I just need to do this." Bruce stood looking at his wife of nearly sixteen years, wondering what in the world was happening. Oh, he knew she was restless; she had started losing weight, working out and buying new clothes that were "in style." Normally, his wife was conservative, attentive and, above all, crazy about him. Their children were in the thralls of teenage behaviors, but he knew they could handle anything they confronted — at least that's how he saw it. But with the changes in his wife, he knew she was having problems dealing with the stress of it all.

"I think we can work this out, Fay, I really do; we've had worse situations," Bruce had tried to convince her. Yet, he knew in his gut something was different; something had changed drastically. So Bruce kept busy as Fay stood firm in her determination to leave. Within another month Fay had moved out and Bruce was confronted with the worst pain he had ever felt — a broken heart.

Now, being a "good ol' country boy," Bruce felt being busy was the best way for dealing with most anything. At least that's how he had gotten through most everything in his life prior to this event. So, Bruce grabbed his hammer and set out to "knock out" anything that was ailing him. The problem this time was, it didn't work. Fay had moved out and Bruce could barely deal with the pain.

With a hammer in his hand he did his best to reconstruct something in his life. After being a framer for twenty-one years, he felt something else must be calling to him. So, he began working for his best friend. The job was easier, less stress on the body and he figured, "it's gotta be better" than what he'd been doing.

It didn't matter. Bruce was defeated on a level much deeper than his body; his heart was aching. So, one night he did what he remembered doing as a child. He went into the woods behind his house and he gave it all to God. "I'm done, God; I surrender it all to you. I can't do my life without you any longer!"

And, with that, his life changed forever.

Shaking his head, Bruce said out loud, "Stop! Do you hear me, head? Stop! I cannot and will not continue to rehash the past. It is time to move forward."

As he looked straight ahead, Bruce saw smoke rolling out of the chimney of a quaint cabin in the clearing. He took a few deep breaths, adjusted his hat and said, "Let's get'er done," as he moved closer to the cabin.

Inside the cabin the old woman finished up the last few details so that a neat tray of biscuits and hot coffee would be waiting for her guest. As she stoked the fire and placed a few small logs on the hot coals, Bruce knocked on the door.

I believe she said to come in, Bruce turned the knob and slowly entered the cabin. "Did you say to come in?" he asked, and the old woman nodded her head. "Sure feels good in here," he said as he placed his hat and coat on the pegs by the door. "Nice use of antlers," he continued, as he inspected the way in which they were attached to the wall. *They did a good job putting those up. Darn it, guess old habits die hard; I can't help but notice good work,* he mused as he removed his boots, placed them on an old rag rug and walked toward the fire.

"Mighty nice of you to have that fire going. Do you need any wood brought in?" Bruce asked as the old woman pointed to a very large wooden box filled to the brim with neatly stacked wood.

"Never mind, looks like you have plenty," Bruce said as he watched the old woman take a seat in front of the fire and begin pouring steamy coffee into two mugs. "Man, that smells great. Mighty nice of you to have something to warm a belly on this cold morning."

Bruce and the old woman sat quietly with only the sound of the fire crackling as they sipped coffee and ate buttered biscuits. "I've heard about these biscuits, and you know, they are as good as I was told." He turned to the fire and said, "Mighty nice place you have here, and you certainly know how to make a person feel welcome."

As the old woman cleared away her mug and saucer, she took out her tatting and began the ritual of "curlin' thread." Bruce savored the warm coffee, leaned back in his chair and began his question.

"Reckon I'm here today to find out how I can stop my head from arguing with me so much. Just when I get things figured out, my head starts asking questions. If they were good questions it would be OK; however, they are 'doubting' questions. They make me second-guess what I know about God and what I have figured out.

"Now, I'm a framer and I know how to put things together and take them apart with my hammer; but, you know, that doesn't work with this situation. So, I need to know how to harness this questioning mind so God and I can work my life out."

Without so much as a moment's hesitation, the old woman began her story:

"There's a coyote that lives in the field on the other side of the woods behind the cabin. There have been a lot of people trying to kill that coyote so they can keep getting eggs from their chickens. Mind you, that coyote has never bothered their chickens, but still they are afraid he might. Try as they may, they cannot seem to rid the neighborhood of that 'annoying' coyote. People have set traps, sat in trees, dressed in camouflage and hid, trying to catch that ol' fella. But, try as they will, the ol' coyote is too clever for them.

"You see, the coyote has a spirit of resolve. He is not going to let some two-legged human outsmart him. The ol' coyote watches the humans as they try all sorts of methods to catch him; he watches how frustrated they become when yet another attempt is unsuccessful, and he wonders when they are going to just accept that he's part of the neighborhood. The ol' coyote does not understand why the two-leggeds don't like him;

he doesn't understand what he did to not be welcomed in the community. But, the old coyote knows that, try as they may, he is not going anywhere. He likes it here, and he's doing his best to stay put."

A beautiful white-laced chain emerged beneath the old woman's hands as she continued. "Life is like that. Sometimes people decide they want things a certain way and it doesn't matter what someone else wants. They want what they want and that's all that matters. No regard for another creature's perspective, no pause to consider what something different from them may be adding to the area.

"The coyote keeps lots of creatures out of the area by his sheer presence. That coyote doesn't have to kill something to make it leave; he merely represents something that another creature finds frightening, so that creature doesn't stay in the area. You see, the ol' coyote knows who he is; he knows he is one of God's creatures, and he follows his inner guidance from his Creator.

"The coyote carries his Creator inside, and there are some creatures, including people, who do not have that sort of connection. They are very disconnected from their Creator. When they come around others that are connected to their Creator, they don't like that feeling, so they do one of two things. They run away and avoid being around a God-connected being, or they try to annoy the heck out of that creature in hopes of abandoning that connection.

"You see, creatures disconnected from their Creator are also disconnected from their own true nature; hence, they are unpleasant to be around. As crazy as it may seem, unhappy people don't like to be around happy people. They find no peace with others and instead seek to be the 'winner' who reigns superior over others. It is a vicious cycle that creates havoc for everyone, even the plants in the woods.

"We humans can learn much from the creatures of the woods, if we would just pay attention and listen. Creator designed life to work together; whether it means something lives one place and another lives a different place doesn't matter. There is a respect for all of life and all the different ways of being in the world that allows life to change. With that change they move with the flow of life, rather than fight to keep things the same, or to keep their way as superior."

As the old woman bit the thread and tied a knot at the end, she continued her story. "You might consider that your hammer has helped you change and create many things in your life. You've done this for people who asked for something to be built or reshaped; and, my hunch is, you have done a very good job building what they requested. It is now time to remember who *you* are, to honor the Creator that lives within your heart, and to allow that divine relationship to help you reshape the things in your life that no longer serve you. It is time for you to build a new home on the solid foundation of truth that will bring you security, peace, and an amazing love like no other you have known."

The old woman rose from her chair, leaned over and handed Bruce the chain, and said, "Your self-doubt will disappear when your heart and voice are connected to the divine; and, just like the ol' coyote, you'll find your place and hold steady to what you know for certain." She gently touched his hand with her fingers, then touched his heart and said, "You will be surprised who shows up in your life when there is room for true love." She paused a moment, then added, "These are my words." With that, she turned and left the room.

Bruce kindled the fire, gathered the dishes neatly on the tray, wrapped himself snuggly in his winter gear, bent over and left a gift in the twig basket, then securely closed the door behind him. As he journeyed back to his truck, Bruce noticed the sweetness of the noonday sun. He heard the sounds of the creatures of the woods and the birds that took flight overhead as he felt a strong pull at his heart.

Reckon I am grateful for your unrest Fay; you helped me find my way back to my truth. Tears came to Bruce's eyes as he paused for a moment to breathe in the fresh air. *I so love you, Fay, and I do hope you find what you are looking for. I'm reconnecting to my sacred self as a way to help you find what you need. Sure do wish we could have found it together, but I guess that's not what's going to happen ... at least at this time.*

As Bruce opened the door to his truck, he saw *The Hammer* sitting on the floor board and said out loud, "You have served me well, and you know, I'm with good people: Jesus was a carpenter! Guess if he could change the world, I can do my best to change my little corner of it!"

Dare to Believe

Fur flew as the two cats screeched and hissed, causing Mark to nearly jump out of his boots. Prickly pins seemed to pop through his skin as his heart thumped so intensely it felt as though it would come through his chest. He stopped abruptly in his tracks to avoid being a part of the hostility.

What the heck...? It's a catfight! He stood very still so as not to become part of the conflict. He'd been raised on a farm, so he knew to stay out of the way of animals that were fighting over something. *A mouse, maybe?* he wondered. It didn't matter to Mark what they were fussing over; he just knew to stay clear of a catfight!

It wasn't long before the two cats were licking their wounds a short distance from each other. It all happened so fast that Mark wasn't certain who got the mouse, if either one of them did. As quickly as the thought came to him, he saw a large mouse scamper off into the woods.

"My goodness," he said, "all that fuss over a mouse and neither of you got it! Now look at you two, standing beside each other like old friends and 'cleaning up!'" He shook his head and took a deep breath as his heart rate returned to normal. "Well, better get back to the task at hand," he said.

Mark continued along the path to the old woman's cabin as he sniffed the air and caught a whiff of burning wood. *Man, I love that smell! There's nothing like that scent to take me back to my youth.*

His mind began to wander as mental images of being a boy in the mountains of North Carolina appeared in his head. Summers were spent baling hay, picking apples and stacking wood for the winter. Fact of the matter was, Mark could do just about anything when it came to working with his hands.

Both his father and grandfather had been loggers, and he had learned very early the importance of being resourceful. There was many a time Mark found himself fixing chainsaws and other small equipment while his father diligently worked the heavy equipment. It took guts and brawn to bring down the big trees needed to supply the furniture makers with the particular wood they requested. Mark knew his father was one of the best in the country, which was why he was always busy. His father had a solid reputation for meeting deadlines and supplying precisely what was needed for each of the furniture makers.

The winds picked up as Mark's attention returned to the trail in front of him. As he turned the final corner to the cabin he saw smoke rising from the chimney. *Now we know where that smell is coming from! Looks like she has a sturdy fire burning.*

The sun was rising in the East, as critters of all shapes and sizes emerged from the trees. "Well, good morning to all of you," Mark said softly. "Seems rather late for you all to just be getting up. But hey, we all need to sleep in from time to time, right?" As quickly as he spoke the words, he wondered, *Is it too early for the old woman?* He quickly dismissed that idea. "Nah, the fire's burning too well; she's been up awhile."

Mark stepped onto the porch, scraped his shoes on the mat in front of the door and knocked lightly. *I don't want to scare her.* Within a few seconds, the door opened, and a small, petite woman stood before him, wrapped snuggly in a purple, wool shawl.

She motioned for him to enter, then moved to the fireplace where she sat in a small, overstuffed side chair. *I guess she wants me to follow her? But then, I've learned to ask.*

"Good morning, Ma'am; mind if I join you?"

His question was met with silence as the old woman poured two cups of coffee, and then carefully opened a napkin-covered basket, revealing freshly-made muffins.

"Wow, those smell great!" Mark commented as he took the empty chair next to her in front of the blazing fire. "That coffee smells rich and bold; that's how I like it. And those muffins! Why, only my granny could make muffins like that." He paused a moment, then corrected himself. "I mean, I'm sure yours are just as good."

Mark added a lump of sugar to his coffee, but no cream, and generously placed two muffins on the saucer beside his cup. He noticed the lace-trimmed napkin that sat beside his saucer and wondered, *Am I to use such 'niceties?' I sure hope I don't ruin this napkin.*

Mark glanced over at the old woman and noticed that she was using her beautifully laced napkin. *Looks like she's using hers, so I guess it's OK if I use mine.* He carefully laid the napkin on his lap and began his feast of homemade muffins and hot coffee.

Mark had been brought up to pay attention to such details so as not to do something "wrong" to upset someone. Sure, he had made some blunders along the way, but he had learned to watch what others were doing so he would do what was "appropriate."

After a few minutes of eating muffins and drinking coffee, Mark began with his question. "I'm here today because I'm concerned about the state of affairs I see in the world." He looked at the fire that burned brightly and continued, "Sorta like that flame, I suppose. Sometimes it feels like people are on a slow simmer, just waiting for more 'wood' to be added. Then, when the wood has had a chance to catch hold of the hot coals, it takes off with a fury."

Mark poured another cup of coffee, added his usual lump of sugar, but no cream, and then took a sip. "Whew, that pot sure keeps the coffee hot," he said as he blew on the brew to cool it a bit. "I've been taught to think before I speak and to consider how my actions affect others. But you know, I think that might be a bit old-fashioned, because I see the generation behind me not thinking about such things. I mean, they seem to only consider what they want, with little regard for the consequences, either for themselves or for those around them. Makes me wonder what's going to happen to this world if we think only of ourselves."

Mark watched the flames dance along the logs, as some portions seemed to "catch the fire" more quickly than others. He carefully considered the large piece of wood that sat on top of the hot bed of burning embers, *Guess that log is like our world: some parts catch hold quickly, while other parts just do a slow burn.*

Mark once again remembered what it was like when he was a boy. His younger, Ned, seemed to think only of himself. Ned was always in trouble with someone, as if he hadn't learned from his past actions. Mark had no understanding of that since he didn't care much for the consequences he received, so he "considered" those punishments when he started to do something he wasn't certain about.

Mark readjusted himself in the chair and said, "I guess the question is, what is going to happen to this world if we don't get back to some basic personal guidelines? I suppose the word is 'ethics,' but I'm not one for knowing the 'politically correct' words! I'd appreciate any suggestions or advice you can give that will help me know what to do. You see, I was taught that you are either part of the problem or part of the solution, and I've chosen the latter."

The old woman began her story:

"Not so long ago, people were coming out of the Great Depression. It was a very dark time for our country, as some people found themselves flat broke after living lush lifestyles with little regard for others. Back then, a great deal of money was made at the expense of others who were less fortunate, and many of the wealthy found ways to run illegal activities to support their lavish lifestyles. For those individuals, there was little regard for anyone other than their immediate friends and family. And, if truth be told, they couldn't really trust them, either, for these were very unethical, greedy people. I wouldn't call them 'rich' folk, because by my standards, there was nothing 'rich' about them.

"Times were tough, food was scarce, and the worst part of it all was that no one knew whom to trust. It's one thing for a family to live in a small, crowded space, and quite another to be scavenging for food to feed their children.

"So, the natural order of life finally had to realign. The playing ground was leveled since everyone was in the same struggle to find a new way of living his or her life. What had been the 'norm' for families of all types was no longer clear, and, the differences between people who had money and people who didn't became blurred. Everyone was hungry, scared, and wondered what would happen to his or her family.

"It is during those times such as those that humankind's *true* nature comes into action. It didn't matter what the previous status of a person's income had been; everyone was hungry, and everyone needed clothes and a place to live. So, strangers became colleagues, families moved in together, and entire communities offered what they had to help one another."

The old woman bit the end off the thread, tied a knot at the end and put away her shuttle as she completed her story. "You see, it is during those times we have the greatest need that we really *see* our commonalities with others. Everyone understands what it means to be hungry, to hurt when their families are brokenhearted, and to be willing to do almost anything to ease the pain. It is the *true* nature of humankind to care about others, if we dare to believe it will!"

She rose from her chair, handed Mark the tatted chain, and said, "Never worry about humankind; it has a way of realigning when it is truly important. Perhaps one day everyone will realize this and not wait for a tragedy to *remember* that truth." She straightened herself, picked up the tray, turned to walk into the kitchen and said, "These are my words."

Mark glanced down at the tatted chain in his hands. *What is this? I didn't see her making anything.* He looked at the delicate chain and whispered, "It sure is beautiful. Wow, I'm impressed, and I didn't even notice her doing anything. Hmm, I generally pay better attention."

He rose from his chair, checked to make certain everything was as he had found it when he first sat down, then stoked the fire and added a few logs. *The least I can do is leave her warm,* he thought as placed the poker back in its proper place, wiped his hands of any residue and headed toward the front door. He dropped a gift in a twig basket as he said, "Thank you!"

The wind blew sharply from the North as Mark paused to button up his wool shirt and lift the collar to protect his neck from the cold. *Brrr, it's gotten cold! I'd better make this a quick walk!* He reached into his shirt pocket and pulled out the tatted chain.

As he looked at the chain, he noticed something furry moving in the distance. When he moved his eyes upward from the chain, he realized it was the two cats he had witnessed fussing along the trail. *Well, for heaven's sake! Guess you two have become friends?* "Now, isn't that a perfect ending," he concluded.

Mark giggled as he slipped the chain back into his shirt pocket. He picked up his pace and thought, *I knew there had to be a simple truth; something I just couldn't quite see. Wonder why I make things so difficult? I mean, things always work out; maybe not exactly as I think it needs to be, but who am I?*

He had to laugh as he considered that he *was* a person who looked for the best in everyone, hoped for a positive outcome, and did his best to offer a hand when someone was in need. Mark knew he was not the only person in the world like that; and yet, there were times when he felt like he was. *What a silly goof I can be. Pops was a good man, Mom always gave of herself, and I know Gramps and Grandma were kind, so what was my concern?*

Mark arrived back at his truck just as snow began to fall. He paused and looked up at the sky as the snow fell onto his face. *Hope springs eternal if we dare to believe in a source greater than ourselves.* As the snow melted on his face he felt the crispness of the frozen drops from heaven and his heart recalled a teaching he'd heard years before in church. *How did that go?* He allowed his mind to "call up" the teaching. *Oh yeah: "Snowflakes are the frozen dreams of the humans that pray to Creator; they come back to us to moisten our hearts so we have the rich soil it takes to grow those dreams. All we need is the courage to hold the vision of our dreams until they come to fruition." Guess all we have to do is keep dreaming, and keep believing there is good in the world. And, like the old woman said, it will happen if we dare to believe!*

Secured within the truck, Mark turned the key in the ignition and turned on the heater full blast. "Guess when life becomes cold, we have to turn up the heat, or the 'fire' within ourselves. Then we can bring warmth to our surroundings." He put the truck in gear and headed toward home, feeling lightness in his heart.

"Oh, I really want to remember today. I want to remember that life can be very simple, and when all the confusion comes into place, I can choose to move around it, rather than fuel it with more concern."

Mark turned on his windshield wipers as the snow began to fall with a fury. "Bring on those dreams! I'm ready to help them become possible! I am willing to *Dare to Believe!*"

Not One Word!

Snow blanketed the trail to the old woman's cabin as Tom stood outside his truck and surveyed the path. *What a winter wonderland!* He scanned the landscape. *Not a human footprint anywhere.* Enjoying the stillness of the morning Tom asked, *Why have I not bought Nancy and myself a woodland cabin?* Without a moment's hesitation he answered his own question. *Because we have a beautiful home in the city!* He had to chuckle at how his mind tends to answer his questions as quickly as it asks them!

Just then a furry fox scampered across the trail, bringing him back to the moment.

"OK, li'l buddy, I see you," he said as he checked his wristwatch. "Better get going before the next wave of snow moves in." With that, Tom added human prints to the fox's as he began his trek to the cabin.

Meanwhile, the old woman grabbed her oven mitt, removed the three-inch-high golden brown biscuits from the oven, and carefully placed them on a wire rack to cool. She turned toward the fireplace in the next room, placed a few logs on the fire, then cleared the table that sat between two large overstuffed chairs in preparation for the visitor.

The fire burned brightly as the old woman placed a large, fabric covered tray on the table. She moved toward the front door and placed her hand on the doorknob just as a knock was heard. After opening the door, and without saying a word, she turned, and moved to her chair by the fire.

Tom greeted her with a simple, "Morning, Ma'am." He removed his snowy boots, placed them on a very worn rag rug, and hung his coat on a set of deer antlers that were nailed to the wall. *Guess this is suppose to be a coat rack*, he questioned as he placed his hat on the adjoining antler.

As he walked toward the fire he said, "My name is Tom," and he sat down in the empty chair in front of the fire. "This fire feels real good on this cold, snowy morning," he continued as he rubbed his hands together and held them in front of the fire. The old woman poured a mug full of hot steamy cocoa and handed it to him.

"Well, thank you very much, Ma'am; you certainly know how to make a person feel welcome." Tom snuggled himself into the chair, blew on the hot cocoa and took a sip. "Oh, man, that's some really good stuff!"

As if she heard nothing, the old woman lifted the towel that covered the hot biscuits, placed one on a saucer, then handed it to Tom. He placed the mug on the table between them, accepted the biscuit and said, "Oh, man, that smells as good as it looks. Thank you, Ma'am."

After smothering the biscuit with butter, Tom took a bite and muffled, "Mmm," as he swallowed the first bite, then added, "I do believe that's the best biscuit I've ever eaten."

Upon finishing the biscuit, Tom looked at the old woman and saw that she was working her magic with a thin white thread and a small piece of wood. *What did Granny call that craft?* He pondered for a moment. *It's not knitting or crocheting ... oh, I remember, it is tatting!*

He watched her move her hands at warp speed as he picked up the cocoa and said, "How did you know I was coming?" When the old woman did not reply, he said, "Never mind that question; I hear you know all sorts of things. You must be one of those psychics, or fortune tellers, or whatever they call it." When his words were again met with silence, he spoke again, "Do you know the future, or are you one of those people that talks to spirits?"

Tom's mind was in full throttle as all sorts of things flashed through. *How'd she know someone was coming? Well, maybe she makes biscuits for herself without someone coming. Still, there were mugs and saucers for two people. Maybe she's just one of those people who is always prepared. What if she puts something in the cocoa that makes you dizzy? Oh, don't be silly! She's a nice old woman who is probably lonely and just hopes for people to come by.* The thoughts picked up speed until Tom said out loud, "STOP!"

Jolting himself back to reality, Tom felt a bit embarrassed. He looked over at the old woman to see her reaction. *Wouldn't you know it, not so much as a flinch,* he thought. She just kept tatting away as a beautiful chain emerged beneath her hands.

"Sorry 'bout that; guess I was off in space somewhere," he said as he smothered a second biscuit with grape jam. "Truth is, that's precisely why I'm here today. My mind is always running full throttle with thoughts. Why, if there was a race for mind speed, I'd surely be the winner, hands down!"

He settled back in his chair, feeling the need to slow down and give his racing mind a rest, and to enjoy the tasty morsel in front of him. Savoring every bite, Tom became mesmerized by the slow, burning fire. *What a peaceful place,* he sighed. *Sure could use more of this.*

"You have a real nice place here; very warm and inviting. Thank you for your hospitality. To get back to why I'm here, I seem to have trouble just enjoying life; like I said, my head is always talking to me. I'm grateful for how quickly it can figure things out, and overall, it serves me well. Lots of good ideas have been birthed in this head." He said as he tapped his forehead and straightened himself in his chair.

"Problem is, I haven't found the shut-off valve. Why, even at night I'm dreaming about problems, solutions, analyzing this and that, trying to figure out what somebody meant by what they said. It's always something."

Tom stretched his legs out in front of him and took a deep breath as he continued, "Not often do I slow down long enough to even sit this long." As silence hung in the air, only the crackling of the fire could be heard.

"Wow, my mind hasn't been this quiet in a very long time, if ever!" he chuckled.

There was a hush in the air that seemed to permeate Tom's skin. He felt a slight vibration on the bottoms of his feet that began to slowly move up his legs, to his thighs, and to his belly, as he could feel the chair surround him with warmth. Tom felt a quickening in his chest as his heart began to beat with the rhythm of the stillness. His thoughts stirred. *Is that my heart?*

A deep breath quickly brought him back to the stillness. He felt a tingling in his fingers that moved upward to his hands, arms, shoulder and neck. As though a gentle veil was moved across his face, he closed his eyes allowing yet another deep breath to open his mouth and release a hum that seemed to harmonize with all of life.

Several breaths followed, and Tom found himself in a place he had never been; he was "at peace." *So this is what peace feels like,* his mind noted. *OK, I'll remember this.*

Sitting in the stillness of all that is, a tear slipped down Tom's face as he became one with the silence, *Thank you my friend, thank you,* his mind seemed to say. *Thank you.*

As moments passed, Tom allowed *grace* to enter; it came in the form of an image of his "mama." She had left the planet several years prior and Tom had done what he did so well; he had buried himself in activities in order not to feel her absence. As a boy he cherished his mama, and thought she was the most beautiful woman he had ever seen. He remembered sitting in church snuggled close to her, knowing this was the safest place in the world. There was, in his eyes, no stronger person on the planet; and, sitting next to her, in "their" pew at church was the most peaceful place on Earth. Being there with her always made him feel connected to something "greater than life."

Another deep breath released as Tom felt the floor beneath his feet. *Oh, I'm waking up; I don't want to leave!* he cried to her. *Please don't make me leave, please!* He squeezed his eyes tightly so as not to wake up. As his breathing returned to normal he felt life come back into his body. *I promise to slow down long enough to feel your presence, Mama. Thank you for reminding me what peace feels like.*

Tom stirred in his chair, opened his eyes and remembered where he was. Staring at the fire in front of him his thoughts flowed, *I have a baby coming soon that needs to know the peace that comes from sitting next to "Papa" in a "favorite" pew at church. It's been way too long since I took the time to go to church; time for that to change!* As he watched the low, steady flame from the fire, he remembered an old hymn he had heard in church. "*I will cling to the old rugged cross, and exchange it some day for a crown,*" ran sweetly through his head. *Man, Nancy is going to be happy that I'm going to accompany her to church again!*

He spun the gold band on his left hand and thought about their wedding day. They were married in the same church in which he had grown up; his mama insisted they marry where Tom had learned the most about being a good person. She told him, "Always remember to treat your wife and family the way God treats you: with much love and respect."

She was right! Time for me to put my faith in the front seat and get this ol' head mind out of the driver's seat!

Sitting up straight in his chair, Tom glanced toward the old woman to see what she was doing. As his eyes focused, he saw that she was tying a knot at the end of a beautiful tatted chain.

"Guess I drifted off again," he said, "What an amazing place this is." As Tom gathered his senses, he rambled, *What in the world just happened?* In a split second he stopped himself. *I won't spend time thinking about that; it doesn't matter. What's important is that I always remember this experience.*

Rubbing his eyes, he looked around the room and returned to his thoughts. *My mind needs to rest. I must stay alert to feel Mama's presence. I have a hunch she still has a lot to teach me.*

The old woman rose from her chair and stood in front of Tom. She leaned forward, touched Tom's heart with the tatted chain, placed it in his hand, then turned and left the room. Tom sat very still, not moving a muscle as he continued to feel the sense of peace that had eluded him all too long. *Why in the world have I avoided such a peaceful feeling?* He quickly left the answer to that question where it belonged — in the past!

His thoughts quickly moved to his wife, Nancy, their coming baby, and the memories of his mama and her faith that he wanted to share with his child. *I'm keepin' my word, Mama. Let's go home!*

He gathered the dishes from the cocoa and biscuits, stacked them neatly on the tray, covered them with the cloth and placed them by the doorway through which the old woman had brought them. He returned to the fire, stoked it, and added a few more logs to keep it burning warm and bright. Then he stepped into his boots, buttoned his coat, and secured his hat as he leaned down and dropped a gift in the twig basket by the door.

What a place, was all he could think as he closed the door securely behind him. *There's no way I can describe what just happened. And, you know, it doesn't matter anyway. To try and explain it would engage my "mind" too much, and I'm giving that some much needed rest!*

Walking through the snow, he turned one last time to glance at the cabin. "You aren't a psychic or a fortune teller; you simply know how to stay in the moment, pay attention and live from your heart," he spoke out loud. Tom then reached in his pocket, pulled out the tatted chain and said, "My life will never be the same."

Pausing to feel the air, smell the pines and listen to the sounds of nature, he realized something. He never heard the old woman's voice. He looked up at the sky, smiled and said out loud, "My life is changed and no words were spoken. Now, isn't that something? *Not One Word!*"

Unblemished Snow

It was a bitterly cold afternoon as fierce North winds howled through the Forest. Evergreens shook off snow like a dog shakes water from his coat, and snow tossed about on the road in front of Scott's truck as he drove. "What on Earth possessed me to pick such a wintry day to make this trip?"

He wheeled his truck onto the clearing to the old woman's cabin, and said, "Better make certain I have easy access to leave! Hopefully, we won't get too much more snow."

After maneuvering his truck into a good spot, Scott craned his neck to look out of his front windshield and scan the sky. "Doesn't look like we're in for too much more snow," he said. He grabbed his coat and hat and stuck his cell phone into his pocket. "I've made it this far, so I might as well go meet this lady everyone talks about."

As he exited the truck, he looked at the surroundings. *What a marvelous winter day; makes me want to lie down and make snow angels. Hmm, forty-five and still thinking about making snow angels!* He laughed at that thought, but Scott knew he never wanted to give up acting like a kid. He felt "growing up" meant that he would become as boring as his father, and he wanted "none of that!"

He slipped into his hat and coat, surveyed the snow-covered ground, and noticed the unblemished white beauty. *Looks like diamonds! Like millions and millions of sparkling jewels! I wonder if people ever get used to seeing new snow? I know I sure don't!*

Scott glanced down at his watch and mumbled, "Better get my rear in gear so I'm out of here before more snow comes."

Despite the newly arrived snow the path was quite visible as he moved slowly along the trail. Dark brown tree branches stuck out along the trail, as the freshly fallen snow clung to the branch tops.

Scott stopped for a moment, scooped off some of the snow, and quickly shoved it into his mouth. The crisp, fresh taste felt refreshing as the snow instantly moistened the palate of his mouth. "Mmm, how I love fresh snow!" He grabbed some more and popped it into his mouth; it melted like butter on a hot biscuit. "Man, how quenching is that?"

Within a few more strides, Scott stood at the clearing to the cabin. *Look at that place! It looks like something out of a storybook!*

Snow covered the cabin roof as smoke moved upward toward the heavens. He eyed the woodpile to the left of the porch and headed in that direction. He figured he would grab a few pieces and take it in with him to help the old woman.

As he stepped onto the porch he caught a whiff of something very familiar. *Man, I believe she's made some biscuits! What a treat!* His tummy began to rumble. *Didn't know I was hungry 'til I smelled those biscuits. Tom said she made killer biscuits, and if anyone would know, it would be him.*

Scott lifted the worn tarp that covered the split wood and gave it a shake to brush off the newly fallen snow. He then filled his arms with wood and moved toward the cabin. The front door opened as he stepped onto the porch, and a vision of purple held it open for him to enter. He stomped each foot to release any residue of snow, wiped them on the doormat, gave her a nod of thanks and entered the cabin.

Once inside he wiped his boots again on a rag rug at the door, and carried the arm full of wood to the fireplace. He leaned into the fireplace to brush the residue from the wood, then turned and returned to the front door where he slipped off his cowboy boots.

"Good day, Ma'am, and thank you for holding the door open," he said as he extended a hand to the old woman. She simply turned and moved toward the two chairs in front of the fireplace.

"Thank you for bringing in some wood," she said as she removed an orange-colored fabric from the tray that sat between the two chairs.

Scott hung his hat and coat on the deer antlers secured on the wall and moved toward the chairs. Once there, he stood until the old woman handed him a cup of coffee and made a nod in the direction of the chair to the left of the fire.

"Why, thank you, Ma'am," he said as he accepted the cup of hot brew. "This will hit the spot; it's a cold one out there this morning." He held the cup with both hands as the old woman finished pouring herself a cup and took a seat to the right of him.

She placed her cup on the edge of the table between them and removed the napkin that revealed piping hot biscuits. A dish of butter and some blackberry preserves offered perfect toppings to the savory dish.

"I appreciate you seeing me today, and I promise to make this a short visit since more snow is on the way," he said as he eagerly snatched up a warm biscuit and smothered it with the creamy butter.

The fire crackled and popped, no doubt from the seasoned poplar that burned. The scent of sassafras hung in the air as Scott began to feel the peacefulness of his new surroundings.

"You have a marvelous home; it is so quaint and peaceful. It makes me feel quite relaxed just being here."

A slight smile appeared on the old woman's face as she put the remains of her biscuit back onto a saucer. "Thank you," was all she said.

She retrieved her black velvet bag from a basket next to her chair and pulled out her tatting supplies as Scott watched her methodically place white tatting thread around her fingers. *Hmm, don't know as I have seen that sort of handwork.*

He glanced at the various items on the fireplace mantel. Starting from the left, there was an unusually large piece of clear quartz crystal that supported one side of a few small books. An antique black iron secured the other end of the books. About six inches further down the mantel was a pair of jeweled picture frames that adorned the pictures of people the old woman no doubt held dear. A feather with tan leather securely wrapped around the stem, a colorful rattle, and a most unusual piece of wood were next. At the very end of the mantel was a green glass kerosene lamp.

Scott looked from the mantel to the old woman and began his question. "I am curious what you have to say about religion."

A momentary pause that felt like ten minutes caused Scott to adjust himself in his chair. He leaned forward, then back, until he finally broke the silence and said, "I mean, my experience is, people talk a lot about religion; and yet, their lives don't always show that they believe in anything but themselves."

He reached for the coffee pot, poured himself another cup, and then motioned toward the old woman's cup, to which she nodded her head. After he poured more coffee for her, Scott rested the pot on the table, took a few sips and said, "It all confuses me. I was brought up in church; our parents accompanied my sister and me to worship services. Although my father smoked and my mother liked to gamble at bit, they were God-fearing people."

After downing a couple more sips, Scott continued, "When my sister and I were just kids our younger brother drowned, and everything changed after that. Mom and Dad still went to church; however, the nightly Bible reading was out the window, and," he paused for a moment, "the whole feeling of going to church seemed to become mechanical. It was like brushing your teeth in the morning; something you did as a routine, without much thought.

"At any rate, as I've grown older, I, too, have become rather lackadaisical about church. I mean, why go just to be going? Wouldn't it be better to just stay at home than to pretend something that really feels almost 'fake?'"

The fire had settled a bit, so Scott got up and gathered a few pieces of wood. As he probed and prodded the slow burning wood and adjusted the hot coals, he placed a few pieces of fresh wood strategically onto the fire to bring it back to life. He continued, "I guess I just feel religion has become pretty unimportant in my life; and yet, there is a void of some sort that I cannot quite put my finger on."

He brushed the wood chippings off his hands and into the fire, then returned to his chair. As he settled back into the seat he concluded, "So, I am curious: what is your take on religion?"

Almost immediately, the old woman began her story:

"A very long time ago, there lived a man of very humble beginnings who was loved by many. He was born to a couple not yet married, and times were such that they traveled to the city to pay their taxes before their son was born.

"They lived a very simple existence, but with all the basic necessities provided. They did not have a fancy home, or the status of position in the community. And, like most parents, they felt their son was 'special.'

"They were people of faith who knew that what mattered most was the gifts provided by their Creator. To this couple, the son they were given was the greatest gift they could receive. They had no doubt their son was given to them by the Creator, and that he would do great things for many people when he grew up.

"As the years unfolded, the son did grow to be an exceptional man of faith, and, as his parents had predicted, he performed miraculous things wherever he traveled. He was, indeed, the son of God."

The old woman examined the white chain that was now extended beneath her hands as she returned to her tatting and her story. "You know this story, Scott; you heard it when you were a very small boy. It was one that touched your heart in such ways that you asked this One to come and live there. You realized at a very early age that this special 'son of God' was not like any other human being. And, knowing he was in your heart comforted you through your early years."

Scott felt a lump in his throat as his heart raced in his chest. The old woman continued, "The trouble with growing up, Scott, is that today's world focuses on what each person can accomplish, acquire, and achieve, with little regard to the things of the heart. Our world has become so 'accepting' of different points of views that the world has become afraid to really listen to another person's heart for fear of offending them."

Scott sat mesmerized by her words, and the warmth from the fire seemed to pierce through a "shield" of sorts that was around him. He really could not quite understand this "shield;" however, he knew something within him had been penetrated. He could *feel* this in his heart and in his body. *Very strange, Very strange!*

The old woman continued, "You see, Scott, religion is different than spirituality. Religion is merely the way through which we demonstrate what is in our hearts, whereas spirituality is what we *know* in our very core to be true." She paused a few moments, looked at the fire, and took a few deep breaths. It was as though she considered her own heart, and that the breathing in and out was a way to reconnect to something really important.

"Many people today have forgotten that core. They have 'thrown the baby out with the bath water,' and abandoned what their hearts know to be true. Religion provides a structured way to show our love for the divine. It does not matter what we call the Creator; what is important is that we acknowledge the source from which we came and to which we will return. Without that intimate relationship with our Creator, we will walk through life like zombies; and, without being fed with the divine love that runs through our veins, we will die. Oh, we may be alive and go through the motions of living, but without our true connection, we will always feel the emptiness of being cut off from our true source."

She bit the end of the thread, placed a knot at the end, and stood up from her chair. As she turned and faced Scott, she bent over, handed him the chain, and said, "The 'church' is the people who know their connection to the Creator, rather than the building in which people attend religious service. If you want to fill that void in your heart, ask the son of God you knew as a boy to be your best friend."

She folded Scott's fingers and wrapped her hands around them. "There is no more important relationship in the world than the one you have with your Creator. Anything is possible with God at your side. Your father knew that at one time, and, when he is ready, he will return to his Creator. When he reconnects to deep truth he will remember what it feels like to have his friend back. When that relationship is rekindled within his heart and he begins to allow himself to feel the return of his old friend, he will begin to enjoy life once again. When that happens, Scott, he will return to you as a loving dad."

She looked into his eyes, and Scott felt a deep sense of love like he had *never* felt in his life; it was as though she had known him his whole life! She then patted his hand and concluded, "You *will* get your dad back, and you *will* live a life with hope if *you* will allow the Creator to heal *your* heart. It takes a daily connection with the divine to help you overcome the teachings given by well-meaning people who do not have their own personal daily walk with the divine."

With that she released her hands from his, gathered the items onto the tray, replaced the orange-covered fabric over them and carried the tray toward the kitchen as she said, "These are my words."

Scott sat perfectly still for what seemed like forever. Visions of a younger, slimmer dad raced across his memory; horseback rides around the living room, pillow fights prior to settling in for the night, and reeling in "the big one" at the local fishing hole brought a smile to his face.

The next instance a balding, more "stout" version of his dad appeared in his vision. He saw blood vessels that bulged at his dad's neck, and a red face that shouted profanities at him.

"Can't you do anything right? I mean, how many times do I have to tell you to fill the gas tank when you bring the car home? And you are a lazy, good for nothing punk! And I'll be darned if I'm going to support your lazy ass!"

Scott felt tears burn his eyes as he remembered what his relationship with his dad had become. *What happened?* And, then, he looked deeper into his dad's brown eyes and all he could see was pain — plain and simple pain.

I am so very sorry, Dad; I never meant to let you down! I never thought about what was going on in your life — I only thought of mine!

The tears hung at his eyelashes as Scott fought to control his emotions; and yet, all he really wanted was to let them go. *I'm sorry; I'm so very sorry!* With that, he buried his face in his hands and released his tears.

Within a few moments, warmth returned to his heart. It was a tender, gentle, sweetness for the man who really was his "hero," despite the tension and words between them. Scott knew without a shadow of doubt that his dad was the strongest, most generous man he knew; and all he ever wanted was to grow up to be just like him.

Somewhere between middle school and high school the relationship had shape shifted into something neither of them liked. Scott spent time with his guy friends and sports while his dad grew old and tired, wanting only to sit and stare at the television. The closeness they had once shared became only a memory as the chasm between them widened. Try as his mom would, neither his dad nor Scott would take the first step toward each other.

As the warmth in his chest spread throughout his body, Scott had a flash of another vision. This time it was a Christmas tree. Colorful lights dotted the green as lines of bright red cranberries crisscrossed strings of popcorn that embraced a six-foot spruce pine. The scent of pine filled his memories along with a rugged wooden manger that sat on a red and green tree skirt at the base of the tree. *We've had that nativity set as long as I can remember,* Scott recalled. *I believe Dad said Uncle Steve carved that in his woodshop eons ago.*

And then Scott remembered the year he played Joseph in the church Christmas play. His friend, Timmy, had a baby sister they used as baby Jesus that year. *Hmm, that was strange; I remember thinking, how can a baby girl play Jesus?* With a chuckle, he was brought back to the fire in front of him.

"Good heavens, I need to get out of here," he said as he rose from the chair and reached for the poker to stir the fire. He adjusted the logs and probed and prodded the coals as his mind began to wander again. *I suppose it's like this fire; when it's tended, it burns steadily and evenly. When we ignore it, it goes out. Hmm!*

Scott completed his task, went to the door, slipped on his boots and dropped a gift in the twig basket. He paused at the door a moment and looked back at the fire. *I appreciate your warmth. You and that old woman are quite the teachers!* And, with that, he walked through the door and pulled it securely closed behind him.

He pulled his hat down tightly and buttoned up his coat as he moved off the porch. Snow was softly falling as he walked along the trail back to his truck. *Fresh footprints on virgin snow, unblemished by human contact. Perhaps that is what I need to remember. Everything comes in perfection from the divine. It is only when we forget our origins that we allow our human encounters to "blemish" that which is perfect.*

One footprint at a time, he said as he moved along the trail, *one footprint at a time. Surely I can walk my way back to that perfection. Surely I can remember where I came from; surely I can find my way home!*

The snow was steadily falling as Scott returned to his truck. He pulled out his keys, unlocked the door, and brushed the snow off his coat and boots before he sat down in his truck. He started the engine, cleaned the snow off the window with his wipers, and turned on the heat full blast. "What a day!"

Scott picked up his cell phone from the seat beside him and noticed two missed calls from his dad. *Hmm, wonder what's up? Dad hasn't called me in months.* He pushed the call button and within a few moments heard, "Hi Scott, thanks for calling me back."

Scott felt his heart race as he replied, "It's good to hear from you, Dad. Are you OK?"

"I'm fine, son." There was a long pause and then he said, "The truth is, Scott, things haven't been alright, but I'm doing something about that."

Scott felt nervous and yet, something told him it was a "good" nervous.

"Son, if you can see your way to forgive me, I really want to sit down face to face and talk with you. Is that possible?"

The warmth from his heart filled the truck more quickly than the heater. He took a deep breath and said, "Of course, Dad. When do you want me to come by?"

"The sooner the better, son. How about this evening?"

"Sounds great, Dad. How about five o'clock? I know you don't like to get out, so I can come by the house." There was hope in Scott's heart as he cautiously considered his dad's voice. *He sounds sincere.* Another breath. *There is always hope!*

"No, son, how about I come to your place? You have been gone all day."

Scott once again felt tears fill his eyes. "OK, Dad, that sounds great. Now keep in mind, I'm not the best housekeeper."

"Oh, I remember your bedroom here at home." His dad said with a cracked voice. "I guess you get that from me." After a brief pause, "See you at five."

Scott hung up his cell phone and stared at it for a few moments. *Could this really be happening? Dare I get my hopes up?* And, as quickly as the thought exited his mind, he said, "Of course, it can! That is what faith is all about!"

Just as he was about to exit onto the main road, Scott noticed the silver cross that hung off his rearview mirror. "Time for me to come home to my old friend. I've been as hypocritical as those I condemned."

He glanced just past the cross and caught sight of the newly fallen snow. As he looked upward toward the heavens, he said, "Thank you for your forgiveness, and for the *Unblemished Snow!*"

Waking Dreams

"Once upon a time, not so long ago, there was a woman who had a dream — a very special dream. It was what some call a 'waking dream.' First, let me tell you a little bit about Tina. From the time she came into this world Tina was brought up with a deep faith and an abiding love for God. Her family taught the importance of church attendance; in fact, most of their family activities revolved around church functions.

"On a personal level, Tina knew the love of God, the importance of his son, Jesus, and she knew about the Holy Spirit. Like her parents, she strived to live these principles in her daily life. It was the deep love she felt within her heart that led Tina to share these beliefs with her own children. She wanted them to grow up knowing they were part of something greater than themselves and that they were never alone.

"The time came when Tina's children became adults and moved out to begin their own families. The absence of her children weighed heavily on Tina's heart as she struggled to redefine her role in life. Everything she knew to be certain in her life had taken a new form, so Tina did what she did so well: she prayed; and, after a short period of time, she decided to try other denominations. What the heck, everything else in her life was changing, why not 'shake that up,' too? However, she did not expect what followed.

"Tina bounced from church to church, and still she felt a pull to 'something else.' One day while driving home from work, she noticed a sign that advertised a 'metaphysical' bookstore. *Whatever is 'metaphysical?'* she wondered. When she got home she retrieved her dictionary, and discovered that it means, not of the physical; mystical, spiritual. She became intrigued with the discovery and decided to visit the store.

"It was a rather 'quaint' store, full of books, stones, incense, various jewelry, and memorabilia from different religious groups. A petite, older woman offered her much information about the store. She explained that her husband was an intuitive reader and that they offered weekly classes to assist seekers who are curious about other beliefs beyond the 'norm.' That piqued Tina's interest, so she attended the first class available.

"The evening began with one of the bookstore owners reading a section from a book, and then opening up discussion for those in attendance. Some weeks it was quite lively, and the really good stuff happened after the discussions.

There would be a short break, and then those interested would enter a darkened room, sit in a circle and be guided into a meditative state. For Tina, it was exhilarating! She began to see colors and forms that were very familiar to her because she recalled that as a child she'd had the same visions. To her it was a 'coming home,' so to speak."

The old woman paused her story and her tatting as she looked off the porch out to the Forest. Silence hung in the air as Matthew watched her. She sat perfectly still, and he could not take his eyes off her. He felt mesmerized by her state of stillness to the point that he felt carried into a trance.

Colors swirled as flowing energy danced before his eyes. He remembered similar visions he'd had as a child. He recalled lying in his bed at night, staring at the chest of drawers; then in a moment he would see the chest become very small. It was as though he were a great distance from the chest, when in reality he knew he was in his bed. It never made sense to him how or why such a thing would happen, but there it was right in front of him, and his eyes were wide open.

His thoughts brought him back to the moment, *Wonder if that is what she's talking about? Could that be what she is seeing from another dimension?*

The old woman resumed her tatting, then quickly continued her story. "Yessiree, Tina felt very much at home with that group at the metaphysical bookstore, and each week she could hardly wait for the next meeting.

"After a period of time, Tina's visions began to take clear forms, and before she knew it, she was receiving messages for others in attendance. As she gained the courage to share the visions, and as the receiver confirmed the messages, she knew she had found her path. The only thing she needed to do now was to make certain God approved.

"Tina went home, sat in her prayer room, and asked for guidance. Tears of joy filled her eyes, and she told God she would go no further in this work without the blessings of Jesus. You see, Tina had a very deep relationship with Jesus, and she wasn't about to step into some new area without his blessing.

"After a few very short moments, tears streamed down her cheeks as she saw the presence of Jesus. Tina felt her heart fill with love as she received a very personal message of approval from him. Her heart nearly leaped from her chest as she realized she was about to become intimately connected to the third part of the Holy Trinity. After years of walking closely with Jesus, it was time for her to personally know the workings of the Holy Spirit, and knowing she had received the blessings from the Creator of the Universe brought comfort and joy to her heart.

"Tina began to cherish and appreciate this gift she'd had from birth, as she welcomed the visions that came to her. She was guided into this new arena when she was told to go to a familiar place in her mind before each journey into the spirit world. She was always to go to this place as a way to be certain her angelic messengers, whom she knew represented her connection to God, were guiding her.

"Once Tina was at her 'place' she would see a woman dressed in a sunbonnet and apron tending a flower garden. Every single time Tina went to her sacred place that woman was in her garden; it was one of the 'symbols' that she was protected and connected to the divine.

"A few years after establishing this routine, Tina went one day as usual to her usual sacred place, only to discover the woman was not in the flower garden. She hesitated to go any further into her meditation because the woman was not there. As always, she asked Jesus for guidance and was assured everything was as it was meant to be, and to proceed as usual. He told her she would understand later. Because of her trust and connection with Jesus, she proceeded; however, there was a deep sadness in her heart from the absence of the 'flower woman.'

"The meditation group was now Tina's spiritual community and with that she allowed her roots to deepen within this new realm of being. Her family was also changing; she was about to become a grandmother and enter yet another chapter of her life. Tina was pleased that her spiritual family was there to help her herald in this new role."

The old woman paused for a moment, looked over at Matthew, and said nothing. Matthew felt a bit uneasy, as if he was supposed to say or do something; and, yet, he knew something beyond words was occurring. He simply kept his eyes on the old woman until she looked back at her handwork and continued her story.

"Tina's granddaughter was born a fussy baby. It was clear she was a spirited soul who had her nights and days mixed up, which gave her already insecure young parents mixed emotions about their effectiveness as parents. Within a few days of her birth, her parents brought the baby to Tina so they could go home and get some sleep, and wouldn't you know it, the moment that baby got into Tina's arms she fell fast asleep.

"Shortly after the parents left, Tina had a 'waking dream' as she held her granddaughter. She took a few deep breaths and went to her 'special place' and, as she looked into the flower garden, she had a huge realization: her 'flower woman' was no longer in the garden because she was now in Tina's arms. Tina felt joy in her heart, because she knew beyond a shadow of doubt that life was, indeed, a continuum. She thanked God for this sweet soul, then whispered in her granddaughter's ear, 'Welcome to life here on Earth Mother, sweet flower! I promise to love and cherish you, and to teach you all the things you need in order to grow and develop into a strong and loving human being.'"

Matthew felt a lump in his throat as tears clouded his vision. *Oh, Grandpa,* he thought. *Now I understand.*

Matthew felt the wooden boards beneath his feet as he took a deep breath and watched the barren trees scattered among the evergreens of the Forest. Strong winds blew as the three-dimensional layers of life moved in different directions. Large limbs hung low and tall pines swayed as the end of winter drew near. It was a time of reawakening from the long winter's sleep in the Forest as chipmunks scurried around the trees, and as rabbits emerged from their winter homes.

What a wonder this life is, and what an amazing universe! How can anyone ever doubt the existence of a divine Creator? He glanced at the old woman, who had placed her handwork materials into the black velvet bag. Wrapped snuggly in her shawl, she rose from the porch swing and stepped toward him.

"We have all sorts of dreams in life, and it is our responsibility to discern what each of them means. No one can interpret your dreams but you, and certainly no one can tell you what is real or not real." She leaned over and reached for Matthew's hand, and Matthew responded by lifting it to her. She placed the tatted chain into his hand and said, "You have many gifts; honor them and they will serve you well. Dreams are the portal to the divine; without them we forget our true nature. These are my words."

The old woman picked up the tray, and Matthew stood up. "May I help you with that?" When she did not respond, he went to the front door, opened it, and she walked through the door carrying the tray. He hesitated for a brief moment until a fierce wind blew from the North, so he securely closed the door and walked to the edge of the porch. Taking a gift from his wallet, he placed it in the twig basket and placed a heavy stone over it to keep it securely in place.

He paused for a moment to scan the visible perimeters of the yard. *What a marvelous place*, Matthew thought. *Wonder if this is what heaven looks like?* Without a moment's hesitation he concluded, *I know it is. I've seen it before, and I know Grandpa's busy working in the garden there.*

Matthew stepped off the porch with a sense of knowing that all was in perfect order. He had come to visit the old woman after hearing other people's stories about things they had learned while sitting with her. Matthew had always been curious about things "outside the box." Although he had been looked upon as though he were a "strange person," he always knew he surely wasn't the only person who had such unique experiences. *That old woman knew what I needed to hear; I didn't even need to ask a question.* A smile spread across his face. *I love that!*

As he continued his walk along the trail back to his car, Matthew remembered the strong and forthright way in which his grandpa would tell him to not believe everything people tell him. *Grandpa always said, "There's more to life than what you can see, you just need to pay attention!"*

He recalled the sharp words his grandpa would use after some "door to door religion" people would come for a visit. *Grandpa was quick to tell them to "turn right around and head back the direction from which you came."* Matthew had to chuckle as he caught sight of a squirrel that turned and darted back at warp speed. "You look like some of those folks Grandpa spoke to!" he laughed.

As he settled into the car he turned the key, placed the car in drive and headed onto the main road toward home. "Grandpa, you said one day I'd understand the visions I saw, just as you said I'd realize why you told me you'd always known me." He felt warmth in his heart as the smell of his grandpa's pipe became strong. "OK, Grandpa, you know I don't allow smoking in my car!" he said out loud. "But, since it's you, I'll make an exception!"

As Matthew drove down the road he noticed all the beauty along the countryside that seemed to have eluded his sight during the drive to the old woman's cabin. "Sure is a rich land we live in, and Grandpa; I understand why you loved the country so. There's something alive in nature that cannot be replaced by anything in the city."

Matthew had a sense his grandpa had something to tell him, so he said, "OK, I'll be still, Grandpa, what is it you have to say?" Within a few seconds, he caught sight of a deer in the clearing to the right, so he carefully eased his car to a safe spot off the main road. He sat very still and his eyes locked with the deer's. *What is it?*

The deer stood tall with his long neck stretched and his ears pointing toward the heavens. Looking straight at Matthew it communicated to him, "Be swift, graceful, and gentle in all you do, and life will reflect the same back to you."

Matthew sat in perfect stillness as the deer took a different form. His mind wanted to interpret what was happening and he quickly told his head to be still as he kept his focus on the image in front of him. Colors of brown, black and white swirled and turned until a shape took form. Breathing to keep his focus clear, Matthew felt strong emotions as his eyes welled with tears and the image of his grandpa stood in place of the deer. It was a brief moment suspended in time and space as their eyes sent love to one another.

I love you, Grandpa, and I miss you so, Matthew communicated. *I understand all that you told me while you were here, and Grandpa, thank you for being the strong individual that always stood by my side.* Through his tears, Matthew's vision became clear, and his grandpa gave him a wave as his image began to fade.

The colors once again swirled and twisted as the image transformed back to the deer. Matthew watched as the deer's ears moved, his neck shortened, he turned, and the white tail bobbed off into the distance.

With a deep breath, he blinked his eyes several times, then released his breath into the air. His body tingled as he felt his physical form once again. *How very interesting! It has been a very long time since I allowed my heart to reveal such gifts.* He looked in the rearview mirror of his car, saw his reflection and said, "Thank you, for honoring my heart."

Matthew glanced at the clock and noticed only five minutes had passed since he pulled off the side of the main road. "Wow, that was quick!" "I do believe that was what the old woman described as a waking dream. I am grateful for the gift."

With that Matthew headed toward home, knowing that life was never really over, but that it merely shape-shifted into different forms. He was grateful for all the amazing gifts life offered; but mostly, he was grateful for his grandpa and for the gifts they shared that allowed them to reconnect in physical form what was always present in spirit. "May I always honor the gifts given through my *Waking Dreams.*"

Winter Reflections

"That fire is what keeps us feeling alive, and it opens our hearts to all of life's experiences."

— *These are her words*

HEAD TALK

What from this Winter season would you like to know more about?

Or, is there one thing you would like to *"think some more about?"*

Where do you suppose you can go to find out more about questions you still have from any of the Seasons?

HEART TALK

Of the stories in this season, pause and consider what Truths were revealed.

What of these *Truths* apply to YOUR Life right now?

As you consider the Winter of YOUR Life, what "jumps out" as a theme?

What can you learn for your own life from the Teachings of the North?

Head to Heart Talks

Life is a Circle, and, wherever you are in this moment, you are given the same "gifts" every year from each season and direction. Their "gifts" are teachings that are offered to assist you through Life's journey. With that in mind, as the Wheel of Life begins another rotation, it would be most helpful for you to set aside time each year to consider what your HEART wishes to create for that year, and how your HEAD can help it accomplish those dreams. Use a circle (mandala) such as the one above, and allow your HEART to dream as your HEAD writes down the ideas. Once this is completed, place the mandala where you can see it every day. Then "get out of the way," and be amazed as you watch the universe bring you exactly what you need. Your only task then is to remain grateful, stay in the moment, and pay attention, pay attention, pay attention!

Life is a Circle

"*As we journey through the Circle of our lives, we discover that every experience prepares us for the next 'season' of life. There is, indeed, a divine unfolding that mirrors the divine essence in all of nature, including we human beings. If we allow ourselves to step back, pause and reflect upon our lives, we will find the interconnection that binds us with ALL of Creation. Through this connection we find that we really are not separate from any of God's Creation, and that to believe we are is to deny the wisdom of our Creator.*"

— These are her words.

After Words ...

Awareness is the very *first* step to any creation. If we were not aware that something was out of alignment, we would go through life crippled! We would have no new inventions, faster and more efficient technologies, cures for diseases, or dreams of a peaceful world.

It is the old woman's hope that you have found something to "*think some more about*" that might lead you to your heart's deepest desires. Perhaps something said in the stories has stirred an emotion, or offered you the opportunity to pause, take a deep breath, and remember what it felt like to be still. She wishes to remind the reader(s), the *first* step merely "opens the door." The *second* step, revealed once you enter, is to lovingly and tenderly examine your life for what works and what needs to be "recycled."

It takes courage and strength to compassionately look within our hearts, and with *gentle* eyes to see who we *really* are. We must be willing to develop an intimate relationship with ourselves; for the saying, "You cannot give to others what you do not give to yourself," is true! Once that is initiated, cherished, and securely put in place, then, and only then, can we bring into fruition what our hearts truly desire.

Somewhere over the generations, we have forgotten the simple things in life that once brought us joy and laughter. We have replaced those simple acts with the belief that material possessions and personal accomplishments define our worth. We all discover that over time things fade, become obsolete, or ultimately need to be replaced. Yet, the simple memory of a favorite fishing hole, baking cookies, playing board games, counting the stars at night or putting a frog down our sister's shirt are within our hearts forever!

Unlike reading a book, watching a movie or TV show, it takes longer than thirty minutes or a few hours to make changes that last. It takes time, patience, and commitment to make the change a permanent reality in our lives. The truth is, there is no stopping point, and we are "masters" of our own destiny! As long as we breathe, we will have to pay attention to what we are thinking, saying and doing.

In order to be all that we desire for our communities and for ourselves, we must realign with the Creator of all things. For we will all ultimately return to the source from which we came. Peace and harmony are not just words; they are an energy force that can be felt and seen, and like anything alive, they need to be "tended" with love and respect.

So, while this book is over, it really is only the beginning of a new opportunity! It is the "Beginning of the End" for a new world! The "End" is merely refocusing on what works in order to bring harmony, peace and love to the world. To do this requires that we "look over our shoulders" to see what brought harmony, and what created disharmony, and then discern which of those actions to use in the new creation. *Gentleness* always adds to the creation of peace, whereas, judgment and criticism do the opposite.

Rather than the current trend of being guided by "rules," "dogmas," and other fear-based guidelines, it is time for the divine Creator to be visible for the loving being that it is. This can only happen when we honor and respect our divine self and allow it to be seen in our lives. It begins with each of us (that means you AND me!) allowing that divine inheritance to be visible in our thoughts, words and actions. We *are* reflections of our divine Creator.

Let's make this very personal! It is an individual choice you make in every moment. Whether consciously or by "default," these choices are made with every breath you take. Now is the time to wake up and take *personal responsibility* for what YOU contribute to the world. The old woman hopes you choose to BE the loving human being you were created to be. Creator, God, Buddha, all represent Love. *Be that love,* so that more joy, laughter and peace is added to your family, community, and ultimately the world!

About the Author

Vicky Kelm Williams is a retired educator who spent nearly 30 years listening to the hearts of students, parents, and caregivers as her own life unfolded. She also apprenticed with a Cherokee Shaman for 13 years, and from that experience learned the Truths taught by those that walked before us — our ancestors! Through these amazing teachings and those found in nature everyday she offers simple yet profound Truths buried beneath societal programming. From the many stories brought to her by seekers willing to do their work, she offers a cornucopia of wisdom from which to glean truths that can be used to live an authentic life.

This book is a series of stories about an old woman who lives in the Forest. She has developed a reputation for being very straightforward and unpretentious. People who find their way to her cabin know they are to ask only one question, and from that the old woman will tell them a story. If a person talks too much or asks too many questions, the old woman has been known to get up and go back to whatever task she had been tending.

From her heart to yours, she offers the reader an opportunity for some **"Head to Heart Talks!"**

Follow us at:

<www.headtohearttalks.blogspot.com>,

we would love to hear from you!